JILLIAN HART

grew up on her family's homestead, where she raised cattle, rode horses and scribbled stories in her spare time. After earning an English degree from Whitman College, she worked in advertising before selling her first novel to Harlequin® Historical. When she's not hard at work on her next story, Jillian can be found chatting over lunch with a friend, stopping for a café mocha with a book in hand and spending quiet evenings at home with her family.

KATE BRIDGES

is fascinated by the romantic tales of the spirited men and women who tamed the West. She's thrilled to be writing for Harlequin Historical.

Growing up in rural Canada, Kate developed a love of people-watching and reading all types of fiction, although romance was her favorite. She embarked on a career as a neonatal intensive-care nurse, then moved on to architecture. Later, working in television production, she began crafting novels of her own. Currently living in the bustling city of Toronto, she and her husband love to go to movies and travel. You can visit her Web site at www.katebridges.com.

CHARLENE SANDS

resides in Southern California with her husband, high-school sweetheart and best friend, Don. Proudly, they boast that their children, Jason and Nikki, have earned their college degrees. The "empty nesters" now have two cats that have taken over the house. Charlene's love of the American West, both present and past, stems from storytelling days with her imaginative father, sparking a passion for a good story and her desire to write romance. When not writing, she enjoys sunny California days, Pacific beaches and sitting down with a good book.

Charlene invites you to visit her author Web site at www.charlenesands.com to enter her contests, have a chat and see what's new. She also invites you to visit her site at www.myspace.com/charlenesands for more fun stuff. E-mail her at charlenesands@hotmail.com.

Western Weddings

Jillian HART
Kate BRIDGES
Charlene SANDS

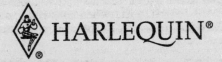

HARLEQUIN®

TORONTO • NEW YORK • LONDON
AMSTERDAM • PARIS • SYDNEY • HAMBURG
STOCKHOLM • ATHENS • TOKYO • MILAN • MADRID
PRAGUE • WARSAW • BUDAPEST • AUCKLAND

ISBN-13: 978-0-373-29495-4
ISBN-10:   0-373-29495-6

WESTERN WEDDINGS
Copyright © 2008 by Harlequin Books S.A.

The publisher acknowledges the copyright holders
of the individual works as follows:

ROCKY MOUNTAIN BRIDE
Copyright © 2008 by Jill Strickler

SHOTGUN VOWS
Copyright © 2008 by Katherine Haupt

SPRINGVILLE WIFE
Copyright © 2008 by Charlene Swink

CONTENTS

ROCKY MOUNTAIN BRIDE

Jillian Hart

Dear Reader,

You may remember the town of Moose, Montana Territory, from my other Harlequin Historical anthology story, "*Rocky Mountain Christmas*" in the *A Season of the Heart* collection. This time, Savannah Knowles arrives in Moose expecting to be united with Nate Brooks, the man she has been corresponding with and has agreed to marry. She is very surprised to find out that Nate has no idea who she is—but his mother does. Will Mary Brooks be successful in marrying off her middle son? I hope you enjoy finding out. Joseph's story is next!

Thank you so much for choosing "Rocky Mountain Bride."

Happy reading,

Jillian

Chapter One

Montana Territory
1881

Snow. Savannah Knowles had never seen so much of it. It was everywhere—sifting through the air and clinging to the roof of the train depot and crunching at the platform beneath her feet. She gathered her courage, gripped her satchel by the patched handle, shivered inside her traveling coat and squinted into the last light of the April evening. She could see only the shadowed impression of dense forests through the downfall, but nothing more of her new home.

A few men stood against the ticket station, veiled by the icy snow. Was her Mr. Brooks one of them, the man she'd come to marry? She lifted her chin, watching each scowling face or curious look, but no one moved toward her.

He wasn't here yet, but he would be. She had faith in him. Of all the letters she'd received from her advertisement, his had been the most sincere. He was her last hope. She was out of options and out of money, which is why she'd come to this strange, rough country with its rugged mountains and unfathomable weather. A keen-edged gust of wind sliced through her layers of clothing, cold enough to freeze the insides of her bones.

Goodness, she'd never felt such cold. Already she missed the sweet gentle warmth of a Carolina spring. Snow caught on her eyelashes and stung her face as she picked her way through the accumulation of snow and ice to the baggage car. Every bit of her ached with homesickness and with hope.

"Hey, there, miss!" A gruff man barked out from the cavern of the opened railcar. "This one yours?"

"Yes, sir."

"Mighty fancy trunk for these parts." The railroader lifted his lip as if in distaste or something worse and tossed down her trunk with a careless heave.

My books. She watched the precious container crash onto the platform. It skidded on the ice and tipped over to rest on its side— still in one piece.

A stroke of luck. The finely crafted side of the trunk was snow battered, but the contents inside were safe at least, and not scattered over the icy platform. All that was left of her family's great library, collected for generations, the volumes with sentimental value too great to sell. Hard times had fallen after the War Between the States.

Suddenly the biting wind hailing against her back seemed to lose its teeth. Before she could turn around, she sensed a tall presence behind her. Her stomach slid to her toes. Mr. Brooks? Could it be him?

"Hope nothing breakable was in that." His gaze met hers and, despite the haze of snowfall between them, she felt a snap of recognition.

Those dark blue eyes were exactly as he'd described them in his letters. Her pulse fluttered in her chest. She'd memorized his features from his self-description, and he'd been surprisingly accurate. He had a granite face, a square jaw and a serious expression just as she'd pictured, but he was taller than she imagined. Maybe it was his bulky coat and the shroud of snow, which made him look like a giant bear of a man, but it *was* him. Her Mr. Brooks.

He'd come for her, just as he'd promised. Happy relief washed through her, warm enough to chase away every chill. At first sight, he looked as dependable as she'd made him out to be. "Nathaniel Brooks?"

"Uh, yep. That's me."

She couldn't breathe as he gave her a simple smile—sincere and respectful. Instead of greeting her, maybe taking her by hand or offering to carry the satchel she carried, he looked past her to the baggage man.

"Hey, there, Roberts." Mr. Brooks spoke in a cozy, friendly baritone. "You got a bundle coming for my pa? Something from Savannah?"

Oh, he had other business, too, she thought, a little disappointed, waiting patiently. Maybe he was preoccupied with that?

The baggage man straightened and gave the small of his back a two-handed rub. "What kind of bundle?"

"Pa said it was a surprise, but I'm not one for surprises. He ought to know that."

The baggage man shook his head, ready to slide closed the cargo door. "Sorry, Nate. I've got nothing else for this stop. Just the woman. Good luck."

"Just the woman?" He looked perplexed as he studied the other end of the platform. It was as empty.

The only other passenger who'd disembarked had already left, and she realized the men who'd been standing in the shadows of the depot had disappeared, perhaps seeing nothing had arrived for them. But why was Mr. Brooks acting as if he didn't know anything about her?

This couldn't be right. Shouldn't the man who proposed to her remember? Maybe she'd better try again. "Mr. Brooks? I'm pleased to meet you in person. I'm Miss Savannah Knowles."

When he looked at her, no recognition sparked in his dazzling eyes. "You're from Savannah?"

"No, that's my name." Why did he seem so confused? "I knew you wouldn't keep me waiting."

"Waiting?" He looked at her as if he didn't understand the English language. "You're Savannah?"

"That's right." This was not going the way she'd imagined. Her heart tumbled to her toes. Shouldn't the man who'd paid for her railroad ticket look less mystified? A knot tightened in her midsection. "You've come for me, isn't that right?"

"For you? You're a woman, not a bundle." He knuckled back his hat with one gloved hand. He seemed to have no recollection of who she ought to be.

She started to shake—from cold or nerves, she didn't know which. "This *is* Moose, Montana Territory? I did get off at the right station?"

"Yes, miss." His gaze raked from the tip of her snow-covered bonnet all the way to her icy skirt ruffle. "Did my mother hire new help? Is that why you're here?"

"Your mother? I don't understand. You don't know who I am?" The wind gusted mockingly, and her high hopes crumbled.

You're a fool, girl, her grandmother's lawyer had told her. *You're chasing after a paper promise, when I'm offering you a home with all the luxuries you could want—*

She closed her mind against the memory and the old man's vein-lined hands, the man who'd offered her marriage and payment of her grandmother's debts. Surely she'd not make a mistake in coming so far. "Maybe we're not talking about the same man. This Nate Brooks owns the feed store in town. He's—"

"I own the feed store in town."

"He's twenty-nine years old. He was born on New Year's Day."

"That's me. As far as I know, I'm the only Nathanial Brooks in these parts anyhow. How do you know so much about me?" His face was hard granite.

She would have thought him angry but for the pain she saw in his dark, kind eyes.

"We've been corresponding." She clenched her teeth together to keep them from chattering as she tugged the envelopes, tied with a gold ribbon, from her pocket. She held them out with a shaky hand, feeling the beat of the snow against her face, hearing it against the arm of her coat as she waited a long moment for him to take the letters. The icy cold crept into the hollows of her heart.

She'd come all this way with nothing to go back to and no other place to welcome her. Surely there had to be some explanation. Some misunderstanding of sorts and then it would come out all right in the end.

But with the way the wind howled like a lonely wolf as it gusted around her, she wasn't so sure.

The bear of a man took the letters. He knocked the snowflakes from the parchments with his leather-gloved knuckles and squinted to study the handwriting. "That's my name but not my address."

"It isn't? I don't understand."

"I didn't write to you."

"Then who did? And why?" Her satchel slipped from her grip and hit the platform beside her with a muted *thunk.* "You proposed to me. I came all this way to marry you."

"M-marry?" He choked on the word. *No. No. No.* It rose up like a wellspring from his very soul right along with a blinding panic. It was so dark, he could barely make out the familiar handwriting on the top envelope. The ink was beginning to smear from the snow, but there was no mistaking the truth. Not only did he know who'd written these letters, but also he could plainly see this woman had nearly traveled all the way across the country. What would prompt a delicate-looking woman to risk a trip all that way?

Sure, a proposal of marriage would. He tried to think past the rush of horror pounding through him and—beneath the panic—the pain of his last and only intention to marry. It was the hurt Adella left him with, that was the reason for the panic, but this little woman didn't know that.

The woman—Savannah—looked at him with pure hurt in her soft sweetheart's face. "I see that idea of marrying me horrifies you. I'll just—"

"Wait." He bit out the word with venom she didn't deserve. Calm down, he told himself and took a single deep breath, which was hard to do considering he was still in a blind panic. Not all marriages were awful; he knew this. But after his experience, he wanted nothing to do with it. "Obviously I knew nothing about this—this—marriage offer. Without warning, a remark like that can scare a man."

"I don't understand. Is this someone's idea of a practical j-joke?" Her soft voice broke on the last word. "I was so sure. The letters were so wonderful. Too wonderful. Maybe that's what fooled me. I wanted to believe—"

The hurt and confusion so honest in her pretty blue eyes chased away most of his panic. None of this was her fault. "This is my father's handwriting."

"Your father's?" She held up her hands in a helpless gesture, so small and alone. "I don't understand."

How could she? He didn't have a chance to answer, for the train gave a loud blast of steam and churned on its way. The rumble of the powerful engine vibrated through the soles of his feet. He watched the cars pull away and the caboose slip out of sight.

Pa had probably laid it on thick, judging by the fatness of the envelopes. Nate shook his head, and snow rained from his hat brim. How could his father—who was a decent man—do such a thing? A bundle, that's what his youngest brother had said. *There's a bundle waiting for you from Savannah.*

He still didn't see how the "bundle" could be the pale, delicate-looking Southerner in front of him looking like a rose out of season. Not that he could see much of her with the snow falling with a vengeance, but she was shivering in the cold, too fine and lacking enough common sense to have worn warmer clothes to this high country.

Nate flicked the gathering snow off the letters and handed them back to her, noticing the dark tips of her expensive traveling gloves. He didn't have to unwrap that cloak to know what he'd find beneath it: the fashionable clothes and shoes, with no expense spared.

If his folks had gone to the trouble of bringing a bride all the way to Montana Territory, then couldn't they have at least tried to find one that wasn't just like Adella? What did a man who worked hard for his daily living have to offer a delicate lady?

Not a damn thing. He swallowed the bitterness and debated

what to do. It wasn't the woman's fault she'd come all this way on a false promise, and he couldn't leave her alone in the cold.

"Why w-would your f-father do th-this?" She trembled so hard, her words trembled, too.

"My parents have decided it's about time I marry." He began unbuttoning his coat. "The trouble is, we've had a difference of opinion—"

"What kind of difference?"

"I'm not partial to the institution of marriage."

"Did your father write me thinking that you might change your mind once I arrived?"

"It wouldn't surprise me. My folks have been talking about taking matters into their own hands. I didn't put much stock in their teasing. I didn't think they would actually find me a woman."

She looked down at her shoes, and he hoped she wasn't trying not to cry. He didn't know how to deal with a crying female. He shrugged out of the heavy buffalo coat and saw there were tears in her eyes. He felt helpless. Too big. Too rough. Too… everything.

She gazed down the empty train tracks. "I wish I w-would have known that sooner."

"The storm's getting worse. We can't just leave you here on the platform. You look mighty cold."

"Cold? Sir, this is hardly c-cold. This wind would fr-freeze the fires of H-Hades."

"True, but you get used to it after a while. I reckon my pa didn't write about the weather here?"

"N-no." She was shaking so hard, she could barely speak. It wasn't only due to the biting arctic temperatures. She lifted her chin, refusing to let this man know how crushed she was. She might not have much left, but she did have her pride. "I'm sorry to have troubled you. It was good meeting you, Mr. Brooks."

"Now, wait one minute." He closed the distance between them, towering over her, blocking the brunt of the wind. "It's nearly dark. You shouldn't be wandering around town alone."

He was close. Too close. She could see the day's growth dark on his jaw. She gulped, taking a step back. "Perhaps you could recommend a place to stay?"

"Sure. I'll take you there myself." He laid his coat over her shoulders. "You look awful cold. Maybe this will help."

The weight of the buffalo coat, the warmth from his body's heat and his pleasant, man-and-wood-smoke scent enveloped her. Overcome, she gaped up at him, touched by his kindness. He really was the gentleman she'd come to know from those letters. The bitter sweetness tugged like a lost dream in her heart.

She slipped her arms into the coat's sleeves. "Thank you."

"Can't have you freezing to death before we give my father the devil for bringing you out all this way."

Emotion burned in her throat and she could only shake her head in an answer. Nate Brooks was perfect, just as she knew he would be.

This wasn't how she'd imagined her journey would end. She wrapped her arms around her middle, but there was no comfort. Not from the wind or the cold or the realization that she had made a terrible mistake in coming. Still, she was a Knowles, and she had the ability to stand on her own two feet.

The storm was getting worse. She thought of the handful of change at the bottom of her reticule, tucked in her satchel. It might be enough to get her a room for the night but little more. If only she had been able to keep her governess position through Grandmama's illness; but in the end, taking care of her grandmother had meant more than the money. The plantation had been sold off in pieces, starting well before the war, but Grandmama's lingering illness had been costly. There was almost nothing left in the end. Now Savannah had nothing to fall back on. Nowhere to call home. No one left who cared.

She watched Nate heft the trunk onto his shoulder as if it weighed nothing at all. The letters in her pocket, by contrast, seemed as heavy as an anvil. Watching him, it was hard not to think about the promises written in those letters and the stories of a large extended family with lots of love to spare. So many hopes she'd had.

Maybe she *had* been a little naive, but she'd wanted to find a new family after losing hers. That was all.

Now, she was alone again.

"Follow me." He headed straight into the thick curtain of snow and nightfall. Into the unknown.

Savannah lifted her skirts, grabbed her satchel and plowed through the ankle-deep snow before the storm could steal him from her sight.

Chapter Two

Nate shouldered the fancy trunk into the store, his angry steps echoing in the quiet store around him. He'd left a single lamp burning when his youngest brother had come with a message from Pa asking him to meet the train.

What a crock. Had he known the "bundle" was a fragile-looking woman whose bonnet probably cost more than his entire year's inventory, not only would he have refused, he'd have hunted his father down and given him a piece of his mind. What was the old man thinking, bringing a woman all this way with promises that he had no intention of keeping?

The cowbell above the door clanged, and he didn't need to look over his shoulder to know she'd stumbled in behind him. In fact, he did his best not to look at her. It would only stir the anger gathering like a blizzard in his gut.

"Lock the door behind you," he ordered more harshly than he intended. The boom of his words echoing in the shadowed, after-hours store sounded harsher. "Follow me."

She didn't answer but the click of the dead bolt did. He wasn't going to let himself feel sorry for her—that would be like a crack in an earth dam, and he wasn't looking for devastation. No, sir. He kept going with her heavy trunk. He let his boots make enough noise to fill the silence and cover the soft, light pad of her weaving through the cold, dark store behind him.

The stairwell that led to his living quarters had never felt this narrow before. Why was he aware of the walls pressing in on him? Maybe it was the woman behind him, so close he could hear the rustle of her skirts. The winter snow and lilac scent of her filled his head.

No good could come from this. He knew that for a fact. He was a man; he couldn't help noticing the woman. Oh, he had self-control and discipline to spare, there was no worry about going sweet on Miss Knowles. That might be his parents' plans, but not his, he realized as he shouldered through the door and dropped the trunk on the floor. There was nothing but shards left of his heart.

He straightened and did his best not to look at Miss Knowles as he grabbed a towel from the closest cabinet. "Here."

"Th-thank you." Her stutter was little more than a soft and vulnerable whisper, and it ate at him.

He dropped it on the corner of the table where he'd left a lamp burning, and headed straight for the stove. "Dry off. Make yourself at home. You'll be staying here tonight."

"H-here?"

He wasn't surprised that she sounded so alarmed at that. He knelt to toss more wood into the stove, and his quick temper raged as the fire's heat. "I suppose this place isn't good enough for your tender sensibilities?"

"No." She sounded puzzled. "This is your home. Where are you going to s-sleep?"

She sounded concerned. He felt his head hang as he closed the stove door and opened the damper wide. The fire grew to a crackling roar. He straightened. Maybe he was jumping to a few conclusions. He was already confusing her with Adella, and that wasn't right. Not right at all.

"I'll head over to my folks." He reached down for a cup from the cupboard, and seeing it was chipped, chose another. It only had a small nick in it. "I suppose I could get you a room at the hotel. You might be more comfortable there."

"Oh, no. I don't want to put you to any more expense, Mr.

Brooks." She paused, and a floorboard creaked beneath her weight. "I cannot afford a hotel room."

"I wouldn't expect you to pay."

"But I would expect to."

That made him turn around, made him forget his fury and his wounded pride and the shattered pieces of his heart. Savannah Knowles stood in the doorway, neither in nor out as if she were afraid to enter, already understanding she didn't belong.

She stood within the reaches of the lamplight. She was white from hat to the tip of her stylish shoes, and the bulk of his buffalo coat didn't begin to hide her loveliness. She had big, blue eyes rimmed by thick black lashes, and a delicate face, prominent cheekbones, a dainty nose and chin and a lush, rosebud mouth. A blond curl of silken hair was uncoiling down her porcelain forehead.

Now that he could see her in full light, his jaw dropped. Why on earth did she need to answer a newspaper advertisement for a husband? She could have her choice of men. His bitter suspicion of women stood up and took note. He grabbed the teapot from its warm place on the stovetop and poured a cup for her. Was she hiding a secret? Running from something?

And why was he wondering? Nate carried the cup to the table. "There. Warm up. I'll be back."

"But—"

"I'll be back."

She winced as his harsh words echoed in the dark corners of the slanted ceiling, and moved out of the doorway to let him pass. She slipped off his bulky coat. "Would you like—"

He stopped on the top step, reached back and snared it. He nodded once, as if that would pass for a mannerly thank-you, and stormed off. His boots struck the wooden boards like thunder, growing fainter until the front door downstairs closed.

What do I do now, Grandmama? She could hear her grandmother's voice, sharper than memory and full of life and heart. Time melted away, along with all the long, hard railroad miles, until she could see the family's home so clearly in her mind's eye that her throat burned with longing. Grandmama was propped up on her carved, high-posted bed with morning sunlight spilling through the Palladian windows to crown her.

"Mind your upbringing when I'm gone." Ever practical, strong as steel, Grace Hamilton Knowles smiled in that gentle way of hers. "Most of all, don't you give in to despair. By the time I was your age, I'd buried a husband and a child, so you listen to me, girl. You hold on to this life, gather up your gumption and look forward to hope. I'll want your word of honor on that."

The tears lumped in her throat blurred her eyes, dissolving the image, fading the memory. She was alone in the shadows where the single lamp flickered and a blizzard's winds howled overhead, and unwanted.

Hope withered up and vanished in the cool air like a curl of smoke, leaving her weak. She sank into the only chair at the table and laid her face in her hands. The new beginning she'd wanted was a dead end. The home she'd wished to find was a bachelor's place with one chair at the table, one armchair by the stove and a narrow bed in the corner.

Everything—from the single plate on the shelf to the lamp—was proof. There was no family to find, no marriage to put her love into and no life to build here. She hadn't realized how much she'd wanted the dream of Nate Brooks until she'd lost it.

The door downstairs slammed with the wind, ricocheting like a bullet in the silence. Nate was coming. She drew herself straight in the chair. His footsteps approached, emphasizing the emptiness and the shadows, until he filled the doorway. The big bear of a man white with snow brought with him the scent of wild mountain air and fried chicken.

"There's wood enough to see you through the night." Not bothering to take off his hat or shake the snow from his coat, he stormed toward her and slid the covered tray he held on to the farthest edge of the table from her, as if he intended to stay as far away as he possibly could. "I hope you don't mind chicken and mashed potatoes. I had my supper ordered up at the hotel right before I was asked to pick you up."

He didn't look at her; he was already halfway across the small space. He threw back the comforters on the bed and tore off the sheets. "There's fresh linens in the cabinet by the bed. Water in the pitcher. The lamp's full of kerosene."

She could only stare at the covered platter numbly. He was giving her his dinner? "What will you eat?"

"I'll head home. My ma will feed me."

"But the storm—"

"I'd rather face the blizzard. No offense." He wadded the sheets up and tossed them into the corner out of sight, where they landed with a muted rasp. "You lock this door here after me. I'll bolt the one downstairs. You'll be safe enough until morning. All right?"

Again, he didn't look at her. He walked away from her, his back straight, his broad shoulders strong, the perfect picture of a man. The lump in her throat ached doubly.

His steps slowed as he reached the door. He paused and turned on his boot heel. "Is there anything else I can do for you?"

With kindness softening his booming baritone and his granite features, he looked like the man she'd dreamed up from his letters.

"N-no," she struggled to say; her voice sounded small and vulnerable and tired, not at all her own. "I'll be warm for the night, thank you. You'd best go before the storm gets much worse."

"Yes, that was my thinking, too." He tipped his snowy hat once before he disappeared beyond the shadowed doorway. He pulled the door close. "Good night."

It sounded like goodbye. The door clicked shut with a final sound. Exhaustion felt heavy on her shoulders as she sat, listening to his footsteps fade. Her stomach growled, the hotel food smelled delicious, but she rose to her feet and crossed to the window. She pulled back the muslin curtain. Frigid air pressed through the panes as she squinted through the dark glass.

There, on the boardwalk below, was the faint shadow of Nathaniel Brooks striding away from her.

She had come a long way, only to be alone again.

* * *

The wind cut through him like glass, leaving tiny embedded shards of ice in his veins that his fleece-lined buffalo coat couldn't stop nor his fury could melt. All he could think about was that pretty, delicate woman and the look on her face when he'd said goodbye. All he could see was her disappointment and the jut of her chin telling him that she was doing her best not to let it show.

The blizzard slammed against him, howling and clawing like a living thing trying to get at him. Trigger, sensible gelding though he was, gave a hop of surprise, shaking his head. His ears were back, meaning he didn't like this weather, either.

"We gotta keep going, buddy." It wasn't much farther—at least he didn't think so. Not that he could make out much in the dark and the storm's swirling fury, but he calculated they would be passing over the bridge any moment.

The *click-clang* of Trigger's hooves told him they were. Not more than twenty yards, and they would be out of this misery. What did Miss Savannah Knowles think of her first Montana blizzard? He liked to think she felt snug enough in the upstairs room that she wouldn't give it much worry. His guts knotted. No, he'd best not wonder if she was afraid or hurting, devastated or at a loss. Savannah Knowles was not his concern—not once he gave his parents a piece of his mind.

There it was—the brief flash of light in the dark. Looked like there was a lamp in the sitting-room window. The welcoming sight only put more misery in his wrenched-up stomach and more fury in his anger. His kid brother must have been keeping watch for him, because suddenly there Joseph was, emerging from the shadows of the storm, swathed in snow, to take Trigger's reins.

"What does she look like?" Joseph had to shout to be heard above the raging winds. "Is she real pretty?"

"Yeah. You'd best marry her, then." None too happy, Nate swung down from the saddle.

"You aren't happy with her? I wouldn't mind gettin' married."

Although it was impossible to see in the darkness, Nate could tell his youngest brother was grinning as he led the horse off at a fast walk toward the barn.

Could the problem be as simply solved as that? To pawn lovely and young Miss Knowles off on his eager brother?

A sudden rectangle of light appeared in the inky darkness—the front door opening. There stood his ma, wrapped in her warmest shawl and graced with lamplight. Behind her the fire roared in the hearth and there was his father, striding in for a look.

"Did you bring her?" Ma demanded, anxiously looking around in the shadows as Nate strode up the steps and into the light.

"Do you see her?" He knew the words were harsh, but he was furious. Having ridden through the teeth of a Rocky Mountain storm hadn't put him in a better mood. He marched into the shelter of the house and began shucking off his layers of snow-driven wraps. "I left her in town, safe and sound, so she'll be convenient to the train depot come morning."

"Son, you mean she wasn't pleased with you?" Ma looked crestfallen.

Pa wrestled the door closed against the wind and glowered. "*What?* What do you mean she's heading back?"

"But she was perfect for you," Ma added. "A lovely girl with a heart to match. It was you, Nate. You offended her."

"Why is it always me?" He couldn't believe this.

"You are rather prickly, Son." Pa came closer, newspaper in hand. "I say be nicer to her, and she'll come around to liking you real fine."

"I don't believe this." Nate tossed his coat over the back of the nearby bench. "Not a bit of remorse from either of you. You made promises to that lady. Pa, she knows you lied to her."

"She'll forgive me in time."

Ma nodded and tapped off to the kitchen. "Savannah will be glad when this comes out all right in the end."

Red. The bold color slid across his eyes and rolled into his head like boiling water. Fury unlike he'd ever known threatened to blow the hat right off his head as he bent to take off his boots. "Glad?

How could she be glad? You should have seen that woman's face when I had to tell her—"

Nate's chest filled up tight remembering how she'd looked so lost and bewildered standing at the train platform, trying to understand that she wasn't wanted and would never be. He remembered how soft her rosebud mouth looked, and the heat of fury in his veins changed to something more. Blushing, he forced the memory of Savannah's lush lips from his mind. Best to concentrate on the problem in front of him, instead of starting new ones. "Don't you realize what you've done? She's expecting *marriage*."

Ma swept into sight, carrying a big steaming bowl of beef stew and setting it on the table. "Yes, that's what we promised her. Have some beef stew, dear. I made it just the way you like it."

He had no appetite. His guts were too tied up, but he sat down anyway. While he poured himself a cup of hot coffee from the pot on the table, he wondered about Savannah. He should have made sure she liked chicken before he left. He should have made sure she felt safe and secure enough to spend a night alone in a strange house. He felt sick, defeated. He should have done a lot of things differently.

Ma brought a basket of sliced bread and an encouraging smile. "Look at it this way, Son. I want you happy and settled to a nice girl."

Anger blinded him. He thought about Adella, how he'd let her into his heart and she'd torn it to shreds when she left him for a rich lawyer. Bitterness flooded him as he remembered standing at her door come to speak to her, just to ask her what he could do to fix things, and there had been that dandy in his tailored, Eastern-made suit seated in her parlor.

His sweet-natured ma couldn't understand. His gentle, loving mother always meant well. She grabbed his hat by the brim and lifted it off his head, carrying it to the wall pegs where it belonged.

Boots pounded on the staircase. Nate set down his cup and there was Gabriel, his big brother, lurching toward the table with a grimace on his face.

"I heard about the woman," he said as he stole a piece of bread. "Tough luck."

Nate nodded in agreement and gave the butter dish a push in Gabe's direction. "Don't worry. I'm sendin' her back."

Gabe grabbed a knife and dug it into the ball of butter. "I'd do it as soon as the trains are runnin' again. The tracks ought to be cleared by noon tomorrow, if this stops sometime tonight. You can always hope."

Nate slurped down some coffee, letting it heat him from the inside out. Pa settled down at the far end of the table and buried his nose in his newspaper. The *clink* of dishes being washed, dried and put away by the hired help made the big ranch house seem cozy, but he couldn't relax. What about Savannah? What was the right thing to do?

Buy her a ticket home to her family? That's what he would do. He dug into his stew, feeling better. His worries were easing a bit, and he set his attention on eating. It was surprising how hungry a man got when he was thinking up ways to get out of getting married. Was there a good chance the storm would let up before morning?

All the evening through, the blizzard raged and the howling winds showed no sign of quieting down. Late that night, tucked in his childhood bed in his room beneath the eaves, he listened to his brothers snoring at either end of the hallway and his thoughts kept drifting to Savannah. Thinking of her luscious golden hair tangled up on his pillows and her lying in his bed kept him, his conscience and his treacherous needs awake long into the night.

Chapter Three

In the morning's after-the-storm silence, Savannah waited and watched the black hands of the wall clock creep toward eight o'clock. She sat in the chair by the stove, unable to do anything but wait for the rasp of the bolt turning downstairs and the impending echo of Nate's step.

She dreaded his arrival. There was no way to measure the disappointment twisting in her heart or the uncertainty filling her stomach. She'd worked things through very carefully during the night. While the strange, wild notes of the powerful wind beat like a rabid animal at the roof, she had passed from devastation to calm, had gathered up her fallen hopes and formed something of a plan. At least, it was the best she could come up with under the circumstances.

There was a faint *click* muffled by the floorboards. Her wait was at an end. Her heart leaped into her throat and beat there in quick, hummingbird flutters. Damp broke out on her palms. The door wrenched open and closed with a clatter. Judging by the stomp of his boots coming closer, he wasn't any happier about the situation as he'd been last night.

How am I going to face him? Her heart twisted; she steeled her spine and sat a little straighter on the edge of the chair. It was hard to know she was unwanted, and it was harder still to meet Nate

Brooks's gaze and see it on his face one more time. She drew in a slow breath as his footsteps paused outside the open door. Nate lumbered through the shadowed doorway and into the light.

"Mornin'." He swept off his Stetson, bringing in the scent of winter snow and mountain air. "You sleep all right?"

Distant and polite, that's how he had chosen to manage this situation—and her. Savannah released the breath she'd been holding. Good, that was how she wanted to handle this, too. She met his shadowed gaze and noted the dark circles bruising his eyes. "It looks as if you slept no better than I did."

"I'm sorry about that. In fact, I'm sorry about all of this. There are some things I ought to have said to you. I'm just not used to a bride arriving at the depot for me."

"Let me make things easier for you." She rose from the chair and discovered her knees were hardly wobbly at all. "I'm packed and ready to leave."

"I expect you've got family back home?"

"Not any longer." She wiped her palms on her skirt. "I only want to get out of your way."

"You'll get no argument from me." Nate took in the packed trunk and the satchel on top of it, all ready to go. It was easier than looking at the woman, pale-faced with worry and lack of sleep. Little wonder, if she had no family, which meant no home to go back to. "I checked at the depot on the way over. The train ought to be running, as soon as they've got the tracks cleared. You can go anywhere and make it your home."

Distress filled her sapphire eyes. "Oh, I couldn't. I simply cannot afford it."

Yep, he knew she was going to say that. Maybe it was the little things, which he was now noticing: the frayed edges of the cuffs on her sleeves, the patch on the toe of one shoe, and the worn look to her satchel and trunk. "I'll be more than happy to pay your fare."

"N-no. That wouldn't be right." She set her chin, and a cascade of golden curls tumbled about her lovely face.

Her mouth was rosy and lush. That traitorous part of him wondered if she tasted as soft as she looked.

"That would be accepting your charity, which is something I cannot in good conscience do." To his surprise, there was no sparkle of greed, no glint of interest as she lifted her reticule from the tabletop. "I would be grateful if you could recommend a reputable but affordable boardinghouse. A-and someone to carry my trunk."

Had he heard her right? He was offering her hundreds of dollars. More than most folks earned in two years of hard work. Why wasn't she taking the bait?

Nate took a step back to consider her. Her clear eyes gazed up at him with unmistakable determination. She didn't want his money. How about that. This here was a decent woman looking up at him as if he'd offended her greatly.

He took a moment to let his defenses down a notch. With the lamplight gracing the delicate shape of her face and her luminous eyes, his opinion of Miss Savannah Knowles rose a step. No need to growl quite so loud at her when it was clear she wasn't interested in a rough mountain man like him.

"I'll give that a ponder over breakfast," he told her. "You want to come over to the hotel with me, let me buy you a decent meal and we'll work this out. Whatever plans are ahead, they are best made on a full stomach. Agreed?"

"Y-yes." Was it pain that pinched the corner of her eyes? Or relief? She spun away from him, her skirts twirling with a whisper that was entirely feminine.

And made his blood heat. Hell, how could he keep from noticing that? Or the way the fabric shivered down across her thighs and ankles to swish over the toes of her shoes?

"I'll just get my coat." Her demure mouth moved sinuously with those words and already she was turning away from him, leaving him to watch her move through the pool of lamplight with her woman's grace.

He squeezed his eyes shut, pivoted on his heel and blindly made his way through the door. He didn't open his eyes until he was perilously close to the top stair.

"I'll wait for you downstairs," he called out past a tight throat. "Outside."

He didn't wait for her to answer. He took off into the shadows, stampeding down the stairs like a bull buffalo. What in blazes was wrong with him that he couldn't look anywhere but at her?

Just another reason to be mad at his folks. They had done this to him, too. His life had been just fine before Savannah Knowles turned his senses atumble. Once he got her on that train, these hot, needy, traitorous feelings would melt like snow on a hot stovepipe.

Savannah hiked across the street behind Nate. The snow had been packed hard by the wind. Solid waves of it had splashed up against the whole sides of buildings. Drifts higher than she was covered the tether posts and the boardwalks on the south side of the street, where the hotel's lamps glowed behind frosted glass.

Teeth chattering, she walked through the door Nate held for her. A potbellied stove glowed red, right in the middle of the reception area. She held out her hands, drinking in the glorious heat.

"Nate!" A woman's voice called from the other side of an open doorway. "Didn't expect to see you here this morning. Fact is we didn't 'spect to see a single soul come through that door. I hear it's close to forty below outside."

Forty below *zero?* Savannah had never heard of such a thing. No wonder she was so painfully and thoroughly cold! She knew that there had been food in Nate's pantry. Coming here this morning in this impossibly bitter weather was a true measure of Nate's feelings for her and of his desperation to get rid of her.

It was hard not to be affected by that. She tucked her gloves into her pocket and untied her coat's sash. Nate's hand settled on her shoulder. Even through the layers of leather and wool and flannel, the shock of it sent a lightning bolt zipping straight to her toes.

"It's warmer in the dining room. Come."

Her body tingled. Her heart galloped in her chest. Did he feel this, too? She searched his eyes and his face and saw only his same stoniness. Perhaps her reaction to him was some strange side effect of such unearthly cold.

The dining room was warmer. She gratefully slipped out of her coat, surprised again when Nate helped her and then held her chair for her. A teapot was set on the table a few moments later. It was for her, since the waitress brought him coffee.

It was the waitress who had spoken to him earlier, and who took their orders now. "You want any hashed potatoes with that?"

Savannah reached for the sugar bowl. "I don't suppose you serve grits here?"

"Not a chance. I'll bring the potatoes. You, too, Nate?"

"That'll do, Thelma. Appreciate it."

Before Thelma strolled away, she gave Nate a hungry look. A rather bold look, Savannah decided, but she understood the waitress's sentiments. Nate was an attractive man. Even more charming and handsome than he had been on paper. As *his father* had put him on paper, she corrected as she swirled a sugar into her tea.

Nate's gaze felt as intense as the cold outside and as uncomfortable as the silence growing louder between them. Savannah laid her spoon on the edge of the saucer. "You must think me the biggest fool."

"Now why would I do that?"

He was polite; she had to give him that. She cradled the china cup in her hands and let the heat seep into her. She took a sip and studied the dark slash of his brows drawn low over his eyes. She took another sip of tea before she answered. "You think I'm desperate for a husband and I don't care who I marry. That's why you are so eager to get me on the first train out of here."

"That would be my standpoint." Nate slurped his black coffee.

No sugar for him, Savannah noticed. He was all hard man, all edges, uncompromising power and action, and he did not soften his life up with sweets. Or women looking for a ring.

His cup clanked in the saucer. His gaze fastened on her, and there was no apology, no softness and no gentleness of any kind. "I can see you're a woman used to being sheltered. Cared for."

Her chin went up. "Leaping to conclusions, Mr. Brooks? You don't know me. The man I poured my heart out to in my letters was not you. If you think I'm marrying so I can have a roof over my head and food in my stomach—"

"Whoa there, filly!" He held up both big hands, as if he were faultless, as if he hadn't been the one to upset her. "You have been in this town for less than one day. I don't know how life is where you hail from, but here in this high country, for most folks it takes a lot of backbreaking work all the day through to carve a living out in these mountains. A woman can't do that here, unless she's got family to help her or a comfortable job here in town. Even then, it's a rugged place."

"I'm not afraid of hard work, Mr. Brooks, I assure you."

"Wait, now, you're starting to get mad and your color is getting high, and I'm only trying to say—"

"You are trying to talk me into accepting a train ticket. Not because you feel genuinely sorry for the trick your family pulled on me, oh, no. You are only thinking of yourself. How you don't want a marriage-minded woman anywhere near to you. How you just want me gone for your peace of mind, and you don't care what happens to me or the fact that I don't what your pity money or your payoff. Either way, I refuse to take a ticket from you. Or, for that matter, anything else."

How did this conversation go so wrong so fast? Nate shook his head at the dainty little woman across the table who had turned into a prim, prickly, sharp-tongued, incredibly beautiful creature. He reckoned he'd best not notice the incredibly beautiful part, as the temper she was showing him was the reason he had thrown off all notion of courting a woman. He'd only been trying to do them both a favor.

He hauled out his wallet and tossed the four crisp hundred-dollar bills onto the table between them. "Take it. It's the right thing."

"For *you*."

Had he ever met such an exasperating woman? "If I say I'm sorry for the high-jinx my folks pulled on you, would you take it?"

"No."

Should he be noticing the way her lush mouth pursed up like a rosebud when she was angry? Or the swell of her bosom as she breathed harder with her fury? His gaze slid a notch lower, and he couldn't help noticing that she had a very pleasing bosom.

He snapped his eyes upward where her jeweled eyes were still looking at him as if she wanted to chase him and his money down the road with a repeating Winchester. Temper flared in his soul. What the hell was wrong with him? Why had he been *looking* at her?

And why was he being overwhelmed with an strong urge to kiss her?

Furious, he shoved his cup and saucer to the edge of the table for Thelma to refill. Why wasn't this all going as planned? It had seemed so logical last night when he'd lain awake, thinking things through. So simple and quick when he'd ridden in this morning.

A familiar voice called across the nearly empty dining room. "Having trouble there with your woman, Brooks?"

Nate gritted his teeth. He didn't need to turn toward the doorway to see who was standing there. Rush Travers. He'd probably been listening for some time, judging by the amused look on his arrogant face. Nate's vision turned crimson and his hands fisted. Every time he saw the man who had stolen Adella away from him, he wanted to come out swinging.

"Mind your own business, Travers." Nate bit out through his clenched teeth. He saw the question on Savannah's lovely face. He felt his own stupidity hit him like the heat radiating from the stove. Overly warm, he unbuttoned his coat and shucked it off.

"Let me get you more coffee," Thelma said as she slipped his breakfast plate in front of him. "Sorry about the wait. We're short-handed since Nellie quit. Miss, would you like anything else?"

"Yes. Could you tell me if you're hiring?"

His jaw dropped. The fork clattered from his fingers. He stared woodenly at Miss Savannah Knowles as she laid her napkin primly across her lap, her attention on the waitress's answer.

"Why?" Thelma took a step back. "You interested?"

"Yes. I'm looking for work."

There was a quiet strength to her, Nate realized. He retrieved his fork and tried to act like she hadn't surprised the hell out of him. She waited with a quiet dignity, now that her temper had abated, and she looked every inch the regal, genteel Southern lady he knew she was. Yet here she was, down on her luck but not afraid to stand her ground and earn her way.

His throat tightened, like someone had just set a noose around his neck. He couldn't let her work here, where any number of men could grope her or admire her with their eyes.

"Did I hear you right?" Rush called out from his table. "Is the pretty lady looking for work? I can help you with that."

There was the crimson again, falling across his vision like a see-through curtain. Firing in his veins like an inferno. "No need for that. Savannah will be working for me."

He dug his fork into his omelet and didn't look left or right. He could feel Savannah's amusement as she shoved the four hundred-dollar bills across the table in his direction, accepting his offer and sealing his fate.

Chapter Four

"You sure this room will be good enough for you?"

Savannah set her satchel on the foot of the bare mattress and tried to gaze around the room. Her senses seemed strangely attuned to the mountain of a man who was shouldering her trunk to the floor. There was a *thunk* as the trunk touched down and a slight scraping as Nate positioned it beneath the window.

That was thoughtful of him. His surly and disconcerting behavior aside, he did have moments where he was greatly thoughtful. The kindness was back in his eyes as he straightened and glanced around the room. "This probably isn't much like what you're used to."

"I'm used to a great deal, Mr. Brooks." She wasn't exactly sure what he thought of her, but he did not seem to have the best opinion about a woman's capabilities. Perhaps there was a good reason for that, perhaps not. It really wasn't her business. "I'm grateful for your help."

"I know, and you don't need to be." He rubbed the back of his neck, as if he were weighing what to say. "I think you got the wrong impression of me. I *am* sorry my father duped you. He had no right bringing you out here expecting so much."

It was hard not to see his sincerity. He might be gruff and disagreeable, but he had a good heart. She thought of the man from the letters. She could see a glimmer of the deeper man written there. "I did have rather high expectations, but this isn't the first disappointment in my life."

"You wanted to be married that badly?"

"Bad enough to marry a stranger?" Oh, she could see what he was thinking. She opened her satchel and pulled out the thick stack of parchment. "We corresponded every week, you and I. For nearly a year. There are exactly sixty-nine letters from you."

"From my dad, you mean."

"Yes. He has about the same number of letters from me."

Nate fingered the edge of the bow. "This was a courtship, wasn't it? This was no rash decision to come marry a stranger."

"No." She sank onto the edge of the mattress. "I already miss that man."

"You mean my dad."

"No, you. I think your dad posed as you. He didn't write me as himself. He told me everything about you—"

"Everything?" Nate rubbed at his forehead as if it were paining him. "What exactly did he tell you?"

"About the time you were ten and you decided you were running away from home to go live like a mountain man."

That put a crack in his granite face. A little hint of a grin tugged at his unforgiving mouth. That mouth no longer looked as hard as stone. She wondered if those lips knew how to smile. Knew how to kiss.

Kiss? Heat flared across her face. Where had that thought come from?

"I packed a bag and took the ax." He lifted the stack of letters from her hands, looking at them as if they were a curiosity.

"You had packed two books, a batch of your ma's oatmeal cookies and your dog Puddles." Savannah had loved imagining the ten-year-old Nate trekking off, dragging the heavy ax behind him. But this big grizzly of a man didn't look as if he had ever been a child. "I know about the time you broke both arms and a leg protecting your little brother from a mountain lion."

Nate ran his thumb down the stack of letters. His dark hair fell forward, hiding his eyes. "I got in a lucky shot, or we both would have been dead."

"You still have the scars from the lion's claws."

"I do." He looked surprised as he rolled up his sleeve. His scars were like a house cat's scratch but ten times wider and deeper. Even softened by the down of his hair, the scar tracks were thick and webby, as if they'd had a hard time healing. They disappeared up his arm, under the fold of his sleeve.

"You know my secrets." Nate leaned closer as he set the bunch of letters on the bed at her side. "I don't like that."

"No, because you don't know mine." She thought of the other secrets she knew of his; the ones his father had shared with her. More painful ones. Ones of loss and heartache. If she mentioned them, would he open up to her? Or would he pull away?

He crouched down on the floor in front of her, and the stance only emphasized the coiled strength in his broad shoulders and hard body. He looked all man. Savannah gulped, realizing that he had blocked her in, and her pulse kicked faster in her chest. Every inch of her seemed to warm, as if aware of his masculinity.

No, she thought in dismay. *I don't want to be attracted to this man.*

He splayed his hands on the mattress on either side of her thighs, caging her in, bringing with him the warm male scent of his skin. "What are your secrets, Miss Knowles?"

"You and I are well-acquainted, Nate. Perhaps we should be on a first name basis."

"You know I haven't read a single one of your letters, which means I've got a few questions about you."

"Oh, are you wondering about me?"

"Not like you think." But a light came into his eyes and twinkled, showing a softer side to the mountain man. "I want to know something about the woman who will be working in my store. Handling my money. Waiting on my customers. I have a business to think of."

"As I'm desperate enough to court any man who sends me a

letter, I can see how you might be worried." Savannah heard the coy tone of her voice and could not believe it. Was she really teasing this man? Wasn't that like playing with fire?

A tiny crook of amusement curved his mouth. "That's a good question. Tell me why."

She brushed her hand over the letters, lingering over the ribbon she'd tied so lovingly around them. "I saw something into the letters your father wrote for you. Something real and wondrous and rare. My grandmother was dying, the rest of my family who cared about me had passed on, and here were your letters, so full of love for your family. And I thought—"

There were darker blue specks in his blue irises and they were all she could see. His magnetic pull had drawn her closer so that she could notice the texture of his stubble dark against his skin and the compassion crinkling the corners of his eyes. She couldn't seem to look anywhere else.

"And your grandmother?" he asked.

"She passed away three months ago. It took a while to settle her estate." She heard her voice falter and forced the dark memories of that time from her thoughts, but not fast enough.

Nate's eyebrows arched in a question, and there was surprising gentleness in his gravelly baritone. "You had a hard time. I can see that in you. You loved her very much."

"I adored her. Letting her go was the hardest thing I ever had to do. She raised me after—" She dropped her gaze. "After the war."

"You must have been very young."

"My papa and brother fell on the battlefield. My mama and my older sister were—" She fell silent.

"I was an infantryman under Grant when he marched through the South," he said into the silence. "I was young even for a soldier, but I can guess what happened to them."

"Mama locked me in the attic. We had been upstairs making the beds. She told me to sit still and be quiet, and went down to check on my sister ironing downstairs."

He could see it all, how it probably happened, the brutality of some villains who masqueraded behind the uniform, and what happened to innocent women. "I want you to know I was never one of those men."

"I know." A single tear hovered in her thick lashes. "I know there are two kinds of men in this world. The ones who do whatever they can get away with, and the kind who stand for what is right."

"Now don't start thinking I'm the noble sort."

"No, of course not. I won't let anyone know that your bark is worse than your bite."

So, she had him figured out, did she? Nate would have to be on guard against that. He drew back and stood, but he couldn't pretend that he wasn't affected by her and what she had been through. She was alone in the world. Thinking of his brothers and his doting—even if they were sometimes meddlesome—parents, he couldn't imagine what that had to be like.

She looked like a picture, sitting on the edge of the bed, with her hair a tangle from the wind outside and the stray strands curling in the heat around her delicate face. She had the bluest eyes. As she blinked away her tears, they sparkled like little bits of a Montana sapphire. His chest fluttered with feeling.

Don't let yourself start caring, man. He tamped down the flutter. Stilled the feeling. Caring led to all kinds of trouble, and he was a smart enough man not to take the first step down that road. He forced his feet to carry him to the door to make his escape.

"I've got it arranged with both the boardinghouse's dining room and the one at the hotel we ate at this morning to put your meals on a tab. That way, if you're short on funds until payday, you needn't worry about it."

"That was thoughtful of you, Nate." She smiled, just a little, just a touch, but there were dimples in her cheeks.

Her rosebud-soft lips drew more than his gaze, so that he stumbled as he stepped into the hallway. His pulse went crazy, right along with his breathing, and his thoughts, his traitorous thoughts, had him wanting to slant his mouth to hers and taste that sweet smile.

Oh, hell. He'd best get out of here before he started to imagine her doing more than sitting on the foot of that bed. The way she looked, so sweet and wind-tossed, was a heady combination. But she seemed unaware of her beauty and of her effect on him, a poor, lonely man. That said something good about her, too.

For some reason his boots seemed nailed to the floorboards. "You need me to light the fire for you?"

The question came out abrupt, more like a bark than anything, but Savannah's smile became bigger and more dazzling. His crazy pulse kicked into an all-out gallop.

"No, thank you." She stood and the fabric of her skirts cascaded downward to twirl around her ankles, giving him a hint of long, lean thighs beneath those layers of petticoats and ruffles. She unbelted the sash of her unbuttoned coat. "Should I come over to the store after I get settled?"

"Come. To the store." Her request ricocheted around his head like a bullet in his brain.

"You hired me, remember?"

Remember? Sure he could, if his mind started working again. He couldn't think beyond the realization that she would be in his store all day long at his side, making his pulse thud like a herd of stampeding bison.

"Nate, you haven't changed your mind, have you?"

He read her concern like the beat of his own heart. Why did the cute crinkle in her forehead trouble him so much? Make him want to reassure her? To take care of her?

"If you would rather wait until tomorrow morning to start, that would be fine with me. It'll be slow today, anyway. Folks don't come to town much in cold like this."

"Forty degrees below zero? No, I would think not." She swept toward him as she shrugged out of her coat. The dress she wore, a soft pink wool, draped her like a glove. Hugging her carved shoulders and slender arms, caressing her fine bosom and clinching her narrow waist. The fall of fabric over her hips and thighs made his teeth ache with fascination.

Why this woman? He'd never experienced this instant fire— not lust and not heat, but something deeper, something more—

before, and it was likely to panic him. He took a few stumbling steps backward down the hall, wanting to get away from her while he still had all of his wits about him.

Still unaware, she followed him to the door and laid her hand on the door frame, her soft, slender, lovely hand. Why was his runaway libido taking off like a train down a mountain slope and imagining that hand on his chest?

"Nate?" She watched him innocently. "If the store is quiet today, wouldn't it be a better time for me to learn?"

More panic cannoned through him. "You don't want to get settled?"

"I have this evening to unpack and get situated."

If a tiny part of him deep inside wanted to like her, to be kinder to her, he was too afraid to do it. When a man cared like that about a woman, it made him weak. It made him vulnerable.

So if his voice boomed like angry thunder when he answered her, he couldn't let that bother him. He hadn't written her. He didn't want her. He wasn't a marrying kind of man.

"I don't want you there today." His words echoed around him as he turned and walked away, alone and safe, once again. "But I'll probably stay upstairs most of the day unless a customer happens by. Weather like this means a rare day of rest for me."

"I see."

"Tomorrow morning will be soon enough."

"Fine, then." He could have it his way. Savannah's temple throbbed and she rubbed at it a few times with her fingertips. A headache was building. "You open at eight o'clock?"

"Sharp." He had reached the stairwell at the far end of the hallway and spun on his boots, as if he had something on his mind, something he wanted to say to her. His throat worked. His jaw ground. "You'll be okay on your own?"

"Don't waste any worry on me. I'm a grown woman and I can take care of myself." She had done it before. She would do it again. His message could not have been clearer. He gave her one last look, one of pity, before he disappeared down the stairs, out of her sight.

Not out of her thoughts. He'd given her the job because he had felt sorry for her. Her chin rose up. Her jaw clenched. She closed the door behind her. There sat his letters on the bed where she'd left him. The look on his face when he had touched that stack of his father's stories had lingered in her mind. There had been love in his eyes—for his father.

Love. Now she understood better. Nate's father had written her with love in his heart for his son, for Nate had been wounded by love. The father's hope was that another love could make Nate whole again.

Yes, this she could see. She crossed the small room, weaving around the trunk he'd set against the wall and pulled back the edge of the crisp, white curtain. The glass panes were wreathed in ice, but there was a clear spot she could see through. Tiny flakes of snow fluttered like lost wishes to the ground below. She had a view of Second Street and the vacant lots across the road, and beyond to the white-frosted evergreens and jagged mountaintops knocking against the icy, mantled sky.

There Nate was, on the street below, striding through the high drifts, blazing a new trail through the downfall back toward his store.

There goes the man I wanted to love. She could not stop the yearning or her heart's memory of Nate Brooks. A memory she had to let go of. She was safe, she was healthy, this was not the end of the world. No, she thought as Nate held up one hand in greeting to someone driving by in a horse-drawn sled. She'd had her world end many times before—thinking of Grandmama, of her mother and sister, of the news when her father's and brother's deaths came. This was nothing, nothing like that.

She took in one last look at Nate, her spirit aching in places she did not know existed, and let the curtain fall. She had come so far with hope in her heart. With wishes for a bright and happy future full of love and family.

She would not allow those dreams to fall like snow to the ground. In memory of her grandmother and of the family she had lost, she would not let this disappointment defeat her. She knelt before the hearth and looked around for the match tin—it was stowed on a small stone ledge—and struck the match. The moment the flame caught the crumpled newspaper in the grate, fire leaped and danced and celebrated.

As from one tiny flame the fire burned, so would her wishes, too. It was just going to be a different future than she imagined, but there was no reason she could not eventually find the love and family she wished for and the right man to share it with. She would have to trust what Grandmama always said, *Life takes you down a different path than you expect but to the right place in the end.*

This was the end of one path, she thought as she climbed to her feet, but not the end of her journey. Determined to take her grandmother's words to heart, she gathered up Nate's father's letters and stowed them in the corner of her trunk. Wind gusted cruelly against the window, driving cold straight into the room as she opened the wardrobe and began to unpack.

Who knew what good things lurked up ahead, and what path her life would take next? She couldn't wait to find out.

Chapter Five

She'd had worse jobs, Savannah thought as she swept the floor bright and early Monday morning. There had been that time she had worked for the Windemere family in Greenville, whose two little boys perpetually kicked everything in existence, including her. That had been a worse job, for those children had needed a lion tamer, not a governess. After constant bruises and endless frustration, Savannah had practically run from that home before she broke a shinbone.

Yes, the Windemere boys made working for Nate seem like a leisurely spring picnic. Although her employer had tersely shown her the coffee mill and the coffeepot, the broom, and then disappeared in the back in complete silence.

The cowbell over the door clanged, breaking into her thoughts. Her first customer? She squinted in anticipation as the low slant of sunlight illuminated a man's chunky form. The door shut, the man stepped deeper into the store and emerged from the sunshine. He had a mop of brown hair and friendly brown eyes, and nodded cordially.

"Howdy there, miss. I'm Austin Dermot. I own the livery stable across the way. I'm the local smithy."

"Oh, a blacksmith. A noble trade." Savannah, having grown up around horses, was acquainted with the skill of the craft. "It's nice to meet you, Mr. Dermot. I'm Savannah, and I—"

"You hail from Charleston. I know all about it." Austin bobbed his head again. "Hard thing to come all this way."

"Y-you know about me?"

"Sure. My brother was hanging around the depot the other night waiting for a delivery, but it didn't come. I hear nothin' did except you." Austin Dermot strode closer and helped himself to a cup on the shelf behind the stove. He poured himself a cup, as Nate said customers were wont to do. "Nate's pa apologize to you yet?"

"No." Savannah leaned the broom against the wall. How many people in this town would know how she'd been duped? Heat grew tight across her face. "What can I help you with today, Mr. Dermot?"

"Runnin' low on oats—"

The cowbell clanged as the door blew open like a gunshot and a tall, rangy man strode in with the jangle of spurs. A cowboy, she thought, as she studied the man who looked as if he'd ridden right out off the range. Another customer? Nate's business must be healthier than his father had let on.

"Miss." The cowboy knuckled back his hat. "I was wonderin' if I mightn't ask for your help with—"

Boots knelled on the floorboards behind her and suddenly there was Nate, his jaw set and drawn up like a bear looking for a fight. "Colby. Grab a fifty pound sack of oats off the stack there by the door, and I'll add it to your tab."

"Nate, no need to be rude about it." Austin Dermot gave Savannah an understanding look. "Add this to my account, Nate. Miss Savannah, it was mighty fine meetin' you."

Savannah thanked the blacksmith and tried to figure out what had put Nate in a worse mood. Maybe she hadn't waited on the customers promptly. Not that he'd mentioned how she was to do that. Yet.

"Keep up with your sweeping." Nate sidestepped her, avoiding her as if she were a carrier of bubonic plague, and went to speak with the cowboy at the far corner of the store.

She grabbed the smooth wooden handle and negotiated the broom across the rough floorboards. Sweeping was a long way from governess work, but she supposed there was little need for governesses here. Maybe she would travel out to California, where there were prosperous families who would want private instruction for their children. When she earned enough for a train fare, that is.

Poor Nate looked as if he didn't understand she really would be out of his life as soon as she could manage it. She watched him as she worked, noting the hard set line of his shoulders, the tensed muscles in his neck and jaw and the appalled look darkening his face.

Tenderness tugged in her heart. She could not help caring about him. What harm could come from that? It wasn't as if she were going to fall in love with him all over again.

The cowbell clanged and a third man stumbled in from the bitter cold, flocked with a fine layer of white, as if he had been riding for many miles.

"Mornin'." Tiny flakes of snow sifted from his hat brim when he removed it. "If I had knowed such a purty woman was comin', then I reckon I would of written for one, too."

She supposed that was a compliment of sorts. "Thank you, sir. Would you like some coffee? You look quite frozen."

"Yes'm." The man's eyes widened like saucers, watching her with a dazed look about his round, clean-shaven face.

Getting him a cup of fresh brewed coffee was the least she could do, since the floor was not about to get any cleaner with these men tracking in snow and ice. She would see to the floor later. Nate had his back to her, speaking intently with the cowboy near the door. She filled the battered blue speckled cup and handed it over.

The cowbell clattered again, and this time it was a man with an Abraham Lincoln beard and a wad of tobacco tucked against his protruding cheek.

"Howdy, miss." He tipped his hat, speaking around the plug. "That coffee smells mighty good. You make it?"

"Guilty." She handed the cup to the frosty man and reached down for another cup. She filled it, feeling every eye on her. The cowboy had turned to give her one last look and a nod over the top of his burlap sack of oats. The frozen man was watching her with that same dazed expression over the top of his rim—perhaps he had become too chilled on his ride in to town, she supposed. And the Mr. Lincoln look-alike was a tad shier, keeping watch on her through his lashes.

None of these men had the impact combined of the big bear of man who watched her with a scowl on his face as he stalked in her direction. No, Nate did not look pleased.

"Get your own coffee, Burton." Nate bit out the words, but instead of being harsh they were tempered with something that sounded like amusement.

How, Savannah wondered, could a man look both annoyed and amused at the exact same moment? She replaced the coffeepot, hung the hot pad on the wall hook and left the men to their drinks. The frosted man looked deeply grateful for the warmth as she swept by, following Nate, who looked even more irritated. Perhaps he had noticed the broom hugging the wall and the snow clumped all over his floor.

"It's not your job to serve them." That was gruff, too. "They're grown men perfectly capable of pouring their own coffee."

"I only thought to help."

He braced his wide palms on the scarred wooden counter, surveying his store and his customers. "We're mighty busy for ten minutes past eight when it's twenty-five degrees below zero."

"I hadn't realized you had such a thriving business."

"I hadn't realized it, either." Was he watching her out of the corner of his eyes? He was no longer scowling. "This is the busiest my store has been. Ever."

"Are people stocking up in case there's another storm?"

"I doubt it as we get storms like that all winter. It's April."

"Surely there won't be too many more storms."

"You never know in Montana's high country."

Was that a hint of a grin softening his stern mouth? And why was she noticing? Savannah shook herself. Didn't she have work to do? Nate's nearness blew through her like a penetrating blizzard's wind, although instead of being icy it was warm.

Yes, it was best to do anything to keep well away from Nate. She snatched up the broom, but suddenly he was there, his hand clasping the wooden handle, too. A scant inch separated their hands, and she felt his heat, hotter than her own.

"If you go wandering around for all of those men to ogle, they will never leave this store. Go look over the account book. It's there beneath the counter. I reckon a lady with a trunk full of books can figure out how the accounts work."

Why did her every nerve ending tingle from merely watching his mouth quirk up in the corners? "How did you know I brought books?"

"It takes one to know one." He pulled the broom from her grasp, stomping away from her, leaving her heart quivering.

Every bachelor in town had crowded around the stove to sip coffee and jaw, hoping to attract the lovely Savannah Knowles's attention, and Nate was sick of it. These men were friends, fellow townsmen and store owners. Didn't they have any dignity? Or at least anything better to do? What about their businesses?

He turned his back on Savannah, who looked pleasantly flushed as she took a partial payment on James Hadley's account. James sure looked like he was charmed by the pretty, dainty Southern belle marking down his five-dollar payment in the books. Never mind that he'd already made his monthly payment last week. Never mind that he was talking up his run-down ranch, sounding as if he owned the biggest spread in four counties.

Smitten. That's how Nate saw it. The big, dazed eyes. The puffed up chest. The straight-shouldered strut. There were ten men in his store, and all of them the same, talking louder over each other, each one with a bigger story to tell, watching Savannah with hope and a whole lot of love-struck foolishness.

Am I the only one immune to her charm?

Then he spotted the family sled pulling to a stop beside Burton's bay gelding. If it wasn't crowded enough in his store, Nate thought that it was about to be. He crashed through the door and into the vicious cold, mad at winter. That's what he was. He was sick of this weather and ready for spring. It was the stubborn snow *still* falling that had his temper whipped up into a fury. And nothing to do with the way Savannah smiled at James Hadley, listening intently to whatever the hell the man was saying to her.

Oh, hell. He was seeing red again. He didn't know what this hot, spiky feeling crammed into his chest was, but he didn't like it. He ought to be glad he had a circle of enamored bachelors in his shop. He *ought* to skip and sing down the damn street that Savannah had her pick of available men in this town. Maybe she could just take a shine to one of them, accept his ring and then Nate would be rid of her without a shred of guilt or a single regret.

"Son." Pa looped the reins around a hitching post. "Looks like you haven't cooled down none. Still got your temper up?"

"You know I do." Nate took over for his father, tying a knot as their cantankerous mare showed her teeth. "My temper's not likely to simmer down anytime soon."

"Just give it time." Pa seemed supremely sure of himself as he circled around to offer his wife his hand. "Spring comes, no matter how hard the winter."

"What exactly is that supposed to mean?" Nate gave the reins a tug; they would hold if the mare got feisty as she was known to do. "Are you thinking I'll come to my senses and marry that woman?"

Ma popped out of the sleigh with her hand firmly in Pa's and a smile on her apple-cheeked face. "That's our dearest hope, Nathaniel."

Oh, hell. "And you admit it. That's the worst of it. You're actually proud of what you've done."

"Is that Savannah?" Ma froze on the boardwalk, staring openly through the window. "She's lovelier than her tintype. Jake, can't you just see our little grandchildren with those blond curls?"

Grandchildren? Panic hit him like a spring avalanche. What was wrong with his parents? Was this a new sort of brain fever, of which the first signs of illness were delusions of grandchildren?

"Enough." Nate bit out the command. "I don't want one word about this to Savannah. Since you're here—"

"We had to see her," Ma interrupted.

"—You will apologize to her for bringing her all this way." He went on as if his mother hadn't interrupted him. "She's devastated that you lied to her. You made her hope—"

"For a family." Pa slung his arm around Ma's shoulders. "We know. Don't you think she's a beauty? We did good, Mary."

"We surely did. Such a sad story how she's lost all of her family. Nate, here, I have something for you." Ma stopped to fuss with his collar and then slipped something into his pocket.

A very thick something. He stared down at the folds of parchment, feeling the horror burn like fire through his skin. "Are these Savannah's letters?"

"She wrote them to you, dear. All her love for you is right in there. All the proof you need."

"She wrote them to you and Pa. You take them back."

"Sorry, but no, or you're not invited to Sunday suppers for the next year."

"What?" This lunacy had gone far enough. Ma was actually smiling, and as for Pa, he looked like a peacock strutting toward the store's front door. "Promise me you'll apologize to her."

All either of his parents did was grin at him and hurry into the shop. The door swung behind them—in his face. Had they shut him out? Nate stared at his reflection in the glass. Had they forgotten him in their haste to meet their beloved Savannah?

"Hey, big brother." There was Joseph, striding up behind him. "What are ya standin' around for? Gee, is that Savannah? Is that her?"

Did he have to say it as if she were an angel who had fallen down from heaven right along with the snow? "No," he ground out. "That's some other woman I'm burdened with."

"Don't see her as much of a burden. Nosirree!" Joseph let out a whistle. "Are you sure you don't want her?"

There was the red haze again, staining his eyes, staining everything. He wasn't sure of a single thing—not anymore. His head buzzed as Joseph shoved past him and through the door, the cowbell clanging like a warning. Through the glint on the window glass, there was Ma, wrapping her arms around Savannah and holding on as if she were her long-lost daughter. Were those tears in Savannah's eyes as she accepted the woman's loving welcome? The sight drew him closer, out of the winter's cold and into the store's warmth.

She melted right before his eyes like butter on a hot skillet. Her careful poise, her set chin, her graceful demeanor all slipped away as she held on to his mother, nodding in acknowledgment to whatever it was the older woman was saying. The sadness slipped from her eyes and the loneliness from her soul. He longed to hold her like that and comfort her until all her sadness was gone forever—

Whoa there, man. He put the rein in his feelings before they could turn into thoughts. No, best just to let them die a silent death. He was not about to start caring for a woman who was as sure to leave him as Adella had. Savannah was prettier, sweeter, finer. Didn't all the men in his store prove that to him? She could have her pick of them. So, best just to let her at it, stay out of the mess and resist any feelings for her.

"Nate." Joseph clapped his hand on Nate's shoulder. "Looks like you've got a bushel of trouble. Look how much Ma loves her. You can deny it all you want. It's my guess Ma has you married off by June."

"Let her try." Nate opened the door for his brother. He wasn't afraid. Ma could do her worst and *nothing* was going to break his resolve.

He was never going to love Savannah Knowles because he refused to. He was staying in control of his feelings. And it didn't matter how pretty or nice or fine Savannah was, he was going to be untouched by her. He was frozen tundra in winter. He was the deepest heart of the strongest mountain in the Rocky Mountain Range. He was immovable.

Nate followed his brother into the store, refusing to feel the tug in his chest when Savannah found his gaze over the top of his ma's head and smiled.

Chapter Six

"You're just adorable." Mary Brooks clung to Savannah's hand as if they'd just met, although they were just finishing up lunch at the hotel's dining room—Jake, Nate's father, had insisted. "I can't get over how perfect you are for our dear Nate."

Savannah blushed. Mary's high hopes for a marriage had not dipped at all. Since there was no way she could wrench her hand free without being rude, she let the woman cling to her a moment longer. "I'm far from perfect. Did you hear the news that Nate has refused to marry me?"

"I did hear something along those lines, but I don't believe it." Mary's blue eyes twinkled as if with a superior knowing. "I do hope you can forgive us for our deception."

"Don't do it. Don't forgive them." Nate glowered from across the table, as intimidating as she imagined a snarling male cougar might look. "They aren't sorry. Not one bit. They don't deserve your forgiveness for what they did to you. To both of us."

A secret little wish swelled up from her soul. Impossible, and she knew it. Hadn't she decided that she would look forward and not back? And certainly not at Nathaniel Brooks? She drew herself up straighter in her chair. "Not to worry, Nate, for I am also determined not to marry *you*."

Reaction to that bit of news traveled around the table. Vaguely

Savannah heard the younger brother's, "Tough luck, Nate!" The bellow of surprise from Jake and the laugh of amusement from Mary. The look of admiration and gratitude that marked Nate's handsome face hooked her like a thread in a needle.

"Thank you." He mouthed the words, and his silent thanks cut like a blade through the chaos around the table.

A tiny little glow burst to life directly beneath her heart. Affection surged through her. She didn't want it. She had to stop it. She tried to tamp it down, but the bright tenderness she felt stubbornly took root.

Look forward, Savannah, and not at what you've lost. She took a steadying breath and gathered up every last scrap of her resolve. She did not want a man who did not want her; it was as simple as that. What would happen if she could not stay the affection in her heart?

Mary spoke above the noise at the table. "I know our Nate can be as growly as a bear rousted from his cave come spring, but you have to know he's got a good side, too."

"A good side?" Savannah fought to keep solemn. "I've seen no evidence of that. Certainly I've seen his bad side."

Across the table from her, Nate's mouth fought to keep from breaking into a grin. His eyes glinted with amusement.

"Nathaniel James Brooks!" his mother scolded. "I raised you better than that."

"Son, you and I need to have us a little chat." His father's deep baritone resonated with gravity.

Savannah had to bite the inside of her lip to keep from laughing. "After meeting Nate, I've decided he simply will not suit. It's just as well that you wrote the letters, Mr. Brooks, as I would have rejected Nate anyway. Even if he had wanted to marry me."

"Sad," Nate agreed as he took one long pull of coffee. He set the cup down with a clatter, joining her in turning the table on his parents. "It's a good thing we didn't really correspond. My heart might have been broken."

Savannah loved the way his eyes filled with life and laughter. Gone was the stone-cold man with the granite heart. This was another glimpse of the real Nate Brooks with an actual sense of humor. She couldn't help but like him more.

"But *I* wrote the letters." Mary's confession brought silence to the table.

"You?" Savannah shook her head. "No, the handwriting was very manly. You couldn't have faked that, Mary. I'm sure you have dainty, lovely penmanship."

"Thank you, dear." Mary blushed. "I mean to say, I made up the letters and Jake copied my words down in the letters. Bringing you here was something we decided to do. We chose your advertisement out of that hands and heart newspaper together."

"As partners of a true marriage ought to." Savannah nodded with what looked like understanding. "I see why I fell in love with your letters. They were written with such love. I thought it was love for me. I was mistaken."

Now Nate knew why Savannah had come all this way on a hope and on a written promise. She hadn't come to marry; she had come for love. To be loved. Shame filled him. Compared to her open, willing heart, he felt too hard and too cold, as remote and as lifeless as the mountains in winter. With all her losses, she still sought love. She had known a different kind of pain in burying so many loved ones, and still she'd come to risk more.

She's braver than me by far. Respect brimmed through him, leaving no room to breathe. He sat mesmerized by the willowy wisp of a woman in her dainty spring-green dress and rose-pink ribbons. Her golden hair fell in ringlets, full and free, cascading over her shoulders and firm breasts, a place he could not seem to look beyond. He closed his eyes, tucked his chin and when he opened his eyes, he had the relief of looking at his plate.

He had not expected to be so attracted to this woman his parents had picked out for him. To make matters worse, his desire for her was growing, so to speak, in a whole new way.

Maybe it was his mother's earlier mention of grandchildren, or maybe because if he had met Savannah on his own, he would want her. He had slept last night in the bed she had lain in. Picturing her on his bed, with her hair fanning his pillow, with her naked beneath her nightclothes on his sheets still was driving him beyond reason.

Rein it in, Brooks. He swallowed the hot burst of anger. If he kept going like this, he'd find himself a weak mess of a man who was a victim to his treacherous needs. Still, he had a feeling it was going to be hard to resist this overriding desire for Savannah.

"I did write those letters with love," Ma was saying, clasping Savannah by the hands again until her knuckles were white. "I put all my heart into those words. I wanted you to love my boy as much as I do. I wanted you to feel the affection this family has for you."

Savannah's eyes filled but not one single tear fell. Nate sat captivated by it and by the longing that seemed to light her from the inside. She was luminous, too lovely and rare to be real. Too wonderful not to believe in.

This was not a woman who toyed with a man's tender affections. He thought of all the men who had patronized his store all morning, who had hung around hoping for encouragement from Savannah. All of them had, of course, already heard the gossip that she was not his fiancée. Not once had she shown anything but polite interest and regard in any of them. She had been courteous and prim and polite and not coy. No, never that. She was not just a quality lady and a nice woman, but she was good to the core.

That goodness looped like a lasso and cinched around his heart. He braced his feet on the floor, fighting to resist it. He *had* to resist it.

"I'll get the bill." He spotted Thelma at a far table and gestured to his empty cup. "Why don't you all go on? I'll just take a minute to have another cup of coffee in peace and quiet."

Ma scolded him. Joseph chuckled as he climbed to his feet. Pa gave him another disapproving look. Nate didn't mind. What mattered was Savannah's quiet understanding as he pulled out the store key from his jacket pocket and leaned forward to place it in her palm.

She had such small hands. So soft and sensitive. Hands he could imagine stroking across him in the dark of the night with a sensitive brush of fingertips and a rasp of fingernails and the caress of her satin skin against his. Heat flared in his veins, and he gulped in air.

"I think you're safe now," she whispered beneath the noises of his parents rising from the table. "They believe that I don't want you."

His gaze locked on her petal-soft lips, so lush and full. A zing of heat spilled into his blood. Would her kiss taste as sweet as she looked? Blood thrummed in his veins and in other parts of his body. Good thing the tablecloth was hiding his reaction.

Her blue gaze was searching his. "You won't be long?"

"N-no." At least he hoped not.

"Good. Please don't leave me alone in the store with all those eager men." There was her humor again, making her eyes bluer and her loveliness more dazzling. "I've already had four requests to come calling."

"With any luck, you won't need to work in my store for long." He tempered his voice, taking care so she knew he meant it kindly.

"I plan to only marry for love. Not convenience. But still, you never know. Maybe I will find my true love in this little town after all." She gave a shrug of one slender shoulder, gathered up her reticule and coat and hurried toward his parents, who were waiting for her.

The swish of her skirt around her fanny drew his gaze like a boulder on a downhill roll. He distantly knew that Thelma was refilling his cup, but it didn't register. All he could see was Savannah as she shrugged into her coat. All he could hear was Savannah's gentle alto as she spoke merrily to his mother. Her lilac scent seemed to cling to him long after she had gone from his sight.

He took a sip of hot coffee, scorching his tongue, drinking steadily until he felt his pulse return to normal. Until his veins quit throbbing. It took a long, long time.

She'd only said that about finding a man here in Moose, Montana Territory, to put Nate at ease. But the thought gnawed at her like a pack of mosquitoes as she crossed First Street, being careful of the snow, and unlocked the store's front door. As she flipped the Closed sign to Open and stowed her cloak and reticule in the back room, his reaction—a dark scowl—came to mind.

Did he reject the notion of true love so completely? The flash of the sunlight on the window winked at her as she emerged into the front of the shop like a sign of hope. Nate was a sad case, and she knew why. *I got my heart good and broke,* Mary posing as Nate had written. *I loved Adella truly, and yet she left me for a richer fellow. Money—not me—was what mattered to her.*

Nate's hurt remained, and this Adella had gone on with her life, finding what she wanted with a richer man. In a mountain town as small as this one, was this woman someone Nate saw regularly on the street? Would this richer man be a customer? Wouldn't seeing the couple together hurt Nate even more? No wonder he was embittered. No wonder he was determined never to trust another woman with his heart.

There was Nate—her gaze found him through the sunbeams. That tough, swaggering walk of his befitted a rugged mountain man. That powerful set of his shoulders and the fall of his strong arms made her stomach flutter. His ever-present scowl marked a face that was strikingly handsome in spite of the downturn of his mouth and the glare of his eyes. Caring for him seeped into every inch of her being.

Caring about him wasn't the same as falling in love with him, she reminded herself as she wrapped her arms around her middle. She couldn't help liking him. Why, she wasn't exactly sure, as he could be growly and distant, but there was no accounting for taste. If her heart ached a little for him when he pushed open the door, she ignored the sting of it.

"I am sorry about my ma." He looked pained. He looked embarrassed. "I don't know what has gotten into her. At first I thought she just wanted to see me married, but now she's talking about grandbabies."

"I counted. She mentioned babies seven times during the meal and twice during dessert."

"Jeez. I wish—" He grimaced as if in pain. "I'm sorry you had to endure that."

"It's not your fault. I can see now why your parents did such a thing. They love you so deeply."

"If they did, then they would understand how much this is tearing at me." His scowl deepened. He shook his head and stalked across the room to the stove. He knelt and went to work adding wood. He worked fast, keeping his back to her.

She saw it in his stance, felt it in the very air, heard it in his silence. He was hurting. "They think if you find someone new to love and marry, then you will stop hurting."

He froze. The chunk of wood he held tumbled from his fingers and thudded against the floor. Shock thinned his voice. "You know about Adella?"

"Those secrets, remember?" She yearned to go to him and lay her hand on his wide shoulders. To caress away the hurt. "Your ma wrote about how she left you for a lawyer."

"A wealthy lawyer." Bitterness flavored his words.

It wasn't only bitterness she heard, but the broken pieces of his heart chinking together like shards of glass. How deeply he must have loved this woman. Savannah felt a touch of awe and respect for this man with such a big heart.

"Ma had no right telling you about that." He looked rigid as he picked up the fallen piece of wood and tossed it into the fire. The flames writhed greedily and he shut the door against them. When he drew himself up to his full height, he seemed even taller somehow, and stronger. "Life goes on, and I'm glad I found out what she was like before it was too late."

He's hiding the pain, she thought. Denying it. Making it sound as if he were past it. What did you do when your heart was nothing but pieces? How could it go back together again?

"You look so sad." He towered before her, watching her with unmistakable concern.

He really was a good man. Her chest filled with tenderness for him. This was more than simple caring, she realized. It was definitely more. "I wish there was something—anything—I could do for you. You didn't deserve to be hurt like that."

"No more than you deserved to lose your grandmother or

your entire family." He leaned closer still, until she could see the pure gentleness in his intense, dark blue gaze. "Your heart is in pieces, too."

He knew. Her hand flew to her chest as if to hide the rest of what she didn't want him to see. "We have this in common."

"We do. Maybe that's why I like you so much."

"You l-like me?" Her chest tightened. "I thought you hated me."

"I want to hate you. There's a difference."

The glimmer of a smile, mixed with the endless gentleness in his eyes, hit her like a speeding train. Her heart gave a single bump of warning before it fell impossibly in one long, slow glide.

You don't love him, she told herself resolutely. She took a step back and bumped into the counter. "I've decided I don't like you, either. As least, as far as your parents are concerned."

"That was a brilliant tactic." He leaned close, so close she could see the texture of his skin and the softness of his firm lips. "I owe you for that."

"Just trying to do the right thing."

"Yes, the right thing." His gaze slid across her face, searching the deep-set eyes and the curl of lashes. Her skin was like cream. And her lips were as ripe as wild strawberries in midsummer. Heat spilled into his blood and skidded through his veins. His mouth tingled with the wish to lean a smidgen closer until their breaths mingled. Until his lips settled on hers with a hungry kiss.

Need hit him like a summer storm. Desire bolted through him like lightning. His pulse thundered in his ears and for one tempting second he imagined kissing the pretty, proper Savannah Knowles until she clung to him with her gentle hands and moaned his name.

The cowbell clattered like a herd of steers clamoring through. Nate jerked away just as he heard the rumble of men's voices. One look was all it took to see the next batch of Moose, Montana's, bachelors parade into his store. These were the ones who lived far out of town who, by the looks of them, had taken time this morning to gussy up before making the long ride in to get a look at Savannah. Word sure traveled fast.

"I've got a shipment coming in on the afternoon train." Nate grabbed his driving gloves from the shelf behind the counter. "Joseph will be over in a few minutes. He works afternoons here."

"Yes." She watched him with big doe eyes, so luminous and vulnerable his soul flipped right over.

He grimaced again, hating that he'd almost kissed her, hating worse that she'd known it. That probably half the men gathering around the stove had seen his near attempt through the front windows. "I'll be back in a while. You need me to get you anything?"

"A cattle prod." She whispered the words as she gestured toward the men trying to get a good look at her over the tops of the stacked bags of rolled oats.

"Sorry. All out of those." He had to fight to keep the grin off his face. "But I have a lasso under the counter."

Her chuckle was a soft, musical trill, one that stuck to him like a barb wire as he walked away. He despised the rise of conversation as he closed the door behind him. He loathed the notion that so many men—good men, decent men—were so eager to meet Savannah.

They were in there right now, he thought as he drew on his gloves, looking at her with their hot eyes. Wondering about her sweet mouth. Noticing the firm rise of her breasts and the flare of her hips. Why wouldn't every last one of them be overwhelmed with the insane urge to kiss her for the next thousand years without stopping? It was how he felt. It was what he wanted.

No, accept it, man. You want to do more than to kiss her. He tripped down the boardwalk and crossed the slushy street. The wind hitting him had a warm blush to it. The tinkle of water ran off the roof and softened the ice at his feet. Nate drew in the sweet, unmistakable scent of coming spring and let himself in the back door of the livery stable. Looked like a new season was on its way.

Chapter Seven

He hadn't been about to kiss her, had he? Savannah wondered as she recorded Mr. Langley's purchase in the account book. Little curls of happiness ribboned within her at the notion. Kissing Nate would be…well, she wasn't sure what that would be like as she'd never kissed a man before. If her grandmama could be trusted, kissing the right man was like floating on a warm cloud in a bright sky.

But was Nate Brooks the right man? Savannah set down the pencil and closed the thick book, remembering how his lips had hovered over hers and anticipation beat between them. Right man or not, she wouldn't mind being kissed by him.

"Miss Savannah." Walton Langley tipped his cap to her. "I'd be most obliged if you would permit me to take you driving Sunday afternoon."

Savannah sank at his words. This was the fifth well-intentioned request. The man across the counter was very pleasant looking, with a solid, can-do look to him, but she didn't feel anything for him, nothing at all compared to what Nate Brooks had made her feel. How was she going to go forward with her life if she kept looking back and wanting what she could not have?

"I'm sorry, Mr. Langley. I appreciate your invitation, but I cannot accept."

"You probably already got plans. I knew you did." He gave her a sad smile and shrugged in a masculine, honest gesture. "I lived so far out of town that I couldn't get here sooner to ask."

"I haven't accepted anyone's invitation." She tried to explain as gently as she could. "I need to settle the last of this mistaken business with the Brookses before I can in good conscience start seeing another man."

"That seems right." Walton Langley nodded once, and he seemed steadied by that news. "I'll ask you at a later time."

"Good day to you, Mr. Langley."

"To you, too." He tipped his cap again, looking a little flustered, before hefting the two-hundred-pound sack of corn onto his shoulder. He walked out of the store handily, as if he lifted more weight every day so this was nothing at all.

He looked like just the kind of man she had been looking for. Good, hardworking, honest and kind. Except for one thing: He wasn't Nate.

Footsteps knelled behind her. Joseph sidled up to the counter and leaned against it on his forearms. "Looks like every bachelor in a day's driving distance has visited the store today. How many marriage offers have you gotten?"

"Only two, but five others have wanted to come courting." She understood what might motivate these men, who lived in this small, isolated town where work was hard and the country harder. They wanted love and family, the same as she did. "Isn't Nate back yet?"

"I think he's avoiding the place."

Yes, she had guessed as much. Was he avoiding her because he'd almost kissed her? Was he keeping busy elsewhere, regretting that act with every fiber of his being?

"All the men prancing around you trying to get your attention has put him in a bad mood." Joseph grinned at her. "I think Ma and Pa took great care choosing you from that newspaper. I remember, oh, a year and a half ago or so, I walked into the kitchen late at night, thinking to sneak myself a piece of apple pie Ma had made, and there they were, poring over something with their heads together. I couldn't make out what they were saying, but boy, they sounded happy. I think they were deciding on writing to you."

Yes, she could envision it. Rosy-cheeked Mary and shy Jake conspiring together at the kitchen table. "You and Nate are lucky to have the parents you do."

"No arguments there. They did a remarkable job with you. Nate likes you."

"And I like Nate." Sure, she liked him, she told herself, bracing for the truth. She *more* than liked him. "But I meant what I said in the dining room. I'll not have Nate Brooks. That's my final decision."

"I see." Joseph frowned. "And what's the reason for this reaction? I suppose a fancy Southern lady like yourself might have imagined something grand instead of this little feed store? Nate must be a disappointment, then?"

"How can you ask such a thing? This place is just what I expected. And so is Nate." The back of her neck buzzed, as if someone were standing behind her.

No, she realized, not someone. Nate. She turned, her eyes hungry to see him. "You're back."

"Sure I am, as my ears were burning." His baritone was layered with amusement, his grin wry. "Good thing I got back when I did. You two have been talking behind my back."

"Your brother has misunderstood the reason why I have decided never to marry you."

"Is that right?" He quirked one brow and folded his arms over his chest. "Little brother, what do you have to say for yourself?"

"Not a thing. Just wonderin' why you aren't good enough for her is all."

"You can't fool me." Nate barked out a laugh. He knew how it was to look at Savannah's lovely face and want to see her every day for the rest of his life. To wonder if her kiss might be the sweetest, hottest thing on this earth. To die a little wanting to hold her late into the night and make her cry out his name.

Yep, Nate thought, he knew just what his brother was thinking. "You were wondering that if Savannah doesn't want me, she might want you. Unless there's another reason that would put you out of consideration. Like not being rich enough."

"Wait, now, ah, that's not—" Joseph stumbled along. "Okay, maybe the thought did cross my mind. Savannah, you don't mind too much, do you?"

"I, ah—" She paled.

Nate nodded to her, to assure her. "The last pretty lady who came to this town was caught here in a blizzard on her way West, was engaged before the storm's end and was married within the month. That was three years ago, so you can see how it is around here."

"Even your brother?" She looked a little stunned.

"Yep. And if it's any guess, here comes my older brother for the same reason. You watch and see." He couldn't resist leaning closer to her to grab the inventory book on the counter. "I'll give you a ten cent raise if I'm right."

"And if you're wrong?"

"I won't be." He winked, confident that he would be paying her more than the low wage she'd insisted on—and thereby getting her out of his store faster—as his brother Gabriel ambled on up to the counter. He tipped his hat, eyeing up the pretty Savannah. He'd been on the trail, it was easy to see, covered with snow and damp. "Savannah, I'll leave you to introduce yourself. Let me know how it turns out."

"But—"

"Hey!" Gabriel called out as Nate dragged Joseph toward the door. "Where you going? I just got in."

"We've got oats to unload." And if he had to look at one more man trying to cozy up to Savannah, he was going to explode like a keg of dynamite—even if it was his brother.

Savannah was the last thing he saw as he closed the door. Her dainty profile. Her riot of golden curls. Her sweetness filling him right up. Good thing the back door was wide-open, letting in the blast of cool air. It washed over his heated face. Now if only it could chill his hot blood and drive the want for her from his soul.

* * *

"Well?"

Savannah warmed at the sound of Nate's voice echoing in the stillness. The store was closed—she flipped the sign around in the door and turned the bolt. "You were right. Gabriel had heard you and I were through, so he wanted to ask me to dinner."

"You are a popular lady."

"As you have pointed out, I'm one unmarried woman in a herd of men looking for a wife."

"That about sums it up." A dimple dug into his cheek. "I guess this means you get a raise. How about I treat you to supper?"

"It's not going to convince your mother and father that we are, well, you know."

She had a point, Nate reasoned. But the tally had been five dinner invitations at midday, and that hadn't counted the late afternoon crowd and his brother. He didn't feel right about letting her out on her own. Not that he was jealous—hell, no. But he had the right to be concerned for her. She was still his responsibility, after all. "How about I order out and bring supper to your room?"

"Perfect. Nate, I appreciate the company. I've eaten a lot of dinners alone."

"Me, too." It wasn't right, her being alone like that, without a man to love her and protect her. Without a man to take care of her and make sure she was happy. Why he felt he had to take care of her now only showed something was wrong with him. He would fix it if he could. "You want to come with me or go on ahead to your room?"

"What? And be seen with you? That would only encourage your parents."

She was right. He couldn't begin to explain why he wanted to be near her. She just— He didn't dare finish that thought. Just as he didn't dare look at her face because he was going to start thinking about kissing her again. What was wrong with him? He'd never been like this with Adella.

The memory of his past failure at love haunted him like an especially mean spirit as he followed Savannah out the back door. She had wrapped up in her cloak and he remembered the first night he'd laid eyes on her, in that traveling cloak and looking like no bundle he'd ever seen. In the soft twilight, she was so pretty, his teeth ached, as did other places he didn't much want to think about.

She waved to him as she took off to the music of the melting snow. His heart hitched after her—and he didn't want it to. He thought of that almost-kiss. He thought of the desire raging in his blood—the desire he was doing his damned best to ignore. He thought of what he'd heard her say to Joseph in the store. *This place is just what I expected. And so is Nate.*

No doubt about it, her words had weakened him. What was he going to do about his hunger for her? It seemed to get worse with every breath.

He couldn't escape her, even at the hotel. Thelma asked about her, saying that it was too bad when a couple had troubles and offered to console him. He politely declined. A few old-timers came over to warn him not to let a nice woman get away. If that wasn't enough, Adella was dining with her mother and sister—with her little son swaddled up and sleeping in a basket-cradle on the floor. He caught her glancing at him and he wondered what she'd heard. Another woman had found him less than desirable—less than worth it.

He fought not to give in to the humiliation. That didn't make it any easier for him as he slogged through the snowmelt with the hot package under his arm and went to knock on her door. He hesitated, fists raised. The truth was, love hurt. He was not interested in experiencing that condition again. The memory of this afternoon's near kiss gnawed at him. Why was he carried away by his own needs? He was a man of iron will. Why was she the only female to melt him into a puddle of liquid steel?

Footsteps shuffled in the hall behind him. Old Mrs. Wilkins shuffled down the hallway. "Nate Brooks, as I live and breathe. You are the last man I expected to see at Miss Savannah's door."

"Just bringing her supper, ma'am." Nate tipped his hat cordially. The gnawing sensation in his gut worsened. Did everyone in this town know his business? Didn't anyone have anything better to do than to speculate and gossip?

"Seems to me you're sweeter on the young lady than you want to admit." Her face wreathed into a lovely smile, and he was certain she was laughing as she ambled past.

Laughing at him. More humiliation hit him like snowmelt from a roofline. His knuckles rapped Savannah's door, and the sound felt hollow in the pieces of his heart. Don't make a mistake, he told himself. The two of them would work together to convince his mother her plan was an utter failure—so she wouldn't go doing it again once Savannah had earned the money she insisted on earning for her train ticket out of town. Theirs was a relationship of necessity, nothing more. She was going to leave. Those pieces within him felt emptier, hollower. There had never been any other way for this situation to end.

The door opened and there was Savannah, looking lovely in the lamplight, as golden and as fresh as a spring morning. "Nate. I want to show you this. Your mother left a note down at the front desk for me. Come read it."

Nate braced himself against the gentle trill of her voice. She sashayed across the small room toward the hearth where a newly lit fire crackled and danced. A terrible foreboding bit him like a hungry mountain lion. "What did my ma do now?"

Savannah's eyes sparkled with merriment. "She surely means well, and has such a loving heart."

He gulped. Right now he was getting mad at the woman who had birthed him, but he also remembered that Savannah had lost her ma as a girl. He set the wrapped meals down on the small table next to the window, keeping an eye on Savannah as she lifted a letter and an envelope from the arm of the fireside chair, her skirts swirling around her hips with her movements.

Iron will, he reminded himself. *Be cold, heartless steel.* He took the letter and envelope, careful not to bump fingers. He spied the train ticket thick in the envelope, and the pieces of his heart broke a little more. She could leave now.

"Dearest Savannah," he read. "I cannot begin to tell you how sorry I am that you have decided not to marry Nate. I know he can snarl like a wounded bear and he looks mean enough to bite, but I'm begging you to give him one more chance. He is a good man with a broken heart. I believe your love can save him from a life of loneliness. Please stay and try. But if you cannot, here is a ticket to take you anywhere you want to go. It has been a privilege meeting you and hoping for a time that you might become my daughter."

Nate closed his eyes, fighting against the swamp of emotion he refused to feel. He was like the railroad tracks—colder than the ice and snow, unfeeling. "I'm glad she and Pa finally did the decent thing by you. You can go home."

"I don't feel right about accepting the ticket."

"What?" After all this, she was going to stay in town? Panic ricocheted like a bullet in his chest. No, that wasn't something he could stomach. He saw the future: spotting her in the hotel dining room and knowing she could not be his. Crossing the street to avoid her when he was out doing errands. Watching another man court her. Marry her. Have a family with her.

"No." The word blasted out of him like a bullet from a Winchester.

The light in Savannah's eyes faded. Her smile faltered. She stared at him as if he'd tried to strike her. "I don't understand. It's not your parents' fault that this didn't work out the way they'd hoped."

"It's entirely their fault." He would never understand the way a woman's mind worked. "They should make restitution to you. They should try to fix this mess they made of your life."

"I'm the one who made the mess. I chose Mary's letters. I read the love in them and I misunderstood it. Perhaps I could have seen through the deception if I hadn't been so hungry to find love and a place to belong."

"That is no crime for a woman who has lost the last of her family. I can't stand to think of what that would be like to lose my brothers and my parents. Loneliness is one thing—loneliness coupled with loss and no chance for family is another."

She could only nod. How could Nate understand her so completely? The worst of this was that she'd lost the dream of love. The dream of connection and devotion and ties of the heart. The wish to be needed and to need. The hope of caring for and being cared for. She'd lost the love for another family again.

Her grandmother's words came back to her. *Life takes you down a different path than you expect but to the right place in the end.* Surely that meant she would find the right family to love and the right man to love her back one day. It was a comfort. So why did a voice deep in her heart point out that whoever that man would wind up being, he would not be Nate? Why did sadness creep into her soul?

You do not love him, she reminded herself as she knelt to adjust the fireplace's damper.

There was Nate, kneeling, too, his broad shoulders crowding her and the muscle of his arm granite-hard against hers. "I'll tend this. You want to unwrap our meals?"

Regret. It was there in his eyes, as luminous as a midnight-blue sky. It was in his heart, as deep as the endless ocean. Savannah tore her gaze away, seeing more of the man than she could endure. Nate, she realized, was much more than what those letters had promised. He was so wonderfully and tenderly more.

You do not love him. She would repeat those words as often as it took to keep from falling. She managed to rise on her unsteady legs. Her entire body was trembling. Her entire being was, too.

"How soon will you be leaving?" Nate's question sounded casual, as if he were merely wondering.

Why wouldn't he be in a hurry for her to leave? She was an imposition and, guessing by the way everyone in town seemed to know about them, an embarrassment. "Would you mind letting me work for you for a little bit longer? So I have a small savings to rely on for hotels and meals?"

"Of course." He placed another log on the fire. "But if you're going to be around, we'll have to come to some kind of agreement. We can't have my ma thinking you are staying around trying to give me a second chance."

"Absolutely not." She forced a smile, and she hoped he would never guess how much his words hurt. It was sensible and right not to give Mary false hopes. "I suppose we will simply have to not get along for the next few weeks."

"Yes. I think for once in my life my growling nature will come in handy." Nate rose from the hearth, his full-fledged smile unguarded, and the effect of it dazzled her as he pounded her way.

She'd thought him a handsome man before, but now…he was a dream. Her pulse stopped. Her lungs failed. Her soul stilled. Desire, sweet and hot, coursed through her like warm honey.

You do not love him, she thought, but those words had become a lie.

Chapter Eight

It was hard to imagine they had talked and laughed for an entire hour and a half over a chicken and dumplings dinner three evenings ago—and every evening since, Savannah marveled as she recorded a customer's payment in the account book. Nate brushed past her as if he didn't even see her and barked at Joseph to get busy and stop standing around.

"What's in your craw?" Joseph asked, wounded. "Rush and I were just talkin' seed wheat."

"Didn't look like it to me. We're not closed yet. I want to see you working." Nate stormed off to the back room with a smack of the door.

At the counter, Rush Travers smoothed away lint on his silk tie. "Looks like something is troubling poor Nate. Must be tough working for him."

"Not tough at all. He has been a very generous employer. Would you like to put all five dollars on your account?"

"Need two bucks back."

Savannah made change from the small cash box Nate kept in the top drawer. She handed over the two bills and a courteous smile. "Thank you for coming in, Mr. Travers."

"Sure must be hard for Nate having to look at you all day and know that's another beautiful woman he couldn't hold." Rush folded the bills into his tailored jacket pocket. "Sure you don't want to come work for me? I'll pay you a dollar more than he is."

Dislike flooded her. "No. Good day, Mr. Travers."

"You change your mind, you come find me." He strode away with a confidence that bordered on arrogance.

I don't like that man. Savannah shivered. She couldn't pin down the precise reason, but she was glad he was gone.

Joseph moseyed over. "That's the man who stole Adella from Nate. See? There she is."

Savannah whipped around, squinting through the blaze of sunlight on the windows. The snow was gone, leaving behind a riot of color, and the boardwalks were busy with folks glad to be out in the temperate weather, so it took her a moment to locate Mr. Travers on the boardwalk across the street. Curious, she crept closer to see the woman he was speaking with. She was petite and fragile, carrying a small baby swathed in blue flannel. The proud father lifted his son into his arms as his wife snuggled close.

That was the woman who'd hurt Nate? Adella looked like a prosperous lady with her matching bonnet and cloak and the ruffle of an expensive dress swishing between the hem of the coat and the toes of polished shoes. She smiled up at her husband as he handed her the baby. Jewelry glinted in the sunlight, as bright as her smile. She looked happy with her choice.

Adella was the reason, Savannah realized, that she could never have Nate. Why early next week, she would be leaving town forever, going forward in her life without ever knowing Nate's love. A hard shaft of sorrow struck her and dug deeper than pain. Deeper than anger. There would be no wedding, no loving nights spent in Nate's strong arms and no son of Nate's for her to hold.

"What are you two gawkin' at?"

Nate's gruff baritone brought a smile to her lips and tears to her eyes. How deeply he was able to feel, she realized as she turned toward him, to be so hurt. She filled with a love so strong, sunlight was like darkness.

"Savannah," he growled out in mock anger. "Are you standing around again?"

"It appears so." He was a watery vision through her tears, and it was all she could do hide her smile. "I don't appreciate your tone, Nate."

"Too bad." A grin flirted across his hard mouth as he stomped closer. "Turn over the sign and lock the door. We might as well close up early. I can't take any more of your admirers."

"Me, either." She was only too glad to do as he asked. As she flipped the bolt, she noticed that Adella and her family were gone. Good, she thought, glad Nate had been spared the sight of her.

Joseph didn't need to be told twice, apparently, because he was already heading for the back door. "Nate, you might think that having a pretty woman around would put you in a *good* mood."

Nate tossed a wink at Savannah before he bit over his shoulder. "Little brother, if you're late again, I'm firing *both* you and the pretty woman."

"You're never gonna get married. Ma is right." There was a slam of the door and more stomping in the back room.

"Our plan is working." Nate leaned close, his breath hot and pleasant against her ear. "Same time, same place?"

"Yes." She knew she sounded breathless but didn't care. She was too busy trying to hold back the shine of her love for the man. What would he say if he knew? Fearing it would be a horror to him, she cleared her throat and tried her best to sound normal. "I'll just get my cloak."

Savannah did her best not to watch him through her lashes as she bundled up against the April chill, but her disobedient eyes found him anyway. He knelt before the stove, banking the ashes, his movements sure and capable. She memorized the fall of his dark hair over his collar, his strong proud profile, his raw masculinity that made her ache. She savored the sight of him as long as she could until she'd buttoned every button and pulled on her hood and there was nothing left to do but to let herself out the door.

Spring evenings were a cold affair in the high Montana mountains. Savannah shivered as the last rays of the sun slipped below the western peaks. Their snowy caps glowed lilac and rose in the waning light. What warmth there had been bled from the day, and she tromped along the boardwalks in shadow.

The bakery was empty when she pushed through the door. The chime overhead belled pleasantly, and a cheerful woman with a cap of silver-threaded hair peered around the kitchen in back. "Hello, Savannah. Perfect timing. I just put a pot of tea to steep. I'll be right out with it."

"Thank you, Mrs. McKaslin." She unbuttoned in the warmth and draped her cloak over one of the chairs and settled down. She'd chosen a small table by the back, out of sight from the large windows.

The shop owner bustled out with a tray and an ironware tea service, and placed a small plate of sugar cookies on the table, too. "To nibble on while you wait. A young lady being courted has to keep up her strength."

"Now I thought Nate made this clear. We are just friendly, nothing more. He's doing me a favor eating supper with me, since I don't know anyone else in town."

"Yes." Mrs. McKaslin's eyes twinkled as if with a merry secret. "It's been a shame there hasn't been a single soul in this town offering to dine with you."

"You heard about that?" Savannah's face heated.

"I can see the feed store from my window. I can't tell you how amusing it's been to watch the daily parade of bachelors over to the feed store." Mrs. McKaslin pranced to the windows and began pulling the ruffled curtains over the darkening expanse of glass. "Nothing quite so entertaining has happened in this town for a decade at least! A lot of folks are keeping their eyes out their windows, wondering what's about to happen next."

"Which is why Nate and I are so grateful to you for this little bit of privacy." It really had been Nate's idea to approach the baker's wife, since they closed up shop at five sharp, and their son Mac was a good friend of Nate's. "It would break Mary's heart if she heard a rumor that we were spending time together. She would start hoping, and I can't do that to her. Not when it's impossible."

"Nothing is impossible, dear." Mrs. McKaslin turned from the windows and her smile shone sympathetically. "I think Nate is softening up some. You might get him to marry you yet."

"But I don't want—" She stopped, hearing the lie in her denial. Maybe it would be best to stick with the truth. "I only want a man to marry me for love, nothing else."

His footsteps padded behind her—he'd come in the back way. He set their dinners on the table next to the teapot. "Mrs. McKaslin, is that hot apple pie I smell?"

"Yes, dear, fresh out of the oven for the two of you. Well, I'm on my way out. Looks like a storm's heading in!"

Savannah could notice nothing but Nate. He laid his hand on hers, and the flash of heat from his skin made her senses spin. From far away she heard Nate's answer to the baker's call of goodbye. She sat transfixed by the pressure of his hand and the zing of lightning blazing through every inch of her. Breathing was impossible. Her every nerve ending twinkled like a midnight star. His mouth was close to hers, she realized, remembering how he had almost kissed her before.

She wanted him to kiss her now. It took all her strength to slip her hand from his and reach for the sugar bowl as if her only desire was for a cup of tea.

Nate moved away, talking as he unwrapped their food. "She's right. The wind's rising. I didn't see any storm clouds on the horizon, but sometimes they swoop down from the northwest over the mountains and we don't get a lot of warning."

"Like the night when I came to town?" She struggled to clear her thoughts. He moved closer again to set a plate of meat loaf and mashed potatoes in front of her. Her nerve endings strummed at his warm male scent. She longed to stay close to him and breathe him in forever.

"That wasn't a bad storm by our measure of things." He slid a second plate of buttered and honeyed biscuits in the center of the table.

"That wasn't a bad storm? But it stopped the train."

"True, but it took them less than a morning to clear the tracks."

He couldn't force himself to move away just yet. He lingered, breathing in the magical scent of her golden hair. "We had the train stuck at the depot for two weeks once. Almost three weeks, by the time they were done shoveling. That was last winter. We had snow all the way to the rooflines of the buildings."

"I can't imagine that. Your mother didn't write me about that kind of weather."

"No, she would have left those stories out, fearing you would have decided to stay in South Carolina like the reasonable woman you are."

That earned him a smile. "You think I'm reasonable?"

"Sure. I have a fine opinion of you, Savannah."

"You do?" Pleasure pinkened her sweet face.

"I've spent time enough in your company to see the lady you are." If his throat threatened to close up tight, he ignored that. If his heart gave a panicked *thump,* he ignored that, too. "You have a lot of admirable qualities."

"That's high praise coming from a taciturn man like you."

"Taciturn? I prefer bearlike."

"Bearlike then." The lamplight touched her creamy face like a lover's caress—like he wanted to touch her. Gently. Reverently. Unaware of his thoughts, she gazed up at him with innocence. "We have Joseph fooled, don't you think?"

He ought to be grateful for the subject change. Every cell of his body was strumming with a deep, aching hunger. Nate forced his feet to carry him to the other side of the table. He sat, and although only a few feet separated them, it felt like a mile. "My little brother wants to call on you."

"Why not? We're about the same age."

His jaw dropped. He'd been reaching for a biscuit and he froze, his arm in midair, unable to breathe. Unable to think. There was that red haze again bleeding through his vision.

"Maybe I'll stay on," she was saying with sparkling amusement, "and get to know Joseph better."

So, she wasn't serious. Relief whooshed out of him. Pressure, which he hadn't even realized was building in his chest, broke up like glacier melt. "Don't do it, or I'll be obliged to beat the crap out of my own brother."

"And why would that be?"

"Just stop teasing me and pass me the cup of tea you poured for me." He wasn't showing his hand. He'd learned how to bluff when he'd been a little guy watching poker games at his pa's knee. Good thing, too, because his heart and his jealousy would be showing about now. Jealousy over the thought of any other man hungering after Savannah the way he was. It was a hunger that hurt, that ran deep, and that threatened his mountain-tough self-control.

He wanted to kiss his way down the graceful line of her neck, pop every tiny little pearled button on her dress and lay her down beneath him. An unbearable urge hammered within him, the need to love her with all of his body, to join them as one, to hear her moan his name with love and pleasure.

Savannah slid a steaming teacup in his direction. "Last night you didn't finish telling me about the time you and Gabriel startled that mother bear."

He took a long pull of tea, but it wasn't strong enough to dull the spike of affection taking him hostage. He wasn't sure how long he could go on bluffing about his feelings—to her, sure, but mostly to himself.

She was glowing inside as Nate held the bakery's back door for her. The blast of frigid air couldn't touch the happiness within her. She was happy because of the man who locked the back door with care and stowed the key on the overhead door frame's narrow ledge. Darkness framed him: the black sky and the angry clouds made him seem invincible, primal male. Her soul sighed with a great wish.

A wish—for him—she could not allow herself to make. A wish for a wish that she could not let him see.

"Mrs. McKaslin just earned herself a discount on her husband's next feed order." He joined her in the alley, circling around to her left side to protect her from the blasting wind. "That was some apple pie she left us."

"The best I've ever tasted. She thinks we're secretly courting, that's why she's helping us out."

"I told her the truth. It's too bad she won't believe it. And if she wanted to let us use her shop after hours and ply us with her fresh baked goods, then I'm happy to let her."

"Me, too." Deliciously full and contented, she breathed in the sharp, icy air and the wild tang of the wind. Something stung her cheek. Snow. Sudden, angry pellets of it hurled into her like hundreds of miniature arrows.

"Looks like we'd best make a run for it." Nate's wide hand grabbed hers, hot even through her woolen gloves.

You do not feel that, she ordered herself as she ran with him past back door after back door in the deeply shadowed alley. It was so dark, the snow fell as if black. The wind rumbled like thunder.

Nate's hand gripped hers. "The storm's growing worse. Let's keep to the boardwalks."

They had emerged from the alley, but without the stores to act as windbreaks, she could see nothing. Nothing of the town. Nothing of the street and hitching posts and upstairs windows that ought to be glowing with lamplight. It was as if she and Nate were alone in the storm, in this black wilderness, alone on the mountain.

His hand folded around hers reminded her that she was not alone, even in the dark. Calm filled her as he came close to block the horizontal snow with his body. Heat bubbled up through her midsection. The granite plane of his chest pressed against her backbone. His breath felt lava-warm against her neck.

"At least no one can see us together," he quipped in his rich, forbidden baritone. "I could kiss you until your knees went weak and not a single soul could see."

His hand let go of hers and he moved to wrap his arms around her, shielding her more from the vicious storm. The updrafts of wind tore at her skirt hem like a pack of rabid dogs, the fire of snow bulleting against the frozen world seemed to echo within her very bones. The temperature plummeted like nothing she'd ever felt before; suddenly the iciness turned cruel and the air she drew into her lungs lethal.

"Come." He nudged her along the boardwalk.

She could not see. She had no notion of where they were. The storm had become a roaring monster. Nate steered her abruptly to one side, his arms holding her safe as a barrel rolled down the boardwalk beside them. The dark storm swallowed it. That had been a watering barrel for the horses, she realized. Frozen solid in these temperatures, and still the brutal wind could push it as if it were a dried leaf.

"It's all right." Nate's voice vibrated against her ear, filling her with reassurance, stirring up a heat that was stronger than the storm and greater than the cold.

"I'll keep you safe," he promised, his fingers squeezing into her shoulders for emphasis.

I know you will. Too overwhelmed to speak, she let him guide her. She clung to the reassuring strength of Nate's body; surely his mountain-toughness would see them safely home. Her stomach squeezed violently with the cold, and Nate's arms wrapped around her more tightly, lifting her into his arms, cradling her against the iron shield of his chest. She had never felt safer.

Then they were in the alley, at the back door. Nate set her down on the doorstep, wrestling in his pocket for his keys with one hand. He did not release her. He did not let her go. He held on to her so tight. She could feel the palpable heat of his gaze on her lips.

Wrenching with cold, she waited, heart hammering, the storm and wind silencing. The rugged world slid away when she felt Nate's breath on her cheek. She lifted one hand to lay it against the base of his throat. His heart beat with a force greater than the blizzard. She felt his need like the heat radiating from his body. In utter darkness, she tilted her face just a little, upturning her lips to his, moving by instinct, seeing by a greater sight.

His lips hovered over hers for a long moment. His mouth covered hers in a hot, yielding kiss. Bubbles grew and burst within her middle, sending tingles of sensation and want outward in spirals. How could his mouth, which looked so hard and frowned so much, feel like heaven? She marveled at the heated softness of his kiss, at the way he tasted and caressed, drawing tingling sensations onto her lips.

What a kiss. She clung to him. She curled her fingers into his shirt. She held on to him, unsteady and wobbly, drinking in the pleasure and sweetness. Savoring the heat and the beat in her blood for more. Wishing this could go on forever without end. Yes, she pleaded, don't let this end.

Then he pulled away, the storm returned, ice pelted her face as he unlocked the door.

"Get in," he said, as if he were not happy with her.

Not happy at all.

Chapter Nine

Her kiss burned on his lips as he put his weight into it and shouldered the door closed. Nate hit the bolt, fumbled off his gloves and tried to make his frozen fingers strike a match. He gave thanks for the darkness so he would not have to look her in the face as he struggled with a second match and a third. So she could not see how much she had torn him apart.

That kiss. Nothing had felt as good as that single kiss. Not one thing. He gulped in air, trying to cool down his blood, and broke a fourth match. Look how rattled he was. The fifth match was the charm; light blazed at the head of the match and he lit the lantern. *Now, please,* he thought, *don't let her notice how hard I'm shaking.*

"What kind of storm was that?" Her voice sounded thin and unsteady.

Why hadn't she pushed him away? Why had she clung to him as if with her very life? Why had she surrendered, letting him deepen the kiss with a brush of his tongue into the softness of her mouth? So that now, she was all he wanted, all he needed. She was the desire that beat in his blood.

He blew out the match shakily. "Spring blizzard. They happen now and then this time of year. They hit like hell's fury."

"I see that. We had a hurricane come through once with the strength of those winds. Tore the roof off my grandmama's carriage house. Broke six windows." She was shivering, covered with snow, her eyes wide and vulnerable in her pale face.

Tenderness hit him like the leading edge of that blizzard, barreled him right over, every defense, every guard, every excuse. "You were scared?"

"Not because of you. If I had been out in it alone—" She shivered again.

"You're cold." He hadn't protected her well enough. Fathomless, that's how this tenderness felt, as if it welled down through his heart, through his soul and further still. He caught her face in his hands, so dear, bowed by her, vulnerable to her, and the magic of their kiss thrummed through him. *He wanted another.*

Down boy. Remember, she's not yours to kiss. He hated it. For the first time, he *hated* it. He tugged at the ice on her hood's tie until it came loose, her hood fell back and bits of snow tinkled to the floor. "You're head-to-toe ice."

"So are you." Her rosebush lips curved into a bewitching grin. "You look like a polar bear."

"Sure, but my bark's worse than my bite."

"I've noticed." Her grin widened, spellbinding him.

He had to resist it. If he gave in to one more kiss, who knew what would happen from there? Another kiss? And another? They were alone here, trapped. What then? Where did it stop? Desire pulsed heavy within him and he refused to think of the room upstairs. Of the two of them alone in it. Of the bed just wide enough to lay her down in, her hair falling across the pillows and reaching for her buttons.

Don't even think beyond that, man. He squeezed his eyes shut, willing the image away before it could take root in his mind. Because if it did, if he pictured himself undoing Savannah's buttons one by one, revealing the lace of her chemise and the swell of her bare breasts, he would—

Damn it. He was rock hard. Good thing he had a coat on, or Savannah would know it, too. He grabbed the lantern by the handle and stalked through the darkness, leaving her behind without realizing it. He stopped in the middle of the stockroom, flanked by stacks of bagged wheat and rolled oats, and held out his hand. "Come with me. We'll get you warm. Your teeth are chattering, Savannah."

He saw her answer in her eyes, luminous and bare. He could see right into her. She was smarting a bit because he'd stalked away from her. She had no notion of the fine edge of control he was grasping. She had no idea how the tree-leveling wind outside was tame compared to the fury of his need for her.

She stayed near the door, shadows and light flickering over her, with the ice driven into the weave of her cloak glinting like diamonds. "I should probably go. It's terribly late for me to be here, and—"

She shrugged her shoulders, the movement sending more snow feathering off of her, leaving her thoughts unspoken. He didn't know what she meant to say, or was too afraid to say, but it was clear she didn't understand the situation.

"Baby, your lips are blue." Since she wouldn't come to him, he came to her. Took her hand in his and brought it to his heart. If she could feel it beat, then she would know what he was going through. What he was fighting. What he was struggling not to do. "You can't go back out in that cold. It'll kill you."

"But it's only blocks to the b-boardinghouse."

"It was only blocks to here, and look at you. Shaking and half-frozen. The temperature's falling fast. This is a worse storm than the night you arrived. Trust me. I'm telling you the truth. You can't go out in that again. I won't let you."

"How can I st-stay?"

"It's easy. You just come upstairs with me." He knew what she couldn't say. He could feel it in the air between them. A nice lady did not spend the night with a man who was not her husband. A nice lady did not go upstairs with a man who wanted her with every fiber of his being. Who wanted her so much, there wasn't a storm cold enough to lessen the heat he felt for her. There was only one way this could end between them, and he knew it. She must, too.

His boots rang like a death knell in the night as he led her through the store and into the unbearable cold of his upstairs room.

She held on to him so tightly, and he could feel her misgivings as he brought her to the top of the stairs. His pulse rattled to a stop. This was it. There was no going back. He set the lantern on the table and eased her onto the chair. She looked so cold, he broke a little inside.

"Believe me now?" he asked her gently, because he knew what she was giving up. What they both were.

She nodded, unable to meet his gaze. Her lips were a darker shade of blue, and her hand through the wool mitten felt like ice. He hated letting go of her, but he had to stir the embers in the stove. Every second that passed, Savannah was getting colder.

He worked fast; soon the embers were giving off a puff of heat that grew as he added slivers of cedar. Flames burst to life, crackling and popping, and the ice frosted on the stove melted off in slow drips. He left the damper wide-open and piled in the driest chunks of wood, and to make sure they caught quickly, he left the door open, too.

"That feel good?" he asked her as he went down on his knees.

"Y-yes."

She didn't pull away as he peeled off her gloves and rubbed her hands between his. They were colder than ice; tenderness bowed him. He felt like a branch with too much snow on it, bending beneath the weight. Any moment now, he was going to break. It was inevitable; he had to prepare for it. He had to take it like a man.

When her hands were warmer, he put them in her lap. "Keep your coat on until the room is warmer. The teakettle's finally rumbling. I'll get you some tea."

"That would help."

He rummaged through the cupboards until he found the right tin. "I'm sure Ma in her letters didn't warn you about these storms."

"She didn't warn me about a lot of things."

"No. You wouldn't have come if you knew."

"About this incredible weather?" she asked. "Or you?"

"She should have told you I was no prize." He pried the top off the tin and loose tea leaves scattered across the counter. He worked, keeping his back to her, making it impossible to see what emotions were on his face.

But she could feel them in the air, and see them with her heart. "You are right, in that your mother was not exactly truthful about you. I got a certain opinion of a man from those letters."

"I know you did." Nate snared an ironware cup from the drainer and dropped the tea ball into it. "I'll always be sorry to disappoint you."

"No, you have that wrong." Couldn't he see? She watched him as he filled the cup with steaming water and set it before her on the table. He added wood to the fire, closed the stove door and checked the damper. Didn't he know what she saw in him? The man she knew him to be? He came to wrap a quilt around her shoulders and captured pieces of her heart.

"Wrong? I don't think so. My mother's blind when it comes to her boys. My brothers and I have pulled the wool over her eyes since the day we could wink at her."

Yes, she could see Mary's love for her sons, and how it must have been to grow up in that household graced with love.

His hands, which were so big and rugged, marked with calluses and hard work, were gentle as he wrapped her up snugly. Tender as he knelt before her and gazed into her eyes. Love for him burned like dawn breaking through the worst of storms so brilliant and unwavering she could not hold it back.

"When I look at you, I see someone who is much more than those letters." She wanted him to kiss her until she was warmed to the very tips of her toes. "The real Nathaniel Brooks is more than I ever dreamed he could be."

"Growls and all?"

"Yes, especially the growls." She wanted him to wrap her in his brawny arms and never let her go. She wanted him to cherish her with kisses until she was so in love with him that he couldn't help loving her right back. Like the pull of the tide, like the tug of the moon, she wanted to pull him into love.

Being all alone with him, being so close she could hear his heartbeat, she felt as if it would be so easy. As if all she had to do was to lay her hands on his face, feel the wondrously male texture of his day's growth against her palms and claim him with one kiss, and they would fall, irrevocably, together. She loved him so much, she ached with it. Every inch of her hurt with an unquenchable need.

"We've got to talk, Savannah. If I—" He stopped, his throat working, tendons standing out in his neck. "If we—"

So, he felt this, too. Relief left her giddy. Joy soared through her like a bird in flight, leaving the earth and all its rules and restrictions and rationales behind. She understood how frightening it was to take a leap of faith; she quaked with the fear of risking that he would reject her when her heart was utterly exposed.

"We can talk later," she whispered against his lips. "After."

She kissed him, brazenly, boldly, as he had kissed her on the doorstep. His mouth was hot and hard; unyielding. She felt every muscle tense as he drew up straighter. His hands gripping her forearms were ready to push away from her. The cracks in her heart shattered. Didn't he want her?

Then, with a growl, he let go. He deepened the kiss, sweeping past her lips, opening her mouth with gentle force. His velvet tongue caressed hers. His arms banded around her as he hauled her against his chest, lifting her to his bed, never breaking the kiss, deepening the connection. She clung to his iron-hewn shoulders as she lay back on the pillows.

When did she tell him how she felt? That she was in love with him? His rough hands swept away the quilt and yanked at the sash of her cloak. The shadows could not hide the reverence in his eyes or the great tenderness on his face as he stretched out over her.

Her stomach fell. She was breathless with anticipation. He was going to love her. He was hard everywhere, yet his fingertips on her skin, his kisses traveling over her intimately as he pulled back layer by layer of clothing were exquisite. Of course, she had to return the same. Unbuttoning his shirt, unbuckling his trousers. Kissing his hot, salty skin until she was melting into him, until he rose over her and joined them as one.

So this is what love feels like. Such sweetness. This was no ordinary love, she realized, wrapping around him, holding him to her, holding on. She gazed up at him through blurry eyes. His tender kisses did not stop even when she broke into a thousand blissful pieces nor when he cried out her name with his release.

She lay in his arms, a changed woman, delighting in his delicious weight as he lay over her, still kissing her. Her chest split painfully for all the emotions brimming up and over. It was as if her heart were breaking, she hurt so much. Don't let this end, she pleaded silently to him, and, as if he understood, he began to love her again. Slowly this time, reverently, making the pain in her chest end. Making the pieces of her heart whole. Love, she discovered, was not what she expected.

It was more.

Chapter Ten

The instant Nate woke to the still darkness, he knew his fate was sealed. There was no hiding from it. No altering it. Nothing to do but to face it. His mother was going to have a heyday with this. His pride would always take a hit that his ma had found his wife. He was never going to live that down. Just like he would never recover when Savannah got a good look at him one day and left him.

She slept beside him like sweetness itself, her lovely face shadowed by dawn's mellow light. She was on her side, her fragrant hair across his pillow, like silk against his jaw. Nestled against her softness, he lingered for one long moment, listening to her quiet, slow breathing. Feeling the peace of being awake at her side. Thinking over the night with her, every dream he had ever had was nothing compared to the reality of loving Savannah. Contentment spread like melted butter through his veins. Heaven had to be like this.

She stirred, opening her eyes slowly, and his chest expanded with intense tenderness. His arm was hooked around her waist and he drew her more tightly against his body, watching as consciousness returned and a smile crooked the corners of her amazing mouth.

He couldn't resist kissing her enchanting lips. "Good morning. Sleep okay?"

"Hmm." She rolled in his arms, snuggling against his chest, so small and precious, his heart gave a wild thump. "That was the best night of my life."

"Far from it." He loved how warm she was, how her skin was satin against him. "Wait until tonight."

"Oh, you think this is happening again?"

He loved that grin in her voice and the way she surrendered without a word or a look, and melted against him. "I intend to make damn sure of it."

"Lucky me." She kissed him, luring him to her like an irresistible siren. Her fingertips traced the crest of his shoulders. She stretched out beneath him, restless as he was.

He brushed the tangle of hair from her face, blown apart by the raw edges of pure emotion he could not give in to. His hand trembled. He kissed her again, wanting, just wanting to be lost in her, to love her hard enough to make her his forever; to love her as if he could hold on to her forever. Need pounded through him; it was more than need, but he wouldn't let himself think the word "love." No, that would be foolish. He had to stay tough, stay strong and keep his heart invincible.

The clang of the cowbell echoed through the floorboards. Who was downstairs? Nate broke their kiss, lifting up to listen for the crack of the downstairs door shutting. His heart hammered, knowing full well they were about to be discovered.

"Nate?" Pa called out. "You here, Son?"

Nate groaned. Why did it have to be his matchmaking father? Was it too much to hope that it might be Joseph, whom he could send away with a terse command and not leave this bed?

"Oh, no." Savannah was just realizing that they were about to have company. Her eyes darted to her clothes tossed haphazardly on the floor. He could see her calculating if she had time or not to look presentable before his father opened that door.

"You stay here, baby." Loath as he was to move away from his sweet Savannah when he was half dizzy from wanting her, he had to handle this the right way. They would have plenty of mornings together after this, and he intended to take full advantage of every one he could, while he could. He was already missing her as he slipped from beneath the quilts. "I'll take care of this."

"Your father is going to start celebrating, and that's not what I want."

"I know." He did. He could see what she expected and what she needed. He was determined to give that to her. Not that he was deluding himself, but he couldn't walk away from her. Not after last night. He was a man who did the right thing.

Always.

He yanked on his trousers and grabbed his shirt from the floor. "I'll talk to him. Sort this out. Make it right."

Relief had her sighing back onto the pillows, the quilt falling down to reveal her creamy shoulders, slender arms and the rise of her breasts. With his heart too swollen for his chest, he yanked open the door and beat his father to the top step.

"Nate." Pa came to a halt in the stairwell. "I worried about you when you didn't answer. That was a mean storm. Word is Walton Langley got caught it in on his way back to his ranch. Thought you'd want to help with the search for him."

"Sure. Yeah." Nate thrust his arm into his sleeve, confused. His mind was on a one-way track to Savannah, of figuring out how to spare her any embarrassment and of the inevitable step of having to marry her. "Pa, come downstairs. We need to talk while I gather up some things."

"Don't forget your buffalo coat. It's staring to thaw out some, looking like rain on the way, but for now it's in between. Falling something fierce." Pa leaned to one side, as if trying to get a look into the room.

"I don't need it." No possible way was he going to go back into the room, leaving the doorway unguarded. Two more steps and Pa would have a perfect view of Savannah in his bed, and all trouble would hit. "Go on downstairs."

"You seem awful quick to shoo me away." There it was, that flicker of mischief in his father's eyes. "Your ma has a theory that you're in love with Savannah. Now I'm thinking she might be right, and you have something to hide in your room. Like Savannah."

"Pa. Downstairs. Now." His temple throbbed with a sudden, blinding pain. How had his parents outmaneuvered him? He closed the door firmly and marched after his father, down the steps into the cold, shadowed store. Cold, gray light spilled in through the windows on a gray, slushy world. Sort of like his heart—half melted, half thawed and a complete mess.

"That's it. Savannah's up there." Pa clapped his hands together, looking like he might break into a jig. "Do I need to have a talk with you about doing the right thing? Savannah's a nice lady. You've got to put a ring on her finger."

"I know." Boy, did he. It was tearing him apart, knowing she was as close to paradise as he was ever likely to get and knowing that he had no chance in hell of truly keeping her. That she was city-bred and far too fine of a lady to be content with the life he had to offer her. The edges of his heart keened with defeat. "I intend to do the right thing."

"I had a feeling about the two of you. Although I expected you to wait until after the wedding."

"If this hadn't happened there wouldn't be a wedding." Grim, Nate had to face the truth. The woman upstairs in his bed might be his notion of heaven, but she could hardly be hers. "I don't want you to get the wrong idea. You and Ma never should have meddled in my life. You think you did what would make me happy, but it'll only bring me more misery."

"Son, you've got that wrong—"

The creak of a floorboard echoed in the morning quiet. There was Savannah, in the act of turning back around on the bottom stair, her long, loose hair swinging from the swiftness of her movement. She'd heard what he'd said. That truth struck him dead center like an ax's blade. The pain blinded him. He never would want her to have heard that.

"Pa, I've got to go. Tell the sheriff I'll join in the search later."

"But Mac's got you assigned—"

"It doesn't matter. Later." Savannah was hurting; he could feel it as if her heart was his. He waved off his pa, hurrying to catch up with his bride-to-be. This was certain disaster. All he had to do was to look around for proof at his store—not fancy, not lucrative and not nearly good enough for her. For what he wanted for her.

She was probably crying. That wrenched him as he pushed open the door and braced to deal with her tears. They were going to be his undoing. He could growl and bark and tell himself to stay strong, but he knew damn well he would break at the sight of a single tear on her face. He'd do anything for her happiness. Anything. Even let her go when the time came.

The door whispered to a stop against the wall, giving him a clear view of the room. Savannah's back was to him as she made the bed. Her unbound hair tumbling down her back made her somehow seem more frail.

"Savannah? I know what you heard down there. I'm angry at my folks. There's no secret about that. It could have sounded as if I was mad about marrying you."

She straightened, so stiff and still. Hell, was she holding in all her tears? All her hurt feelings? That was even worse. He could barely breathe past the notion of her hurting like that— because of him.

He came toward her, his feet taking him there without thought. Suddenly his hands were on her shoulders, her hair tickling his jaw, his soul beating with such tender regard that he had to work at keeping his heart cold and set. "I didn't mean that marrying you would be a misery. But that it would end that way."

"I-I'm s-sorry you believe that, Nate." She shook, fine little shakes, vibrating through her body and into his hands. "The last thing I want to do is hurt you."

"You're not. I'm doing the hurting here, and it's not what I mean." Frustration clawed at him. Love teased him, as if it were fighting to get into his heart. "See why I'm not the kind of man who ought to get married? I'm not good at this. I mean what I say, but it's not always what I mean. I've hurt you. Savannah, tell me how to make this better."

"You can't. I didn't s-stay last night to try to trap you into marrying me. I can leave town. My reputation isn't likely to follow me, so you can r-rest easy." When she turned, tears filled her eyes, but there was not a single tear track on her cheeks. "Perhaps I ought to be on the noon train."

"No, that's not what I want. After last night—" She might have smoothed away the tangle they'd made in those sheets, but he had not forgotten the pleasure they'd found together, or the lasso she'd tightened around his heart.

"I can't stay and work for you by day and love you by night without a commitment, Nate."

Didn't he know that? "That's why I'll marry you. We can have something quick. We can walk down to the judge and have him do it."

There was a good side of this marriage thing, he realized. Savannah in his arms every night. Waking up to her. Coming home to her. And if there was more than tenderness building in his soul for her, he refused to acknowledge it.

Her blue eyes, translucent with tears, searched his. "I'm in love with you, Nate. Please, tell me the truth. Do you love me?"

Panic rattled around in him like a loose stone in an empty boot. There was that word he was trying to avoid. It was a word that made a man weak. That could bring him to his knees. That could make him surrender all his strength and will. How could he travel down that road? "I'm a hardworking man of humble means. One day you're going to miss that city life you used to have, and you're going to move on."

"Like Adella?"

He gulped, seeing only more pain on Savannah's lovely face. He wasn't saying the right thing, although he was sure trying to. "I'll care for you as long as you'll stay."

"Care for me?" One tear brimmed over and trailed down her cheek. Just one. "After last night, after how I loved you, you still only care for me?"

He squeezed his eyes shut, refusing to watch that tear fall anymore, refusing to see the image of her laying beneath him as they loved, shadowed by the night, holding him as if he were the greatest man to her, clinging to him as if her life depended on it, wanting only him. How his name sounded loving and precious as she cried out in surrender.

Love beat at the gates of his heart. Love that he could not—should not—*would* not let in. He quaked with the effort to hold it back. How did he tell her? He treasured her immeasurably more than he'd ever loved Adella, so look how much he was risking? What he stood to lose?

Remembering that darkness and pain when she'd left him, he only had one choice. He had to be smart. Safe. Do this the best way for both of them. "I will cherish you."

"Not love me?"

"I will honor you."

Not love me. Savannah felt her heart crumple with agony, and it was worse than any heartbreak. No, her heart was whole, she realized, or it wouldn't be hurting so much. It was her soul shattering, that would never be whole again. Not without Nate.

Last night she had given herself to him—all she was, all the love she had. It had made no difference, in the end. Her love had not been strong enough to breach the defenses around his well-defended heart. "Perhaps you feel that way now and you aren't ready. But in time…?"

"No." He looked so sad towering over her, but invincible and tough, as if nothing could ever bend him. Sad, and not angry. Not in denial. "I'm sorry, Savannah. I'm not going to change."

Deep inside, she knew that was the way he intended things to be between them. She felt empty. Destroyed. She drew in a slow breath, careful not to give herself away. "I'm not Adella."

"No, you are far better than anyone I've ever met. You're amazing." He stumbled over the word. He looked tortured. "You're far better than I deserve."

That was his way of rejecting her. Of telling her that she had a better chance of reaching into the heavens and plucking down a star than of convincing Nate Brooks to love her. There was only one thing to do now. She held her feelings still and fisted her hands. This would take all her courage and all her might to do the right thing. She took her first step away from him. "I heard your father say that Mr. Langley is missing?"

Nate released a pent-up breath, as if he thought everything was all right. "I need to go join the search. He might be holed up in an abandoned claim shanty or miner's cabin, or he might have come to a worse end."

Savannah remembered what he'd said about the temperatures last night, cold enough to kill. "I hope he'll be found alive."

"Me, too." He looked uncertain as he took a step after her. "I'll be back in a bit. You might want to start thinking about how you want the wedding to go. I want the judge, but I know weddings are important to you ladies. Know what you want when I come back and that's what we'll do."

He had no notion how every little thing he did, especially his kindness, left her bleeding. She lifted her cloak from the floor and shook the wrinkles out. "I already know. There won't be a wedding, Nate. I didn't come here to marry someone who didn't love me, or who didn't want to try to. I don't want a convenient arrangement. I don't want to give my heart to a man always expecting me to walk out the door one day. I don't want a man who sees so little in me."

"No, Savannah, you've got it all wrong."

She saw the sincere emotion in his eyes, so impossibly sad. He was the one who had it wrong. "I'm not going to waste my life on something that will never happen."

"I'm marrying you, damn it." He sounded angry, but there was heartbreak cutting into his granite face. "That *will* happen. I'm not the kind of man who uses a woman."

"I'm not the kind of woman who uses a man. I know you will never be able to see that." Her chin shot up and she let the anger come, because it would wash over the agony like a rising river did the bank. "I gave you all the love I had last night. Every drop. Every measure. Every essence. All I want is your love in return, *not* a wedding ring."

"But—" His jaw worked, and no more words came. Misery dug into him like cracks in a mountain wall as he fisted his big hands and stood helpless.

It only hurt more that he wanted to love her and couldn't, for now she saw his loving her would truly be impossible. She did what she had to do and walked through the door. She turned back to drink in what she loved about Nate one last time: his mix of gruff and kind; the straight, dependable line of his shoulders; the wind-tousled hair and dark, soulful eyes; the unyielding presence that came with a truly good and strong man.

"Adella didn't really love you, Nate. I thought you should know." She grasped the door frame for support. The wood was cool against her palm. The icy chill rising up the stairs from down below felt like a sign of her life to come; always cold without Nate by her side. "A woman who really loves her man loves who he is, not his pocketbook. I really love you. I wish you could see that. I hope you find happiness, Nate. I'll be wishing that for you every day."

"But—"

"Goodbye." She kept walking and didn't look back.

Chapter Eleven

Now what did he do? Nate raked his hand through his hair and yanked open the window. Savannah was upset and hurt, he could see that. But he cared about her. Wasn't that enough? Did she want his heart and his soul, too?

Slushy snow slopped down the windowpane, making it impossible to see the street below. Impossible to see which direction Savannah was going. His chest felt like it was stuffed full of dynamite and ready to explode. He rubbed at his breastbone, trying to breathe past the obstruction. No luck.

He let the curtain fall. She *had* to be going to the boardinghouse. She would be safe there. She would get some breakfast, settle down with a cup of tea and start thinking rationally. She would see that her leaving was a ridiculous choice. It was an uncertain world out there for a woman alone. Didn't she appreciate the security he was offering her? And why did she have to go and bring Adella into this? *A woman who really loves her man loves who he is, not his pocketbook.*

Fine, he couldn't argue with that, but he couldn't trust another woman with his heart. Even if he wanted to, he didn't know how to drive out the blinding panic that would take him over if he tried. He didn't know how to change. It was better to lose her now than later, right?

What if she had told him the truth? What if she was never going to leave him? Nate hated that contrary voice, the one that seemed to come from deep within him. He sat down and covered his face with his hands. He didn't want to search through his soul and see all that was wrong with him. There was a man out there maybe freezing to death, needing help. That's what he ought to be doing instead of ruminating over what might or might not be.

What mattered was now. He rifled through the stack of clothes on the floor for his warmest things. His heaviest flannel shirt. An extra pair of wool long johns. He put those on and went in search of his best gloves and his buffalo cap. With each passing minute he felt grumpier, as if something were missing. Maybe it was Savannah's lilac scent that seemed melded with his skin. Perhaps it was the memory of the unbelievable night spent with her on his bed, a piece of furniture that was within his sight as he donned his buffalo coat.

Don't think about last night. His stern self-command had no effect. How could it? He remembered every touch, every kiss, every sigh. His soul felt bound to her although she was nowhere near to him; even though she was determined to leave him. Need kicked him like a stubborn mule; except it wasn't need alone. There was also the deep well of emotion he was trying to ignore and avoid. Some wells were best not looked into.

He went to button the coat, but two-thirds up, one of the buttons wouldn't meet with its loop. There was something in his pocket. He recognized that thick bundle his ma had tucked into his shirt pocket the day Savannah had first started working for him.

She wrote them to you, dear. All her love for you is right in there. All the proof you need, his ma had told him.

He took out the bundle, his pulse knocking, his breath rattling, and studied the pile of envelopes that held Savannah's words to him. It was their courtship. Their slow dance toward one another. Did he open them? Did he hope there was a chance in hell that he could take the risk? Jumping off the highest peak of the Rocky Mountain Range would be easier for a man like him.

A hammering knock on the front door saved him. He wrestled

open the window and spotted the burly town sheriff on the board-walk below. Wet slush spattered his face as the slush storm continued. "I'll be right down, Mac."

"No need. We found Walton safe and sound at widow Brown's house and much warmer than the rest of us." The surly sheriff frowned his disapproval.

Nate shook his head in agreement and slammed the window shut. He swiped the wet from his face with his sleeve, glad all was well and that he didn't have to go out in that cold, messy weather. Nope, he could stay here, safe and snug and alone and do his best not to think of Savannah out there in it, trudging back to her room.

Would she keep her threat? he wondered. Would she really be packing to leave on the noon train?

I really love you. I wish you could see that. Her parting words tortured him. What if she meant it? What if this was true, this dream of hers? He didn't know if he was a man who believed in dreams.

With the stove stone-cold and a storm battering the roof and eaves, Nate sat down and began to read.

Savannah shivered on the train platform, miserable, but not from the cold. No, she was numb clear through from the quiet agony of broken hopes and lost dreams and a soul that could never be whole again. So numb and hurting that the sharp bite of slush and the marrow-freezing damp felt like no hardship at all by comparison. The wind gusted cruelly, sending a cascade of freezing slush against her, but it was not strong enough or bitter enough to drive out the memory of Nate's painful words. *If this hadn't happened there wouldn't be a wedding. You think you did what would make me happy, but it'll only bring me more misery.*

She hated that. She hated that he equated marriage with her as a misery. As punishment for last night. Pain burned behind her eyes and gathered like a lump in her throat. Why did she only love him more? She was not only hurting for herself, but for Nate, her beloved Nate, who could not love. Who would not love.

I'll care for you as long as you'll stay, he'd said, content to spend their life together holding back his affection for her because he expected her to leave for greener pastures. She pressed her hand to her mouth and smothered a sob. Couldn't he see who she was? If he loved her, then he would know her heart. He would know she loved him, only him. There had been no one before him, and there would be no man after him.

The train's whistle pierced the roar of the terrible wind, the chorus of the bending, tortured forest of trees and the slop of the falling wet. A few more minutes, the train would appear, she would climb aboard and Nate Brooks and the little town of Moose, Montana, would be a memory. The pieces of her soul stung with unbearable pain. She braced her spine, drew in a slow breath, gathered her strength to fight it, but it was a deep wound that would never heal.

"Savannah?"

Nate? Her pulse fluttered in her chest. She was twirling toward him without realizing it. Suddenly she was facing the big bear of a man veiled by the shroud of ice. It was him. Her Nate.

She wanted to wrap her arms around him and feel safe and protected against his powerful chest. She wanted to kiss him until they were both breathless and filled with need for one another.

But why had he come? Reason kicked in, and she took a step back, away from him. He hadn't come to declare his love for her. She took in the serious set of his eyes and the grim set to his hard mouth.

No, of course not. He had either come to say goodbye, or to talk her into his ridiculous sham of a marriage.

"I read your letters, Savannah. The ones you wrote to me." His rough baritone dipped dangerously low, bringing to her mind the way he'd spoken to her when she had been in his arms.

She fought against the memory, for dwelling on what could not be was a mistake. "You mean the letters I wrote to your mother."

"No. You wrote them to me." Lower this time, although he did not move closer. The veil of wet slush hid him well from her sight, allowing only an impression of a frown, the hint of a cold-eyed gaze and the set line of his invincible shoulders.

Disappointment slid through her. He had come to force the issue of marriage. Why had she thought he would rather be free of her? He was a stubborn man, and an honorable one. He would not allow her to leave with a ruined reputation or the slight chance that their lovemaking had resulted in a baby. Her eyes burned again and she blinked hard. She refused to let him see how much his rejection had hurt her. She had honor, too. "I don't want to argue with you, Nate. I don't want our last words to be harsh. Please, just say goodbye and let me go."

"There's not a chance in hell of that." He closed the distance between them, the indistinct shadow of the man becoming flesh and blood, staunch resolve and tender love as he laid his warm hands against her face, cradling her gently. "I love you, Savannah Elizabeth Knowles, and I'm begging you to stay. To give me one more chance to get this right."

"Wh-what did you say?"

"I love you." Was it easy for a man like him to admit to those three little words? Hell, no. Nate gulped in air, squared his shoulders and shielded his chest. He had to stay tough. There was no telling if she still felt the same way. Had he hurt her too much? Had he come to his senses too late? If only he had thought to read her letters earlier. Then he would have known. He would have saved them both this anguish and this torment of standing in the unknown, facing a future without her. Without his better half.

He searched for her answer in her fathomless eyes. Tried to glean her feelings from her lovely face. She gazed up at him, shielded, her jaw slightly open as if he'd given her a good shock. He could feel her trembling. He could feel the warmth of her and the strength. Had he lost her? He couldn't breathe. His heart stopped beating. More anguish than he'd ever known racked through him. Was it too late?

Tears filled her eyes, threatening to break him apart completely. "You said my whole name." She smiled at him through her tears, a heart-starting, healing smile full of love for him. "You read my letters."

"Every last one." Maybe it wasn't too late after all. He could see now Savannah was right about Adella—the woman had never loved him, and what he had felt for her wasn't the kind of love that deepened with time and devotion. He knew because what he felt for Savannah was far different: true love.

Love terrified him, but not now that he knew what it was. It wasn't warm and syrupy and weak at all. It didn't bring him to his knees. It lifted him up, made him stronger, made him tough enough to see.

"Last night changed me. Your love changed me." It was time for her to see that, too. "I read every word you wrote. From your shy first letter telling about how you had quit your job to take care of your dying grandmother and felt hopeless, to the last one where you had sold most of her treasured books to pay the last of the medical bills."

"I can't believe you did that. That you would care enough—"

"Care? No, I never should have said that word to you. It is nothing compared to what I feel. For what I will always feel for you. I was in love with you before I read your letters. But then I got to really know you. To see the woman you are down deep, one who would give up everything to take good, loving care of her dying grandmother. Who sat up endless nights with only a few winks of sleep to keep a loved one comfortable through her last months of life. Who gives without taking. Who doesn't leave when the going gets rough. Who loves with all of her heart."

"But I didn't write about those things." She'd mentioned her devotion to her grandmother and of Grandmama's needs, of course, and her grief of losing her. But there was so much she had left out, for it was too sad to write about.

"I could see what you didn't say, Savannah. I can see your heart. I can see you." A muscle tensed in his jaw as if he were struggling with himself, fighting for the right words. "I love who you are. Please stay. Give me the chance to show you the man I am. A man who is strong enough to love you the right way forever."

This was the Nate she had fallen in love with. A man strong enough to be tender, tender enough to stand strong. A man with a heart of gold. "What about that convenient marriage you wanted?

The one where I stayed until I got tired of you, and you would be careful not to love me too much?"

A deafening whistle kept Nate from answering. Savannah had to wait as the train chugged into sight, and the rumble of its powerful engine vibrated through her feet. The engine churned past, bringing the cars behind it to a screeching stop. Smoke puffed. Activity broke out on the platform. Passengers began disembarking and travelers jostling by.

Nate stood unmoved, as if untouched by it all, and she watched the corners of his mouth quirk up in the corners. He didn't have to say a word, because she could read his heart like an open book.

"Bad idea," he said. "What I want has nothing to do with convenient. I fully intend to ply you with adoration by day and passion by night. So if you reckon that's not what you want from a marriage, you could always get on that train and leave."

He was smiling. His dark eyes twinkling with laughter. Love was in his touch as his lips claimed hers. This was no convenient kiss, no hesitant kiss, no safe kiss. No, it was passionate and warm and demanding, a promise of a lifetime of tender and exciting love. The kind she had dreamed of. The kind that would make her happy beyond measure.

"Or," he breathed against her lips. "You could stay, take my heart and be my wife. Please. I swear I will love you forever."

"Yes." She didn't have to think about it. She was absolutely certain. She could see their future together. Blissfully happy together living on that patch of land he owned, which his mother had written so lovingly of, and the house they would build there. The life they would build there together. She could see their children— two boys and two girls—growing up happy in the sunshine of their love. "A hundred times yes. I would love nothing more than to be your wife."

His ardent kiss was his answer, sealing their love. The wind gusted hard against her, as if trying to drive her more closely against her beloved. Something wet hit her face. The snow had turned to rain like a perfect sign. Spring had come to her life and to Nate Brooks's heart.

Epilogue

It was a perfect day for a May wedding, Mary Brooks thought, standing in her garden at her husband's side. Spring had finally come full force to Montana's high country. The sun was warm, the air fragrant with green grasses and budding roses and green pines. Birds trilled with delight as she watched her son lift Savannah's veil and kiss her right and proper, as a husband should.

Pride filled her at the couple she had brought together. Had she ever seen Nate look happier? If he had, she couldn't think of a time. And look how Savannah radiated happiness. In fact, one might say she was glowing. It led Mary to believe—and she was often very right in her beliefs—that a grandbaby was already on the way. What luck! Not only did she have a wonderful new daughter, but there would be a grandchild before year's end. Why, it was a dream come true.

"You did a good job, my love." Jake put his arm around her to whisper approval in her ear. "You were right. They are a perfect match."

Beneath the arbor at the gate of her rose garden, Nate took Savannah's hand gently within his own and they turned to face the gathered crowd. Mary waited until the minister pronounced the couple as man and wife before she let the first happy tear to fall.

"Now, now." Jake nuzzled close, even though they were not

alone, and kissed her cheek. "No need to cry. You know they are going to be as happy as we are."

A long, happy marriage was a great joy, as she well knew. It was exactly what she wanted for Nate—for each of her sons. Warm tingles traveled through her heart. She leaned into her husband's embrace, unable to take her gaze from the happy couple. Savannah was a complete dear with her golden curls and big blue eyes and her gentle soul. And with the way Nate seemed alive with happiness, still stubbornly gruff and growly, but with eyes full of heart and tenderness, she knew Jake was right. Theirs would be a true happily ever after.

She spotted Joseph in the crowd, and whispered in her husband's ear. "Why stop at one successful marriage? We have two more sons."

"Mary! You aren't thinking—" He looked shocked, but there it was in his eyes, the sparkle of interest and of hope.

"I most certainly am thinking of doing it again." Was it her fault there were hardly any young marriageable women for her sons to choose from in this part of the country? Of course not. But it *was* something she could rectify. "I'll put an ad in the paper first thing tomorrow morning. We'll have Joseph married and happy by year's end."

"Mary, you aren't fooling me." Jake kissed her soundly. "You want a whole passel of grandbabies."

"You know I do."

Laughing, she watched as Nate took his bride in his arms and kissed her like there was no tomorrow. Joseph gave a whistle, and the whole family broke into laughter. Yes, Joseph needed someone who could be quiet like he was, but who saw the bright side of every cloud. The perfect bride was out there, and Mary intended to find her. But for now, she would enjoy this perfect day.

With Jake's hand in hers, she went to help her son and his bride celebrate their true love for one another.

* * * * *

SHOTGUN VOWS

Kate Bridges

Dear Reader,

In the late 1890s, during the Klondike Gold Rush, springtime was always celebrated. With the thawing of rivers, people could travel more, ships came in with new passengers, and there were more opportunities for courting and the possibility of new brides.

Imagine how one such bride feels when her plans for the Spring Fever Ball go horribly wrong. Intending to dance with one man, she winds up with another. Permanently. Hardworking Milly Thornbottom is looking forward to weeks of dances and spring socials to select a proper groom, but when she's caught in a compromising situation with Corporal Weston Williams, her father forces them to marry at gunpoint.

I was inspired to write *"Shotgun Vows"* by the many tales I'd heard over the years of real-life shotgun weddings. I always imagined these marriages would be emotionally charged.

It was a lot of fun to write Milly and Weston's story, from the humor to the more dramatic elements, and I do hope you enjoy it. They're ongoing characters from my Klondike series. Milly made her first appearance in *Klondike Doctor,* on a ship traveling to Alaska. She met Weston when they were stuck in quarantine together in *Klondike Wedding.* And now they have their own story.

For more information, and photos of my research trip to the Yukon and Alaska, please visit my Web site, www.katebridges.com.

Wishing you a happy spring.

Kate

This story is dedicated to my family.

Chapter One

⚭⚭⚭⚭

Dawson City, Yukon
May 1899

"I think he's going to ask you to dance."

"Hush," said Milly Thornbottom to her good friend, Cora Vandenberg. Heat of embarrassment rushed up Milly's neck. She smoothed the pleats of her ball gown in the bright evening sun that blasted through the community lodge for the annual Spring Fever Ball. "I dearly hope not."

Her other friend, Rose Addison, whispered. "He's attracted by your wicked hat, no doubt."

Milly glanced across the crowded dance floor to the tall man in the red uniform who wouldn't let go of her gaze. A cool evening breeze ruffled the tiny hairs at the back of her knotted bun, dark brunette hair she'd carefully pinned up for the biggest event of the year. She fiddled with a lose strand.

The lace trim on her sleeves swirled through the air. Beside her, Cora leaned against Rose. The two friends were such a contrast—Cora with her ruddy complexion and short golden curls, Rose with long black tresses.

"Can't you two behave?" In order to break away from the

Mountie's gaze, Milly adjusted the brim of her hat, a wine-colored burgundy that matched her dress.

She'd stitched the organza to the brim only last night at eleven o'clock because it had been so sinfully busy at the hat and tailor shop where she worked. She'd volunteered to stay extra late to help her dear older neighbor, whose vision was going. The grandmother had needed help to hem a dress she'd attempted to fix on her own. Milly had restrung the loose beads across the waist while she was at it.

The customers had all dropped in at the last minute it seemed, women boisterously preparing for the coming week of celebrations.

The Yukon was celebrating its spring, the thawing of its rivers for passage and the endless sunshine that would soon bake the north. Milly couldn't wait.

Across the room, the door opened again and caused another breeze. More folks entered the lodge. The fluttering white sash on Milly's hat tickled her back, where her neckline plunged in a fashionable swoop.

She wondered if the man in uniform was truly coming for her, and dared another glance his way.

They hadn't spoken the entire winter.

Weston Williams. Recent recruit for the North-West Mounted Police. He maneuvered his muscled frame through the crowd, aiming his blue-eyed gaze on Milly. To her annoyance, he still made her pulse rush. Dark blond hair brushed his shoulders, a bit longer than the other Mounties'. Although she and Weston had been quarantined for measles together last summer for two whole weeks in a group of strangers, they'd rarely shared an entire conversation. No matter how hard she'd tried.

He'd treated her as though she was far beneath him; a young child compared to his maturity. Ha. He wasn't that much older.

The flecks of black in his blue eyes added to their depth and mystery. His lips seemed always on the verge of expression, yet never seemed to give away what he was thinking.

His red wool jacket tugged at the corners of his broad shoulders. Dark breeches spanned long legs and tall leather boots added height to his already-huge physique.

Did the Mounties dress to intimidate? She supposed the uniform and boots did that. Or perhaps the shoulder harness and gun.

Judging from the other men nodding at her, it seemed Weston was not the only one who'd noticed how much she'd changed from last year to this. Changed on the outside, she thought, but not on the inside. She was the same she'd always been, only he'd been too haughty to notice when it had really mattered to her.

Tonight, she appreciated the others in the room who had more manners and kinder things to say to her as a woman, not a child.

"Pardon me," said a male voice behind her.

Milly twirled around. Her long skirts flashed across the plank floors, exposing the pointed black tips of her new boots. When the mercantile's handsome son, James Yakov, nodded his dark head at her, she beamed. "James."

"Your father said I might have this dance."

"Absolutely," she gushed. "I was hoping you'd ask."

She'd stitched this dress for James. He'd once complimented her on a burgundy-colored blouse, and so she'd chosen burgundy linen for the gown tonight.

"You look pretty," he told her, causing her pleasure to deepen.

"Thank you. I've—I've never seen you in a suit before. It makes you look quite dashing."

He boldly took her hand and whirled her around the floor to a waltz, awkward at first, then synchronizing steps.

She glanced in her parents' direction. Theodore and Abigail Thornbottom, owners of the rope and broom shop in Dawson City, were watching her carefully, even while shaking the hands of Reverend Murphy. Her thin father, in his tight plaid suit and white ponytail, squeezed the plump shoulder of her mother, whose own golden ball gown Milly had worked on in secret for a solid month, and then surprised her. It had been well worth her mother's delight.

Tonight, her mother's skin was flushed with pride, her eyes sparkling as she said goodbye to the minister. The man was leaving on a journey in the morning to visit the camps that dotted the river-banks, for those in need of religious services that had been stymied by the impassable winter weather.

Milly reveled in the feel of James's loose hold on her waist. She wished he'd press tighter so she could really feel his grip. She also wished her folks would let her make her own decisions regarding dance partners, but she was working on them.

Thank goodness they'd said yes to James.

It was spring and Milly, Cora and Rose would blissfully take their time deciding on men. Potential husbands, even. The thought made Milly's stomach flutter. Like Cora and Rose, Milly was ready for courtship—for the year ahead, meeting all types of gentlemen she could thankfully choose from. Perhaps she didn't have to look far. James was here.

He squeezed her waist. She lowered her lashes and held back a smile, not wanting to be too obvious. Then to her utter shock, he twirled her around right at the base of Weston William's feet. She held her breath and didn't dare look up.

Weston had been snubbed by James already, if he'd intended to ask for the dance first. However, it was Weston's loss. He'd waited too long. Ever since last summer, to be frank.

When the waltz ended, she was panting with enthusiasm. "Thank you so much, James, I—"

"Her pa said I was next." A heavy-set older man interrupted them. Mr. Dirk Slayton. He'd apparently missed a patch of dark stubble on one cheek when he'd shaved this evening.

Queasiness rolled up her spine. Must her father direct every moment? In his late forties, Mr. Slayton was nearly as old as her folks. And as big as a giant.

She nodded goodbye to James—for the moment—and slipped her hand into the palm of this rich gold miner, one of the Klondike's newest millionaires.

He waltzed her into the crowd. She held her face away from his sweaty neck.

It was said Mr. Slayton had more gold than he could carry. More than he could spend in a lifetime. But his problem was the same as everyone else's who'd struck it rich, here in the middle of nowhere at the end of civilization.

Nothing to buy. No place to spend his massive fortune. The shops and tented stores couldn't keep up with the demand for clothing, utensils, furniture and everything else that most folks back home in Montana took for granted.

"Been a long, cold winter," said Mr. Slayton.

She nodded. Her hair tugged from its bun as he spun her around a little too freely. "Yes, sir."

"Fella gets awful lonely."

"Yes, sir."

"A wife is what I need."

"Yes...*no*...I see."

Her temple throbbed. Her fingers, moist with perspiration, slipped against his grip. She dreaded what he might say next.

"And in case you're wonderin', my nuggets are the size of eggs."

Good grief. How crass.

Milly's gaze darted about for a means of escape. Cora and Rose were also on the dance floor, being whirled about by a shopkeeper, and another gold miner even older than Milly's.

To her rescue, one of the youthful Baldwin brothers appeared. "Your parents suggested I come say hello."

With great relief and giving the pleasant bartender her best show of welcome, she moved forward, intending to place her hand in his.

Instead, a familiar figure slid in. Weston snatched her hand and placed his other firmly against her waist.

Firmly.

Her pulse leaped.

"She's mine this time, Baldwin."

Had Weston asked permission from her father?

She stared openmouthed across the floor, searching for her parents, but Weston yanked her back to look at him.

She stared up at the cut of his dark blond eyebrows, the strong lines of his jaw and cheekbone. With a tingle racing through her stomach, Milly didn't know how to stop him from entwining his fingers into hers.

"Have you asked permission?" Milly asked.

"The only permission I need is yours."

He paused for a moment to let her respond while her heart pounded against her ribs.

Piano music filled the hall. Guitars strummed. Banjo pickers added flavor to the waltz.

She should object. She should say no. He gave her precisely two seconds, then taking her silence for a yes, he pressed his warm palm against the plunging back of her dress and led her firmly across the floor.

Firmly.

Weston held her. She was stunning.

He wrapped his hand around Milly's warm, slender fingers and slid his other dangerously low along her bare back. Her mouth formed a silent gasp when he did so, which in turn made the corner of his mouth tug upward.

Fool with him, would she?

He'd give her a taste of how it felt to follow through on temptation.

How much could he expect her to take?

Last summer in quarantine had been almost impossible. She had tagged along his every step as he'd tended to the horses in the stables, always watching with those dark, luscious eyes…but she'd seemed so much younger at the time. There'd been other eyes upon him then, too. Wherever Milly had gone, her father and mother had followed. Indeed, it had been her obnoxiously interfering parents who'd kept him at a safe ten paces. They didn't see themselves as the town's biggest gossips, but everyone else did. Nothing but a headache is what they were.

Good luck to any man trying to get close to Milly.

But…what harm could one dance bring?

Maybe she'd stop making those eyes at him if he once and for all just danced with the woman. He'd get the desire to touch her out of his blood and be done with it.

In one year's time, Milly Thornbottom had matured into a startling beauty. Her brown hair, rich in the fading sunlight, framed clear skin and a pretty upturned mouth. Had her waist gotten smaller and her bosom larger, or was she simply constrained by a tighter corset? In either case, she had blossomed from a shy adolescent into a compelling and competent woman, one training as a milliner.

At least her parents had taught her the virtues of hard work and labor. They owned the only shop in town that sold ropes and brooms.

Surely a Mountie, caged indoors for an icy winter in the Yukon like he'd experienced, was allowed the presence of a beautiful woman if only for one night?

They would dance. He would know how it felt to hold her, then be on his way.

"How's business at the shop?" he asked.

"Busier than ever, now that spring has arrived."

"Does spring fever bring out the desire for colorful new hats?"

Her responding smile affected the rhythm of his breathing. Her cheeks sparkled with light glowing from the ceiling lanterns.

She tilted her head, her crimson hat framing brilliant brown hair. "How are you enjoying your apprenticeship?"

"Very much."

"I hear the veterinary surgeon is relying on you more and more."

It felt strangely pleasing that she had heard—or perhaps even *asked* about him. "We've got half a dozen horses just brought through the pass. Twelve others didn't make it. The ones that did are in rough shape. Two broodmares who'll need delivering soon."

Tenderness melted the lines of her mouth. "Will the foals be all right?"

"They're skinny, but the mares are in good health."

He pressed her close to twirl her through the crowd.

Weston lowered his palm on her back, letting it linger almost at the base of her spine. It was a racy position, and he knew it. But he enjoyed the soft feel of her, the proximity of her lips to his neck, her bosom pressed almost against his chest. When he glanced down, her scooped neckline revealed the white lace edge of her corset, making him gulp a breath.

Her corset had to be a daring new design, in order to expose this much of her bare back without the whalebone being visible.

Her lashes flashed upward at the boldness of his hand. Her nostrils flared slightly, her glossy lips parted. He restrained himself and glanced away. But his body was beginning to react in a manner that would soon betray him.

The dance ended. Weston grasped her hand. "Let's go for a walk, shall we?"

He should leave her. Right here on the dance floor, staring up at him with that feverish look, in a pretty, low-cut gown that exposed the top swell of breathtaking curves.

"Sorry," he said, abruptly changing his mind. "I didn't realize the time. I should really say good-night. Thank you for the dance."

He departed and left her with her mouth open, standing alone among the others.

Chapter Two

An hour later, Weston saw her again.

He strode to the banks of the Klondike River outside the community hall, enjoying the cool breeze that tossed the waters. It was nearly midnight, and only now was the sun setting behind the mountains. He'd only been here a year, like most of the other townsfolk, but wondered if he'd ever grow accustomed to the northern sky, the endless sunshine in the summer and never-ending winter darkness.

Older couples called goodbye, heading home from the dance. Younger couples remained indoors to lengthen the evening. Didn't they always?

Cora and Rose passed by him, hugging their shawls, long gowns rustling.

"Have you seen Milly?" asked Rose.

Weston straightened at the banks. "Not for a while."

"She was supposed to meet us outside," said Cora.

"Perhaps she was tired and went home."

Cora nodded in agreement. "Her folks have left."

"Come along," Rose said to Cora. "We'll be meeting her at the market tomorrow morning. We'll ask about her time with Mr. Slayton then."

The mention of another man's name made Weston clench his jaw. Milly was free to dance with whatever man she chose.

With a wave, Cora and Rose left for home without Milly. So should he. He'd left her on the dance floor, but couldn't seem to leave this spot in the darkness. It was such a blessed wonder to listen to the music after months of solitary living in the darkness of winter, and little contact with the fairer sex. He'd intended to go straight back to the barracks, but sitting here on an old log with the cool wind nipping at his cheeks and the scent of spring blossoms around him was difficult to abandon.

Finally he rose and headed into the lone silence of the wooded path that would lead him to the Mountie outpost. He heard a sound on the deserted path. With a shuffling of skirts, a familiar figure raced past. Milly.

"Good night," he shouted.

She turned, slowed for a moment, then picked up pace. The way she moved—shoulders narrowed, twitching when she heard his voice—unnerved him.

In a few long strides, he caught up to her. "Milly? Are you walking home alone? You really shouldn't—"

She trembled. Her hairpins had come undone and hair was tumbling down her back.

"What is it?"

"Nothing…I'm going home. I suppose I've lost my friends."

He moved toward her. "They were looking for you. But they left. I'll escort—"

"Don't—"

Was she afraid of him?

Milly tugged hard on her shawl, covering up every inch of her neckline. She was carrying her splendid hat rather than wearing it.

"What's the trouble?" he asked, slowing his long stride to keep time with hers.

"How much information would you need to press charges against someone?"

"Charges? What happened?"

"I'm not saying anything did, but if…"

He halted. Darkness engulfed them. Night birds called on the distant slopes. The scent of spring grass and dew drifted around them. Moonlight danced across her shoulders and lit the side of her cheeks, her thick lashes, the mouth that seemed to want to tell him something private.

"Why don't you tell me what happened?"

"It's—it's that Mr. Slayton…he—he put his hand on my backside…grabbed me as if I owed him something for the dance… I screamed and slapped his face and…and he said…he'd be pressing charges."

Weston clenched his teeth. The thought of that son of a bitch… He turned around and stomped back toward the hall. "I'm going to kill him."

"No—" she yanked on his elbow "—please…my father…you don't understand…the man has a million dollars."

"Did he hurt you?"

Her brown eyes softened. Tension left her shoulders. "Just my feelings, I suppose. I kicked him in the shin so hard I think I bruised my toe." Weston glared at her and she at him. "He's hurt more than I am."

"I hope you broke his leg."

She exhaled. Then she smiled, perhaps of embarrassment.

It was comfortable between them. Grateful she wasn't harmed, and feeling protective, he reached out and tugged her shoulder. Surprising him, she leaned into his chest. Entwined together, they set a slow pace toward her home.

"This is the long way back. Can you handle it?"

"It's fine…it'll give me a chance to recover."

"I'm sorry you went through that. I'll have a talk with the son of a…with the man tomorrow."

"Thank you."

"He won't come near you again. I assure you."

"I believe you, Weston."

The way she said his name played with his senses. Blood rushed through his veins. He inhaled the rich loam of the riverbanks, the heady cedars, heard the call of wolves in the forest beyond. With his arm still wrapped around her shoulder, he pressed his fingers into her arm.

She swayed in the crux of his arm and in a daring gesture of her own, reached up behind and touched his back. A simple touch, so fleeting he barely felt it, yet it rocked his flesh so thoroughly he felt as though he'd been pierced by lightning.

He halted and turned to face her.

Eyes cast low to gaze into her face, he was riveted by her looks.

"Weston, why didn't you come near me last summer? Why did you treat me as though…"

With a gentle hand, he stroked her throat, unable to resist. She was so soft and inviting. Milly searched his face as if pleading for an answer.

In response, he cupped her cheek and kissed her lips. At first restrained, tender and exploring the nature of this beautiful young woman, he quickly grew more urgent.

She stepped closer, aching to touch him, and anchored her arms up over his neck, gripping her hat behind his back and running her other hand at his throat.

Her touch was wondrous. She seared his skin, as if branding him with her sex. Weston lost himself. He kissed her lips, her chin, her neck, the base of her throat where the hollow captured the moonlight. She responded with fire, pressing herself against him, her breasts encased in that intriguing corset, her thighs pressing against his own and undoubtedly recognizing how much she aroused him.

Milly gasped at the discovery and broke away for only a fraction of time before he drew her close again and ran his hand along her waistline. He caressed the soft round of her belly, and couldn't help but envision her naked.

"What you do to me is mad," he whispered.

Surely she was a virgin with little experience in this realm, but her heated response to his kiss drove him further.

How little he needed to be pushed over the edge of reason. Of danger. He tried to tear away. He pulled his head up and faced her in the moon's glow, but couldn't fight his desire.

With a moan, he cupped her breast upward till it nearly struggled free of her corset, and kissed the golden swell. She stilled beneath his skillful hand. And then one of the pink tips appeared—a sweet, round circle, a pointed nipple.

His stomach went rigid.

He hadn't meant to go this far and he stopped. What on earth was he doing?

She seemed just as shocked as he pulled away.

"Milly, I'm sorry."

They nearly didn't hear the footsteps behind them.

With a look of sheer terror, she smoothed her neckline. They weren't quick enough for the couple approaching. Weston remained facing Milly to protect her for the seconds it took to adjust her escaping bosom.

"There you are," said her mother.

Then nothing but deep, penetrating silence behind him.

"You scoundrel," said her father. He cocked his pistol.

Mortified by the sound and the situation, Weston put his hands in the air and slowly turned to face her parents.

It was a humiliation no bride should have to bear. To be forced into marriage with her father pointing a gun at the groom.

Outside the chapel, midnight darkness mingled with the haunting call of the loons and echoed Milly's sentiments as she stood at the altar inside. She was cold. Her legs were rigid. Her body shook. Reverend Murphy read from the Good Book, her mother sobbed, her father clutched his pistol and Weston clenched and unclenched his fists beside her.

Milly's eyes stung from holding back the tears. Her ball gown rustled around her thighs. She'd chosen this gown for James. For James.

This wasn't how she had ever imagined her wedding ceremony. She'd envisioned something lovely, something to treasure and remember.

And to be thrust like this in the middle of the night before the reverend… He was leaving in the morning on his journey, and according to her father, this marriage couldn't wait a month—not even an extra hour—for the minister's return.

Anger welled inside her throat in a lump so big she could barely swallow.

How could her father force her?

The reverend looked up from his reading. He pressed his spectacles onto the bridge of his nose. His hair, ruffled on one side because he'd been roused from sleep, needed a combing. She knew she shouldn't lash out at him, but she wanted to lash out at something.

Her protests, and Weston's urging to wait, hadn't worked on either her father or the minister. Reverend Murphy had often married folks right on the spot while traveling his lengthy five months to the Klondike. In dire circumstance, there was always flexibility with the Lord, he'd said, to do things quickly.

"Is there anyone here who objects to this marriage?" the holy man asked an empty chapel. His befuddled gaze turned to the four people standing before him.

Me! Weston! Both of us!

Weston scoffed under his breath. Which made Milly finally release a sob she could no longer hold.

"Then I now pronounce you man and wife."

Head bowed, Milly squeezed her fingers together. She couldn't look up. She just couldn't.

"You may now…um…well, I suppose you've already done that…"

There was no kiss. No touch.

From the corner of her eye, she saw her mother turn and weep into her father's wool jacket.

Her father finally took his hand off his weapon. Still, Milly couldn't bear to look up at Weston.

Through a murky haze of tears, she stared at his tan boots. They'd been newly polished, she'd noticed, for the dance. The weathered lines of wear gleamed in the lantern light, tiny wrinkles caked with brown cream. He had big boots. The big boots stood perfectly still. He was appalled, as she was, at how quickly his life had turned. They'd tried to explain to her folks and the reverend that they weren't suited or ready for marriage, that the kiss had been accidental, that nothing beyond what her folks had witnessed had ever occurred between the two.

It was because Weston hadn't asked permission to dance with her, thought Milly. And her father was too stubborn to allow another man to have the upper hand.

"You'll abide my daughter," her father had finally proclaimed. *"And you'll respect my name. Do I need to go to your commander and file a complaint?"*

Milly watched the boots. Finally one turned in her direction.

She heard Weston pull in a deep breath. She swiped the tears off her cheek, and trembling, turned her head upward to meet his stare.

His blue eyes had lost their warmth, as if they'd been replaced by a slab of blue ice.

Her stomach clenched in her despair.

Stepping up to Weston, her mother sobbed into a handkerchief. "Welcome to the family."

Chapter Three

"**I** knew I would one day have this talk with you." Abigail Thornbottom, her face still puffy and damp from her explosion of tears, sank onto her daughter's mattress and patted the stack of skirts Milly was folding.

It was past three in the morning, and Milly's eyes were so dry and tired they almost squeaked. She propped two suitcases onto her bed and shoved the skirts to the bottom.

Maybe she deserved this.

She took full responsibility for her behavior. She and Weston had been caught in a compromising position. Maybe her father's fury had been justified. But the shame. She'd heard of shotgun weddings and forced marriages due to the woman sometimes being with child, but she and Weston hadn't gotten nearly that far.

To be forced in the dead of night as though they'd done something criminally wrong...

Her throat constricted with hurt and humiliation.

She'd never speak to her father again.

Why, oh, why, had she allowed Weston to kiss her? It was James she'd dreamed of all week.

She barely registered her mother's voice as she tried to come to grips with all that was racing through her.

How could she be married to Weston? Although she'd always

been attracted to him, they'd never had a full conversation about anything, let alone anything meaningful in life. Last summer, he wouldn't look at her other than to almost pat her head, explain something about the care of horses and almost gush the words, *Run along now, little Milly.*

What dreams and goals did he have in life? Did he wish to live here in the Yukon forever? Did he adore children? What did he think of her occupation?

How would they manage, living alone?

Lord, she barely knew how to cook.

Would Weston's river-blue eyes ever look at her again with dignity, not with the glare of sorrow and shame and fury she'd witnessed in the church?

Her mother folded Milly's stockings. "Anyway, it is your wedding eve. A mother has an obligation to prepare her daughter… unless you've already experienced…?"

A tide of embarrassment rushed up Milly so hot her cheeks felt like molten lava. "No, Mother, please. We keep assuring you…it didn't get far."

"Far enough."

Milly pursed her lips together and avoided a response. She told herself not to take her temper out on her mother. She had been as helpless as Milly in begging and pleading with her father.

Her mother played with the edges of her chewed handkerchief. "It will be awkward at first."

Milly cringed at the intimacy of her words.

"Awkward," her mother continued, "but if you learn to position yourself properly…"

Hmm?

"And it really does get better. If your husband is aware of…of… oh, dear, how can I say this?"

"Perhaps it's best if…if Weston and I…perhaps it's best if my husband and I figure this out on our own."

"Nonsense. My mother had this talk with me and I insist on having it with my only daughter. My only and dearest, dearest child."

"Yes, ma'am."

"You see, it can be rather painful."

"Marriage?"

"The marriage night."

Prickling with heat, Milly pivoted to her blouses and averted her focus. She folded creams with whites.

"The pain is usually brief."

"Yes, ma'am."

"And the trick is…the trick is…"

Oh, please don't have my mother teach me any clever skills.

"The trick is, you see, that your husband must care for you. That you care and love each other. It's easy to remember this when your marriage is faring well and you're happy, but it's more important to remember to look out for each other when things are not going well. He's your husband now. Abide his word. I'll pray he abides yours."

Her dear mother was trying hard to be kind. At any other time, perhaps Milly would have welcomed the conversation, but under these circumstances, she only wished it would end. Her hopes of courtship and happiness had been shattered.

With a thud, she tossed her shoes into a second suitcase. Her father had no right to treat her as if she were his property, his to decide who and when and where she'd marry.

Of course, these were the blasted laws. Her father had more legal rights over her life than she did.

She muttered a few choice words as she shoved her dresses and thrust her nightgowns into bags.

Her mother left the room and returned with five threadbare sheets. She held the pile toward Milly. "On my wedding night, my mother offered the same advice I'm going to offer you. Always keep your bed clean and fresh."

There was no further explanation, no wise words of advice, so Milly tucked the sheets into her bag. Restraining tears, she hugged her mother goodbye.

Then she trudged out of the house to meet her groom as though she was walking to the gallows.

* * *

Weston stood beside his horse and buggy outside the Thornbottoms's home, trying to control his simmering temper as he waited for his new wife.

Wife.

He knew nothing about her other than the surface things, things that didn't matter. He tried to tell himself she was no longer a timid adolescent, but a grown woman. And there was no denying she was attractive and stirred his desire.

When he'd gotten dressed to go to the dance this evening, he had no idea how much trouble one waltz would bring.

A cool wind kicked up. The mare snorted. Weston turned up the collar of his long, leather duster, adjusted his wide-brimmed Mountie Stetson, and stroked the mare's nose.

"Easy now."

His pulse was still hammering. Had he lost his mind? How could he have gotten so stuck in a situation that another man had held a gun to his head? Every time he thought of old man Thornbottom, Weston gritted his teeth.

To threaten to go to his commander... Weston was a new recruit, had little say in the police force, and a soiled reputation could earn him a swift booting. It was either marry Milly, or if her father chose to press charges against him, be forced to leave the Mounties.

He braced himself in the wind. No one else mattered in this entire mess except he and Milly.

What they wanted should be his focus.

But what sort of a man allowed himself to be led like this?

Hell.

Milly hadn't done anything more than he had to deserve this sentencing, but he was damn angry.

What the hell had he been thinking, and why hadn't he been able to control his urges?

What kind of a man...of a Mountie was he? She'd come to ask for help in dealing with Slayton, and in the end, Weston had been the worse culprit. He'd taken advantage of her alone in the woods.

But not enough to be forced into marriage!

Yes, they'd gotten caught up in the heat of that kiss. Her breast had slipped out by accident, and for that he was truly sorry, but to pay for it with the rest of his life?

The house door opened and three shadows loomed on the porch. Weston refused to go closer to speak to her parents.

Her mother called goodbye to her daughter, her father stood with his arms crossed, watching, as Milly hauled her suitcases toward Weston.

The bags slapped against her legs.

"Good luck, Milly," her father said rather sadly.

She didn't answer. Indeed, it appeared she refused to acknowledge the old man. Weston didn't blame her.

He jumped to the gate and opened it for her. Without a sound, he shoved her luggage to the backseat of the buggy and went around to help her get in, but she slid up and onto the seat without waiting for his aid.

He tugged on the reins. The mare moved off. The buggy clomped along the hard dirt.

Wordless, they stared ahead at the passing buildings and tents of Dawson City. Banners above them proclaimed Medicinal Cures, Mining Equipment, Canned Goods, Jewelry Repair. Milly ignored them all, but he saw her head turn slightly as they passed the newly painted storefront where she worked, Genevieve's Hats and Suits.

"Are you cold?" he asked his new wife.

"I'll be fine," she said stiffly. "Where are we headed?"

"Three streets down from Main. There's a small cabin belonging to my friend Jack."

"Right, I've met your friend Jack. Is he still out in the gold fields?"

"Wanted me to look after his cabin while he was gone."

"You sure he won't mind?"

"It's a temporary place to stay till we sort out where we'll go permanently."

Permanently, he thought. A life sentence.

"Right," she said, head bowed.

"I'm sorry, Milly."

"I regret what's happened, too," she whispered.

He felt as though he'd failed her, as well as himself. She still seemed so overwhelmed by the turn of events she couldn't stomach looking at him.

What did he expect?

He could barely stomach the situation himself.

Like guilt-ridden thieves, they crept along the quiet streets in the cover of darkness, wondering how on earth they would tell their friends tomorrow.

Weston wondered how he would report himself to the commander. Commissioner York.

Milly wondered how on earth they would make this forced marriage work in any way that resembled normality.

But as the mare and buggy came to a rolling stop in front of the darkened log cabin, they were both stricken with the immediate thought of how they would get through this.

Their wedding night.

Chapter Four

Weston grappled for something to say to his new bride that wouldn't reflect his growing indignation.

"I've got the bags."

Whipping the luggage out of the buggy with more ill temper than he'd intended to display, he followed Milly as she bolted into the cabin.

Now that their initial shock had worn off, resentment set in. He could tell fury was building in her, too, by the stiffening of her neck, the manner in which she snapped away from him, even the sharp bite of her step.

For pity's sake, she wasn't making this any easier.

The less he said tonight, the better. They were both tired. It added to their strain.

When he entered the cabin behind her, the chill inside nipped at his jaw.

With her lips pressed together and cheeks twitching with unspoken accusation, she whipped her shawl over her shoulder and scanned the items in the room. There was a cold cast-iron stove, a kitchen counter cramped with jars, pots and utensils, a cramped parlor area with a sofa and chair and bookshelves undoubtedly stuffed with last year's newspapers.

The moon's glow from the window streamed down on her

dark head, accentuating her disapproving stare on the tattered carpet.

He shoved past her with the bags. "I'll put these in the bedroom."

"Will you now?" she snapped.

Irritated by her tone, he dropped the luggage at his feet, dangerously close to saying exactly what was on his mind. He towered so high above her there was little connection between them. "Let me understand something. Are you blaming *me* for this?"

She swung around, her skirts fanned the air. "You could've asked permission for that dance!"

"It's not the dance that got us into this situation."

"It's what started it."

He ordered himself to stop, to say no more, but it flew out. "I thought what started it was your behavior last summer."

She placed a hand at her throat and stepped back. "What's that supposed to mean?"

He narrowed his eyes, speaking to her in the dark, her silhouette cast in moonlight. "Your father and mother knew very well how much time you spent in quarantine following me around. Maybe that's why they insisted on this silly marriage." He couldn't keep the sarcasm from his voice. "Your dream come true."

She parted her mouth, speechless.

Then, coming to her senses quickly, she fought back. "How dare you suggest I had a hand in any of this. *You* asked *me* to dance, remember? I was perfectly content to spend the entire evening with James Yak—" She bit her lip and said no more, but it was too late.

It was Weston's turn to stare with his mouth open. "James…" So his wife already had a beau!

He took a moment to swallow his circumstances, so different from last night when he'd slept in the barracks as a bachelor. A married man with a reluctant wife.

Milly seemed flustered by her own admission. She unwrapped her shawl and slung it over a sagging upholstered chair and sauntered to the counter.

"I brought sheets." She gulped. "Bag on your right." Then mumbling to herself, "Dream marriage…"

He watched her as she tried to avoid his glare. Maybe a confrontation was exactly what they needed. She was his wife now, despite what either of them wanted, and she would listen to him.

"I'll light a lantern." She removed a long match she found in a box above her, struck it, then adjusted the long, orange flame. The scent of kerosene filled the air. The fire's glow struck the petulant turn of her lips.

This was how it was going to be, was it? Casual talk of lanterns and bedsheets when their entire lives had just been thrown out the window?

And what of his career? Her father…reminding him that he was a Mountie and supposed to uphold standards of decency.

As if he needed reminding.

His words came with a brute edge. "Where would you like your bags, Mrs. Williams?"

She startled at the words, first by her new name, and second by what they implied, and her frustration erupted. "I don't know where you're sleeping, but I'm sleeping in the bedroom!"

She tried to sail past him and yank her bags out of his hand, but he refused to let go.

"This is your dream marriage, remember?" He panted as he stomped into the bedroom and flung the luggage to the mattress. "You're my wife and we'll sleep together!"

With nostrils flaring, she gaped at him. Then her breathing subsided and her face softened. She bowed her head. "All right. If that's your wish."

That was more like it. He was the husband. He would make the decisions from this point forward. "I'll put the mare in the barn and be back shortly."

"As you say."

But as soon as he stepped past the bedroom door, it slammed behind him and he heard the grinding of the lock as it closed.

He winced. Damn it. He'd been had.

Sunlight flooded the feather duvet on the bed, but when Milly opened her eyes, she recognized nothing. For the few seconds before she recalled the disastrous events of last night, she basked in the heat of the warm Yukon sun.

Then the memory of the wedding crashed down on her.

Jolting up, she looked for Weston. No sign of him.

Of course not. They'd argued last night and she'd bolted the bedroom door.

She wondered with trepidation if there was anything a husband could do if a wife refused him in bed. Was there anything in the law books to force her? Weston was a Mountie and he knew the laws....

She cradled her head. What a sorry mess.

Jumping out of bed, she reached for her clothes. She clawed into a skirt and blouse and dashed into the other room. He wasn't there, either.

What was she hoping for? An apology from him? He was harsh and crude, demanding she be subservient to his wishes. Just like her father.

The ticking clock on the mantel declared it was five minutes past seven. The horsehair sofa looked indented, as though a large body had lain there for a few hours.

Guilt crept up her cheeks. So what, she told herself. So she'd had the bed and he'd had this sofa. As a police officer, he traveled great distances in his duties and often slept outdoors on the hard ground. Furniture was a luxury for these men.

Weston had likely been very grateful for this sofa.

But he'd gone to work. It was Saturday; most Mounties worked today.

She, too, was expected at her shop by nine. Today was their busiest day of the week and some women still needed fittings for the dresses they'd ordered late for the week's festivities.

Did life just go on after one was married? Was there no celebration, no joy in waking up together and perhaps, at least, sharing breakfast?

Her stomach rumbled with hunger. What was there to eat? She turned to the cupboards hung on the kitchen's log wall and spotted some coins on the counter.

Weston must have left them for her. Why?

She soon got her answer when she ransacked the empty cupboards. There was nothing in the house to eat except a half-filled jar of honey. She'd have to go to the market this morning. Ravenous, she found a spoon and took a bite of half-creamed honey.

While that melted in her mouth, she tied her hair into a tail and washed her face with the pitcher of standing water Weston also must've hauled in.

Sliding the coins off the counter, she grabbed her wicker hand basket and straw hat and flew out the door.

She prayed she wouldn't meet anyone she knew. Well, she did know almost everyone in town, so that was impossible, but she prayed she wouldn't run into any of her *good* friends. She needed a few hours to find the words to tell them what had happened, to figure out how she'd explain her new status as wife to Corporal Weston Williams.

Her boots pounded the planks of the boardwalk leading to the market. Morning sunshine cast clear shadows in the streets.

Weston should be at her side to announce it. Logic told her he had to go to work, but her heart filled with a longing she couldn't define.

The market stalls were packed with shoppers. She wrapped her shawl around her head and kept her face lowered as she walked.

But she'd forgotten that a paddle wheeler had anchored in last night, carrying wares from the south, the town's first steamboat to get through the river's thaw. Of course the markets would be crowded with townsfolk all vying for the dried fruits, canned vegetables, sturdy jeans, locks and shovels, and other badly needed supplies the vessel had no doubt delivered.

Milly headed for the dried meats.

"Good morning," hollered Cora across the way.

Milly peered up and groaned. Her insides wobbled at what explanations lay ahead.

Plump and smiling in her housedress and kerchief, Cora waved as Rose, beside her, bought withered oranges—already dried out from the long voyage here, but as appetizing and pleasing as anything a person could hope for in the middle of nowhere.

Cora, cheeks reddened from the cool air, puffed to catch up with Milly, who ordered two sausages from the butcher.

"What on earth happened to you last night?" Cora gripped the handle of her splintered straw basket.

"We looked for you for quite some time." Rose puckered her lips, as if hurt. "It would have been nice to let us know you were leaving early."

Gooseflesh rose on Milly's arms. "I'm sorry." She placed her wrapped sausages into her basket, trying to hide the shaking of her fingers. "Two pickled eggs," she asked the vendor, then turned back to her friends. "I—I didn't leave early. I believe you left before me."

Rose sniffed into her handkerchief. "Oh, our apologies, then. We were the rude ones."

"No one was rude."

How could Milly explain this to her two dearest friends?

I was married last night. Dear Weston got caught with his hand in the sugar bowl.

Or, *You'll never believe what happened. I not only danced with Weston, I married the son of a gun!*

Or perhaps what she was closest to feeling. *My father forced Weston Williams, at gunpoint, to the chapel. I don't know what to do or where to run.*

Cora squinted in the sunshine. Her short blond hair, of Dutch heritage, looked almost white in the morning light. "Did you get home all right, then?"

Milly clenched and unclenched her fingers on her packages, trying to find the right words. "No, actually I was with…a *man*."

Rose gasped. "Good Lord, don't tell me it was…"

Cora's eyes grew as round as the coins in her palm. She whispered in a slight frenzy, "You didn't go home last night?"

Milly tried again, "I went home with…a *man*."

The two women looked stricken, as though their hearts had failed. Rose's basket dropped to the ground. Oranges tumbled. After a pause, they scurried after them.

"Land's sake. Don't you ever tease me like that again!" Chuckling, Cora got up from her knees and planted a runaway fruit back into Rose's hands.

Rose adjusted her bonnet around her long black braid. The trauma of surprise faded from her face. "You! You have quite the sense of humor this morning. Care to buy some lard?"

Floundering for more words, Milly tried to speak but her friends, still chuckling, turned their backs to buy cooking staples. Flour, sugar, salt.

Milly glanced timidly at the faces around her. No one paid her any heed. They didn't know. They hadn't heard about the humiliation she'd suffered last night.

Bodies bumped past Milly as she stood frozen, unsure of what to do while her two friends continued shopping.

"Milly, what are you wearing tonight for the barbecue?" Cora asked over her shoulder. "That pretty plaid gown?"

"Don't be silly," said Rose. "She said she'd lend it to me, remember? *If* she finished her new dress on time. Right, Milly? Did you finish?"

Milly's spirits plummeted. Was she going to the barbecue and dance? Likely not. She hadn't discussed any of it with Weston, and in either case, neither of them would have the heart to join in any festivities.

"Morning, miss," said a gent to her left.

She swung around, and to her astonishment, Mr. Slayton, standing tall and wide in a tight wool jacket that accentuated the bulk at his middle, nodded at her.

She moaned. An undercurrent of trouble seemed to follow this gold miner. Three other rough-looking men—he'd hired as bodyguards, it was rumored—accompanied him. How could he pretend to be polite after last night's attempt at grabbing her behind?

"Good morning," she said curtly and stepped away, joining Rose and Cora as they made their way to the spice stalls.

And then, to her utter humiliation, another familiar voice called out on her other side. "Mornin', Milly."

James. Dark-haired, handsome James. How was she to explain this mess to him? She wiggled her fingers in hello, then rushed away.

"Milly!" he repeated. "Hold on a minute!"

Dirk Slayton was faster at getting to her side. She shoved her basket higher to impede him from stepping too close.

"I've come to ask you to the dance this evening." Slayton grinned, exposing a gold tooth on his lower jaw. He'd shaved the spot on his cheek he'd missed yesterday. His long, dark hair, slicked straight back from his ears, had just been soaped, for he smelled clean today.

"Thank you, but I can't."

Mr. Slayton stepped in beside her and Cora. "I could ask any woman I want to. But I've set my sights on you."

"I—I do appreciate the gesture."

"Hell, it's no gesture. I've got a lot of gold to spend. You've got a lot of wishes, I'll bet, on how to spend it." He laughed. "Seven o'clock. I'll speak to your father and pick you up at your home."

"Please...I can't." Milly tried to duck away.

But James appeared on her other side, wearing his work clothes, holding empty buckets for sale. "You heard the lady. Step off, Slayton."

Cora and Rose came to a shuddering halt. Milly held her breath so hard she thought she'd explode in her corset.

Slayton looked from James to her. "I asked first. It's only right she answer me." His loud bellow attracted the attention of the folks around them.

Cora nudged Milly in the ribs as if urging her to say yes to the millionaire Slayton. Rose, on the other side, pinched Milly's elbow and eyed James, indicating the younger, handsome businessman as the better choice.

Feeling cold and weak, Milly peered at the watchful faces in the crowd, then at Slayton. "I'm afraid I don't live there anymore. At my father's house."

The giant was put off balance for a second. "Whaddya mean? Where do you live?"

She nearly fell over when she heard the cool male voice behind her.

"With me," Weston declared, stepping forward in his scarlet uniform. "She's my wife."

Chapter Five

Weston tried to control the pounding emotions running through him. His sleeve brushed Milly's shoulder as he glared from one offensive man to the other. Of the entire group, she seemed the most upset by his arrival.

No smile. No warm welcome in front of the others. Was she or wasn't she relieved to see him?

Slayton, pushing a lock of hair from his brows, blinked from one to the other. "You? She married *you?*"

Weston's jaw flickered with a beating artery. What was so damn surprising that she might've chosen him on her own accord?

James was cooler in his reaction. His grin disappeared. Perplexed, he stared at Milly and her heightening color.

James was the one Milly had her sights on last night. How utterly disappointing it must be for him. *Ha.* Weston felt like kicking the tar out of him but he wasn't sure why.

Weston looked to the other man, Slayton, and hurled back. "That's right. She married *me.*"

Rose wound her arm through Cora's, both women speechless and beet-red. They took a step back from Milly, as though betrayed by their friend for not confiding.

Milly tried to repair the breach. "Cora…Rose…I tried to tell you."

Slayton fingered the guns at his round hips. "When did you have time for a wedding?"

"Last night," said Weston coolly. "We caught the preacher before he left town." He planted an arm around Milly and yanked her close. Perhaps she wasn't expecting it, for her wicker basket of food dipped in her hands and nearly spilled.

"Why didn't you tell me, miss?" Slayton's upper lip thinned with suspicion.

Her voice squeaked with nervous tension. "There was no time."

"You could've told me while we were dancin'."

"I apologize."

Slayton pursed his lips and stuck his chin out of his collar, as though the heat of anger was creeping up on him. He motioned slightly to his two bodyguards, and they took a step closer to Weston, on either side. What was the lug planning?

Weston clenched his fists as he recalled how Slayton had forced Milly last night with his unwanted affections, and then had the gall to say he would press charges against her. Maybe Weston would beat the tar out of him, too.

"We need to talk, Slayton," he said. "Privately."

The scoundrel wouldn't get the best of him or his new wife. Milly tugged at Weston's elbow, as though she'd noticed his physical reaction.

"Please don't," she whispered into his shoulder. "Let's just go."

James shifted the buckets in his hands and narrowed his heated gaze on Weston, making Weston's muscles tense. This man, with his quiet demeanor and his hold over Milly was far more of a threat than Slayton.

But what the hell could James do? Weston had married her. It brought a smile of satisfaction to his mouth.

James seemed to notice it. He struck back with a cutting insult. "Mighty kind of you to lend your intended bride to so many other men last night."

Weston reeled as though he'd been slugged in the gut. It was one thing to attack him, but to insult Milly was too much.

He leaped forward, Milly yelped, Slayton's two bodyguards

staggered back in surprise, and Weston, exploding with all the frustration of the last twenty-four hours, punched James square in the jaw.

Horrified, Milly stared at the two men fistfighting. James leaped back to his feet, spit on the ground, circled Weston and lunged. He whacked the Mountie in the stomach. Weston fell over. The crowd parted and onlookers shoved each other to get a better look.

"What are they fightin' about?" asked one.

"Her," said another.

"Do something!" Milly begged Slayton.

He snarled in smug pleasure, helped himself to a wrinkled apple from a nearby stall and bit into it as he watched the entertainment.

Weston rose to his feet and circled his opponent, oblivious to her pleading. James kicked his knee, Weston swung and crunched the man's jaw again.

Desperate, Milly bobbed in place, searching for other Mounties—or anyone—who might help her. Not a soul. So, she did the only thing she could. She stepped right beside Slayton and just as bold as you please, slid one of his guns from his holster, gripped it with both hands, closed her eyes and blasted a bullet into the air. Her shoulders lurched.

"Damn it, lady," Slayton shouted. "Never take my gun!" He grabbed it back from her shaking fingers.

In the middle of slugging each other, Weston and James stopped.

Weston seemed to gain hold of his senses. He raised his hands as though declaring a truce, stepped back and brushed dirt from his sleeves. "You got anything else to say about me or my wife, you can say it to me alone. Got that?"

James scoffed, scrambled to collect his strewn buckets and headed out without a glance in her direction.

What a horrible thing James had said about her. Milly couldn't believe the words had come from him.

Weston watched her as she stared at James's retreating figure. Conscious of the eyes on her, she lowered her head and straightened the items in her basket.

"Let's go." Weston grabbed her elbow and escorted her firmly from the market. She didn't even have time to say goodbye to Cora and Rose.

"You're too impulsive," Milly told him as they stormed away on the boardwalk. "If you weren't so quick to follow every urge that strikes you, we wouldn't be in this mess."

"Me? Again you blame me?"

"Why did you come here this morning? What good did it do?"

"I checked in with the commander and the stables are quiet. There's a few animals to examine this afternoon, but I thought you might need some help at the market."

"This kind of help I don't need."

They walked in stewing silence.

She brushed away strands of hair that had escaped from her tail in all the commotion. "What did Commissioner York say about your marriage?"

His blue eyes flashed with temper.

"You did tell him?"

"How could I not?"

"And?"

"He said congratulations."

"That was it?" She knew without a doubt Weston hadn't divulged the fact they were forced into marriage.

"He wanted to know if it would affect my duties. If I needed some time away. Of course, I told him no."

"Of course." Again, she felt a mad sense of betrayal. Young married couples were supposed to spend every free moment together. Yearn for it, in fact.

What did Weston yearn for? Her disappearance?

What did she want? She had been looking forward to courtship and choosing her own husband.

She sighed.

They reached the end of the boardwalk and parted ways. Weston tipped his fingers against his brow, Milly nodded, and that was that. He headed toward the outpost, she delivered her food to their home, then made her way to the hat shop.

Another sticky situation awaited her there. Putting aside her embarrassments, Milly grasped the door handle and pushed. Several customers turned their heads to look.

"We heard!" Genevieve, her older cousin and owner of the hat shop, six months with child, waddled toward Milly. She'd married her husband, Luke, also a Mountie, last year and they were remarkably content. A sharp contrast to Milly and Weston. Genevieve gave Milly a big hug, as far around as she could reach and crushed her for a time.

It was nice to be held. The comfort and acceptance from Genevieve was more than anyone had shown Milly in this entire mess.

"You will make a wonderful wife," Genevieve said gently. "I know Weston. He's a good man. Congratulations." She gave her a kiss on the cheek.

"But, Genevieve, you don't know how this all came about—"

Genevieve brushed aside her hair and held her chin in her hands. "I can very well guess," she whispered, "by its quickness. Knowing your folks, I imagine it's not easy for you. Whatever the circumstance, your marriage is cause for celebration."

Before they got too far into their discussion, customers interrupted. Dresses needed to be fitted, and everyone, absolutely everyone, asked questions about Milly's new marriage. She stood her customers before the full-length mirror, pins stuck in her mouth, her fingers grazing the latest cotton prints.

"How long was your engagement?"

"You kept a secret from us all!"

"Corporal Williams is quite the fella. I don't know how you managed…"

"My dear Rebecca was hoping he'd—"

Yes, well, I beat them all, didn't I? Milly wasn't proud of her accomplishment. Last summer, she willingly would have fallen into his arms, but now, it was entirely different knowing he was not a willing participant in his marriage.

Last night had been an utter fiasco.

"What are you wearing to the barbecue?" Genevieve asked close to four o'clock, near closing time.

"I don't think we'll be going."

"Why on earth not?"

"He doesn't really want…we'd have to face my father…James might be there."

James. If she hadn't heard it for herself, she wouldn't have believed he could be so cruel. And what was almost worse…she felt guilty that her terrible disappointment over his true character weighed so heavily on her heart.

She was married to Weston. She had better learn to accept it and to work toward pleasing her new husband and herself.

Perhaps the incident at the market happened for good purpose. It had shown her that Weston would stand up to any man who misspoke or mistreated her.

That was certainly something positive.

"We'll pick you up at six," Genevieve rambled on. "I've been working on hemming your new dress all day."

"I forgot about my dress. That was my job—"

"You were busy with the customers. Here, take it please." She pressed the pretty fabric against Milly. "We'll use our big buggy tonight. Go home to your husband and…and have a talk with him. We'll be by to pick you up shortly."

It was easier said than done.

Milly got home, washed up and brushed her hair. Weston didn't arrive home till five to six, leaving her with the impression he wasn't planning on going to the barbecue under any circumstance. His face was solemn. A bruise was erupting above his left eye.

Oh, wonderful. Everyone at the dance would see.

The bruise added a hint of danger to his powerful physique, and made Milly uncomfortably aware of him. The gruff lines around his eyes indicated his misery. Maybe his colleagues had heard about his fistfight and had given him grief. Or had heard about the true nature of his wedding. If her cousin could guess the circumstance so quickly, then his friends might've, too.

"Maybe we should sit this one out," he said glumly.

She hadn't changed into her dress yet, wondering if she should bother, but with a newfound determination she decided to stand firm. "Weston, I think we need to face whatever it is we're avoiding. If we get this over with…announcing our news and talking about it…maybe it'll get easier."

He thought about that, then apparently came to the same conclusion.

"Don't have any clean uniforms. I'll wear my regular clothes. Give me twenty minutes."

Her nerves twisted into a ball. She could never predict what he was going to say or do or how this evening would turn out.

"All right." She dashed into the bedroom to get into her dress while Weston went outside to the pump to haul some fresh bath-water.

When Genevieve and Luke arrived in their buggy, Milly was ready first and went out to greet them. While she waited outdoors in the fading sun, Weston changed into his casual clothes, then just when she thought he'd changed his mind and would never come out, he strode off the porch toward her.

The cool line of his mouth and stiff cut of his shoulders indicted how difficult this was for him, and made her stomach lurch at what the evening ahead would bring with her new husband by her side.

Chapter Six

$\mathcal{Q}\mathcal{Q}\mathcal{Q}\mathcal{Q}\mathcal{Q}\mathcal{Q}\mathcal{Q}\mathcal{Q}$

$\mathbf{M}$aybe tonight would go better than he feared.

Weston stepped off the porch. His sore eye throbbed, reminding him with each burning step that folks were bound to notice. To hell with them all.

This evening's barbecue was less formal than last night's ball. He wore his newly starched white shirt and blue denim jeans. Milly had apparently ironed them both in anticipation.

His old suede jacket with the fringes on the sleeves made him feel more like himself. And the holstered guns that fit snug on his hips.

Milly was standing behind her cousin and husband at the rear of the buggy, and Weston didn't have a good view of her at first.

Inspector Luke Hunter, also in civilian clothes—black shirt, black tie—gave him a heartfelt handshake. "Congratulations. Take care of her, Weston. She's a good woman."

Genevieve embraced Weston, shocking him with her gushing. "I can't believe it…my little Milly. Oh, Weston…"

Enough of the hearty family welcome. He hadn't come into this willingly. Why go overboard pretending?

Nonetheless, he gave his thanks to Genevieve and Luke. In fact, Luke was his superior officer, the veterinary surgeon training him. Luke had been out of town today tending to a sickly stallion, and hadn't heard the news.

When Weston finally swung around to Milly, he was caught breathless by the vision.

She was dressed in red from head to toe. It was a simple country gown on first glance: cotton fabric that rippled at the bosom, with splashes of cotton lace trimming her open neckline and the edge of her sleeves. But something about the cut of the fabric looked sophisticated. He'd heard she had a talent for sewing and creating her own patterns. The red fabric added a luminance to her skin where the neckline dipped to her cleavage. Her glossy brunette hair, half pinned up at the back, seemed to sparkle against the color of her warm, brown eyes.

"You look nice," he said. The unexpected comment surprised him as much as it did her.

She cast her eyes at the intertwined fingers she clutched in her lap as the mare tore off. "Thank you."

"I appreciate your ironing my clothes."

"You're welcome."

So formal with each other. He wished they'd loosen up, but at least it was a start.

The dreaded whispers started as soon as they arrived at the outdoor festivities. Luke reined the mare by a circle of cotton-woods. The man tending to the animals and buggies took one look at Milly and Weston in the back, then mumbled something to his attendant. They both smirked and looked away.

Folks gathered at the barbecue pits by the roasting corn and frying fish swept their gazes this way, too, then nudged each other. Some of the politer ones had the courtesy to say hello and keep their mouths shut.

Weston placed a hand beneath Milly's elbow and led her to the picnic table where the Mounties were congregating. The ones who were married had brought their wives.

Dr. Elizabeth Hunter, the town's incredible female doctor, and her husband, Colt.

Colt and Luke were brothers—as well as Mounties—who'd traveled to the Klondike together.

Then there were the newlyweds Lily and Dylan Wayburn.

Dylan was an inspector, too, and Lily was starting up a string of visitor lodges along the route to the Yukon.

The other couples were smiling and sharing plates of food. Luke draped his arm around Genevieve.

It made the cool distance between Weston and Milly seem even more detached.

He took his place beside her. The other wives knew Milly, and welcomed her graciously as though nothing was amiss. They chatted about their gowns and the evening's events.

The lump above his left eye was growing and now partially obstructed his view.

Weston scanned the crowd. When he spotted Milly's folks, he stiffened.

What was he supposed to say to them after last night? Was he to bow down to Theodore as if he owed him the world for his daughter's hand?

"Evenin'," said Abigail to Milly.

"Evenin'," said Milly. She kissed her mother's cheek but didn't look at her.

Theodore stepped closer, Weston nodded with all the restraint he could muster, and walked the other way.

He needed time to swallow all of this.

Apparently so did Milly. When he glanced back, she seemed to be battling something inside of herself, trying to control the sorrow and hurt as her father approached. Unable to hold back, she let out a silent sob, broke free of her mother, turned away from her father and bolted to the nearest tree.

Weston felt a tug of powerful emotion. He should have stuck by her. He should have helped her handle her father, even if that meant they would both walk away, but at least together.

He should have been there for his wife.

The games started. There were darts to throw, balls to toss, candies to be won and horses to be raced.

Weston had approached Milly an hour earlier, when she'd

escaped her father, but before he could get to her, the other women settled in around her—Elizabeth and her cousin Genevieve.

Weston was itching to leave, but Milly seemed to be content to sit by her cousin's side and listen to tales of the dress shop.

How much longer? Half an hour? He caught her eye again, and this time, Milly didn't immediately look away. Genevieve was whispering some humorous story in her ear, the other women laughing, but Milly was looking with hope at Weston.

Orange sunshine from beyond the ridge of mountains warmed the glow in her cheeks and heightened the hue of color around her cleavage. He was drawn to look at her shapely figure, the one that had caused all this trouble to begin with.

Last night, he hadn't even begun to kiss her where he'd wanted to. He'd gotten as far as running his tongue along the lovely swell of her bosom. Although he'd seen the beauty of her bare breast when it had escaped her corset, he hadn't been able to get anywhere near it. Not with his hands or mouth.

The vision, the memory of her beautiful breast stayed in his mind. He smiled slightly at Milly, and winked.

She blushed and turned away.

His wife? Shy? It was ridiculous to have to court her as though they were strangers, but perhaps that's what he had to do, for after all, they barely knew each other and there'd been no time for courtship.

The boom of three horses galloping on the distant grass on the other side of the river made him turn his head. The townsfolk had made a track for the races.

"Go!" said the stranger marching past him, urging one of the racehorses. "Cut to the inside!"

The crowd around him cheered, and that's when Weston spotted Dirk Slayton and his three bodyguards.

"I'll supply all winners with free meals at the Casino restaurant!" he boasted.

Weston groaned and turned away, only to catch sight of James Yakov.

He was making eyes at some other young lady, the daughter of a miner, partnered up with her in the sack race.

Cora seemed to be avoiding her friend Milly. When the games were nearly over, Milly joined his side.

"I haven't seen you speaking to one person tonight."

"I'm speaking with you, aren't I?" His grin softened his words. She gave him a slight smile.

"Are you implying that I'm being rude?"

"If the shoe fits." She popped a raisin into her mouth, raised her eyebrows and challenged him. Yet the sparkle in her eyes indicated more of a tempting nature to her challenge.

She was teasing him.

He was about to yank her by the elbow to murmur something private in her ear, when Rose breezed by.

"Very pretty gown," she whispered to Milly.

Weston didn't understand how such a kind comment could turn Milly's expression into one of regret. "Rose, I'm so sorry. I forgot about the plaid dress. I would've brought it over but I completely forgot."

Rose's mouth puckered with hurt. "Heavens, don't worry about that. It was just a dress."

"But I promised it to you, and dearly would've loved to—"

"Yes, well." Rose swiped her hands along her worn country skirts. "I suppose you've got more important things to think about now." Rose turned her eyes on *him* in pointed fashion.

Weston felt the heat of embarrassment creep up his neck.

"Rose, please," Milly insisted. "You're still a major part of my life. Perhaps you and Cora could join me tomorrow afternoon for tea at…at…our new cabin."

"Cora and I have been invited to the Sunday social."

"Oh."

The music started—banjos, guitars, harmonica. One of the Mounties whisked Rose away with no chance for more talk.

Weston and Milly sat out the first dance.

And the second. On the third, folks were turning their heads and beginning to stare at the newlywed couple. Since no one truly knew that their marriage was motivated by a shotgun, and despite his anger at the forced marriage, Weston wanted to spare Milly from folks ever finding out. Which meant they had to pretend more cheer, whether he felt it or not.

He swallowed his pride and asked his wife. "Care to dance?"

They were stiff with each other. They stood two feet apart. His grip beneath her hand was slippery. It felt so different from holding her last night, when there had been tension, excitement and anticipation. It was because everyone was staring, he told himself. If the gawking eased up a bit, he could relax and show Milly that he was trying.

But the dance ended and she stepped away.

That's when Dirk Slayton and his three bodyguards made their move. Slayton sauntered over to them, hat in hand.

"I'd like to apologize," he said to her.

A flash of surprise shot through her face. Weston didn't trust the fellow and wouldn't be swayed.

"It was boorish of me to say what I did to you last night, and then again my bluntness this morning."

"Apology accepted." Milly bristled, smoothed her skirts and nudged her way through the crowd toward the tables of food.

"There's more," Slayton said.

Weston stepped up protectively to her side and waited. This time he wouldn't desert his wife.

"I've been watching you this evening," said Slayton.

Weston startled him by replying for her. "Our life is none of your concern."

The gold miner adjusted his cravat. "What I see are two miserable people."

Folks around them stopped moving. Ears turned.

Weston tried to keep his rising temper in check, his voice on an even keel. "Like I said. None of your concern."

Slayton scratched the back of his ear. "I can read people pretty well. And I'd say you were forced into it."

Milly gasped. The man was simply stating what everyone here was probably guessing, but good manners prevented them.

Slayton was a brazen son of a bitch.

Weston's sore left eyelid throbbed. "Folks, enjoy the rest of your evening." He grabbed Milly's hand and whirled toward the picnic tables.

"I'd like to strike a bargain," Slayton bellowed.

All heads turned. The crowd's whispering stopped.

"I'm not interested in anything you've got."

"How about her father then?" Slayton turned and scanned the crowd. "Where's Theodore?"

Beneath a far tree, Theodore looked up from a plateful of fried fish and biscuits. He set the food down and made his way through the crowd.

"Let's go," Milly whispered. "I can't bear to watch another fight."

"I don't plan on fighting," Weston replied. "It was a mistake this morning and I won't do it again."

Slayton cleared his throat. All eyes were on him. "Let's not pretend your marriage happened because you two were thrilled to get hitched."

Women gasped.

Weston's fist clenched above his holstered guns.

"It's obvious you're miserable," Slayton pleaded at Milly. "I'm the man to help you get out of this terrible arrangement."

Weston's nostrils flared in disbelief. His blood raced. "Beg your pardon?"

"I'd like to buy Milly's hand in marriage."

The crowd went mad.

Weston's heart beat like thunder. Milly turned white. Beside her, her approaching mother clamped a hand over her mouth and Theodore grabbed his forehead in amazement.

"Keep your bloody money," Weston ground out, barely able to control his rage. "And shut your bloody mouth!"

He gripped Milly's hand and pulled her toward the cotton-woods. No, not there. They'd come by horse and buggy but would walk home. He turned and headed past the river.

Slayton called after them. "I'm offerin' you all the veterinary medicine you can buy with a barrel full of gold! Whatever's left over, you can keep to buy some stallions. Animals don't come cheap to travel over the ocean and the mountains."

"Go to hell!"

"For Theodore and Abigail, I'll throw in another barrel of nuggets. I hear they're achin' to build a fine country home. With servants, maybe, and stables. As for Milly, I'll build her the finest dress shop in the Klondike. Imported silks and lace. She'll have her independence *and* money of her own!"

Weston kept stomping, his heart wildly out of control, Milly at his side panting for air.

"That's three barrels of gold! All you have to do is annul your marriage and send her to me!"

Chapter Seven

Milly stood riveted by the scandalous proposal.

The idea was sinking into her mind, still unbelievable to comprehend, when Weston dropped her hand, turned around and marched his way back to Slayton. She withered at the possibility of another fight.

The miner's bodyguards pressed forward but Slayton urged them to back off.

Weston's face was inches from the giant's. "You want to buy another man's wife?" He laughed without humor. "*My* wife?"

Slayton slid his big hands into his wool pockets, as though he were talking about something as casual as after-dinner drinks. "I don't think she's truly your bride. Not in every sense. Not from the animosity I witnessed. Someone forced this marriage on you." He glanced in her father's direction. Her father huffed, stuck out his chest in indignation and tucked his tongue into the pocket of his mouth, as though slightly ashamed.

"Let me be perfectly clear, since you don't seem to understand," Weston shouted. "The answer's no. Not on your bloody life!"

His volatile reaction made Milly silently cheer, even though she was reminded of his comment that she had asked for this *dream marriage.*

"Hear him out," her father called.

Milly cringed. Why did her folks always embarrass her in the most public way? The crowd was speechless, rumblings laid aside, faces turned at the family presenting the evening's events in the most theatrical fashion.

"You see," said Slayton. "Theodore's levelheaded."

Weston threw his hands up in the air and scoffed.

"Since the both of you seem so miserable," said the gold miner, flashing his golden bottom tooth, "I'm offerin' you a way out."

"You're insane."

"I don't hear *her* raisin' any objection."

When the heated faces turned to Milly, she wished the earth would quake and gobble her whole.

Bombarded by the absurd nature of Slayton's proposal, the ludicrous whirlwind marriage of last night, and her genuine lack of sleep in the past twenty-four hours, Milly finally lost her temper.

She trounced across the grass toward her husband, skirts flaring, boots crunching on pebbles, blood simmering.

She pointed at Slayton, her father, then Weston. "I'll have all three of you keep in mind that no one owns my life!"

"Why are you upset with me?" asked Weston. "I had nothing to do with this."

Not wishing to prolong the scene, she couldn't help herself. All Weston had to do was walk away from the man, but he hadn't been able to do it. "You didn't ask permission for that dance!"

"That again?"

"And now you engage in a public discourse with this man!"

"I'm making it perfectly clear it's out of the question! Why don't you tell him the same?"

Furious, she whipped her shawl across her shoulder, turned away in the opposite direction and stalked toward their cabin. All eyes be damned.

Weston raced to catch up. "As my wife, I would like you to tell him."

"As your wife, I shan't be told what to say to whom. Or when."

"Then the man's right. You raise no objection."

"Why don't the three of you play a hand of cards and decide my fate that way?"

"Don't be ridiculous."

"Ridiculous? One man just offered to buy me from another. My father is considering it. And if that's not ridiculous enough, last night I was led gagged and blindfolded to the altar!"

He grew dangerously silent. She stormed ahead of him, crossed the dirt road, tracked her way along the mud, past the trail by the pines, up the porch and into their cabin.

It was late and she was well worn for sleep. He must have waited a spell on the porch, for she was through washing her face and preparing for bed when he entered.

He could darn well face the sofa again this evening.

To blazes with all the men in her life. She clutched her night robe at its gaping neckline and paraded past him.

He leaned against the kitchen counter, boots crossed, biting into one of the wrinkled apples she'd bought at the market, staring at her cross the floor.

She'd show him.

When she got to the bedroom, she reached for the doorknob, fully intending to snap it closed right in his face. Something odd made her blink.

The knob was missing its latch.

Alarmed, her lashes flew up. "What happened to the lock?"

Penetrating blue eyes stared back at her. He chewed nonchalantly on his fruit.

"You dismantled it!" She gasped. When did he have the opportunity? Of course…earlier this evening when he was changing inside the cabin, while she was waiting outdoors with Genevieve and Luke.

He rose to full height, proud and strong, his overwhelming size sucking the very air out of the small cabin, it seemed. "There'll be no locks in this house."

With that, he tossed his apple core in the pail on the floor and marched out into darkness.

* * *

Milly waited all night for her husband to come to her.

Sinking her shoulder into the lumpy mattress, she flinched again at the sound of Weston's boots stirring on the planks outside her door. Were his feet too long for the sofa?

She didn't care. She hoped he was uncomfortable as hell.

Well…maybe it would be *better* for her if the opposite were true. If he were cozy and relaxed, he'd fall into a deep sleep and thus ignore her.

Leaves smacked against the windowpane and she startled.

His boots stirred again. *Here he comes…*

The sound of a heavy weight stirred on the rough cushions, then nothing.

Why was he torturing her like this? He'd removed the locks, therefore she knew he wished to bed her. He was her husband. What did one expect?

The floor creaked outside her door. She braced herself, closed her eyes shut, then nothing.

She pried her lids open again. They stung from exhaustion.

Weston moaned in the parlor and she jolted. She tossed the blanket over her head. Then nothing again.

It was hot beneath the covers. She could barely breathe. Unable to tolerate the heat, she threw off the blankets.

Starved for air, she gulped it. *Come and get me.* Land's sake, she couldn't stand the waiting and wondering one more minute.

Flannel pajamas added to the heat. She wanted to unbutton the high collar but if she did, he might get a glimpse of what he was missing, and jump on top of her.

Silly, really. He'd already seen plenty of her bosom the night they got engaged, if you could call it that!

She thought that night had been humiliating. How about this evening?

Why did men like Dirk Slayton have so much say in the world, simply because they were filthy stinking rich? If a pauper or a drifter had propositioned her in the same manner, the

Mounties would've taken him aside and set him straight in no uncertain terms.

Her father certainly wouldn't have given him a moment's attention.

Slayton was one of those Klondikers who demanded respect and believed he deserved it, simply because of his pile of gold. He'd accomplished nothing in the way of bettering the community, didn't have an education nor was he seeking to read books on his own to get one, said whatever stupid thing popped into his brain, yet believed he was the smartest man in Dawson.

He'd been lucky with a shovel. That was all.

What he'd offered her was preposterous.

Her eyes grew weary. She peered at the door and waited through half-closed lids for the arrival of her husband.

Her mind drifted. Slayton was offering her independence. Granted, it had some appeal. To be totally independent financially, and to run her own affairs. Marvelous, really.

If she married Slayton, could she then apply for a divorce and still keep the shop he'd promised?

No…her lids closed. That would be terribly unkind of her. And selfish.

Would she have to sleep with the giant if she married him?

She groaned in stupor. Surely to God not.

Her parents would get a lovely home. Her dear mother, much more understanding in matters of the heart than her father, would match the kitchen tablecloths and curtains in the same bold pattern. Checkered yellow was her mother's favorite this season.

"Milly?" Weston's voice called out to her.

"Oh," she gasped, frightened the time had finally come.

"Milly, you're snoring. Please roll over!" he called.

With an embarrassed sigh, Milly tugged the sheet up to her burning ears and realized the heartless truth of the matter.

Her husband wasn't coming anywhere near her tonight, and for some reason, this lay heavy on her heart.

Chapter Eight

Weston woke up listening to her soft breathing. At least Milly had stopped snoring. She must've been awfully tired to fall into such a deep sleep for all these hours.

He looked at the mantel clock. Seven. He'd only caught about two hours himself. It was all that damn thinking that had kept him awake. And the thought of Milly, his wife, laying in his bed only feet away.

He strummed his fingers on his bare chest. The cotton sheet drifted around his long legs. He shifted his feet over the edge of the sofa. Sunlight barging through the cabin window warmed his naked thigh.

Thinking of Slayton's proposition still burned him. Of all the gall…to look straight into Weston's eyes and ask for his wife! If Milly hadn't been around, he would've been tempted to smash the smug look off his face.

He might still.

But there was no getting around what this implied.

Milly had several men interested in her before her marriage, and *still had.* There'd been James Yakov, as well as Dirk Slayton. How many others?

She was pretty and energetic and hardworking…a bit hard to tame, but he was looking for a way.

The truth was, Milly Thornbottom had had her choice of men, and being forced into marriage had likely overwhelmed her as much—or maybe more—than it had him. He wasn't the only one whose dignity was suffering.

It must've been difficult for her growing up, her folks ordering her around all these years. True, she had her understanding cousin Genevieve nearby, but otherwise no other family to run to for a kind word of support.

What had Milly ended up with in terms of a husband? He was only starting out in his career. Lived at the barracks, no home of his own; no team of horses, since he could borrow them from work; no title of Veterinary Surgeon behind his name. A simple apprentice.

She could have done better, if one were measuring by the outer trappings of wealth.

But what he *could* offer…if he tried harder…was a partner by her side, someone who'd defend her and care for her, help raise the children if any came along and be a solid husband in every sense of the word.

Wasn't that what marriage was all about?

She was much more mature than last summer. Her thin body had filled out into womanly curves to tempt a man, and most importantly, she carried herself with a lot more pride and confidence since she'd been working in the dress shop for almost a year.

Dress shop. He could never afford to give her that.

Cursing, he ripped off the sheet and rose to dress.

He heard a squeal behind him and Milly stood there, about to pour fresh water into the coffeepot. "I thought you were sleeping," she muttered. She blinked down at his nakedness and dropped the water pot.

It smashed on the floor. She didn't seem to notice.

He made no move to cover up. This was his house, damn it, and she was his wife.

"Why were you sneaking up on me?"

"Could you *please* shield yourself?"

He reached for his rolled-up ball of clothing. He thought she'd turn away, but instead, she gaped at his body.

"Next time, give a man some warning."

Crimson stained her cheeks. "I didn't think...I *did not think*...you were sleeping in the buff."

He stared at the high collar of her flannel gown, the many little buttons that she'd sewn on with delicate care. The flannel reached right down to the floor. Her bare toes, so pretty and small, wiggled under the flounce. A pool of water trickled toward her feet.

The side of his mouth curled up in a slow smile. "We couldn't be farther apart in what we choose to sleep in."

"I'll have you remember...it's Sunday!"

He raised his eyebrow. "People engage in physical affection at all times of the week."

She uttered an exclamation of astonishment. With a firm clamp of her lips, she turned around, found a rag and soaked the water off the floor.

As he slid into his underwear and then his denims, he watched the stain of pink get deeper.

"Do you blush all over?" he asked, intrigued by Milly's obvious interest in his body and amused by her reaction.

"That's something you will never find out!"

Finally frazzled, she stalked out of the kitchen, back into the bedroom and slammed the door, leaving him laughing softly at her predicament.

"Oh, I'll find out!" he called. "And you'll like it when I do!"

They didn't speak about Slayton's offer while they walked to the chapel. Milly couldn't bear to look Weston in the eye after having looked him in the...*well*...no matter.

The minister was away, but he'd arranged for a layman to read the scriptures. Milly groaned when she recognized who it was—Mr. Yakov, father of James. Thank the Lord, James himself was seated at the front and not looking back her way.

Milly had hoped showing up in church with her new husband by her side would stop all gossip, for they'd see how devoted—or how devoted they *seemed* to be—to each other.

But as soon as she slunk in, bowed her head and slid into one of the far pews, heads turned, whispers grew. Folks nudged each other when Dirk Slayton walked in, hat in hand.

Good grief.

Slayton turned toward her, smiled and bowed his head.

She frantically said the Lord's Prayer.

Weston glared at everyone who dared look at them, and gave an especially icy send-off to the gold miner.

She pretended she never saw her mother and father enter. God help her for behaving so wretchedly, in a church no less, but she couldn't help herself, and then had to pray extra hard for her own salvation.

The minutes crawled past. She could barely breathe in the stifled air, and the corset that constricted around her ribs each time she inhaled.

As the congregation listened to the holy words being read aloud, all she could think of was the naked, vivid image of her husband.

It was odd what men looked like. She'd never seen one of those before.

Mr. Yakov added a few words of his own. She tried to listen, but quite frankly, her mind drifted to more interesting topics.

"…resist the temptations…"

How would she and Weston fit together in bed? Would it be pleasurable, their first time?

"…the goodness of our neighbors…"

He was so much taller and…*bigger*…than her.

"…we especially pray for the newly married in our midst. Corporal Weston and Milly Williams."

"Amen!" someone called.

"Bless them both!" called another.

She wasn't paying attention, lost in her own thoughts. The image of Weston's broad chest, the trickle of hair that spanned his thighs and abdomen and lower, still, to the wild expanse of—

"Ow!" She clutched her ribs at the jab of pain. Weston had elbowed her.

Everyone was turned and staring at them, smiling and murmuring words of congratulations. At the front, Mr. Yakov had his arms extended toward them.

Had she missed something?

Was it good or bad?

"Thank you," Weston replied to the onlookers, bowing his head.

Must've been good. She followed his lead and nodded, then looked to the floor.

Toward the end of the hour, she thought everything was coming together nicely. At least, she and Weston appeared to be fooling people about how happy they were. If they could fool them for just a while longer, maybe she and Weston would have a chance at being left alone to discover themselves, perhaps work things out in a more tender and caring fashion.

Perhaps they would even grow to love each other.

He was awfully quiet in church, too, obviously thinking and praying for answers. But as they exited the building and caught sight of Slayton, Weston turned somber and whispered into her temple.

She went ice-cold at his words.

"It's your choice if you wish it. Discuss it with your folks and do what's best for you. The judge in town can annul our marriage before it gets any further."

Chapter Nine

❦❧

The man was infuriating. Just when Milly thought the thunder between them had settled, Weston says this.

"From now on," she whispered at the top of the chapel stairs, "I won't be discussing anything with my folks. You're my husband and I'll discuss things only with you."

Weston, equally exasperated, hiked down the stairs. She followed at his side.

When they were out of earshot of the others, he steered her toward the cottonwoods. The trees behind him rustled; the wind fell softly across her cheeks.

His hair, thick and blond, dipped at his shoulders. "It's not that I agree with Slayton. It's that I think we should discuss it. We never got a chance to weigh our marriage options before it happened, and now look. We're both trapped. I want this matter debated. That's all."

Trapped. Did he feel that way completely? Was there no hope for him in this marriage?

Perhaps he was right. Talking things through might be a refreshing change. "What is there to say?"

"He's got a hell of a lot more to offer than I do."

"Material things."

"He's not a cruel man. He'd treat you well."

"He nearly ravaged me that night at the Ball. Don't you remember? And then he wanted to press charges."

"It was all talk."

"The charges might've been, but his grimy hands were on my body."

There. Discussion over.

She flung off her shawl in the warming breeze and headed home. They spoke no more till they turned the corner at their cabin.

Weston slowed his pace as they neared their porch, his long arms nestled in his pockets, his boots dodging the ruts in the road.

Beneath her simple white blouse, her chest felt heavy with uncertainty. She needed to get it all out in the open. "What has gotten into your dang fool head? Why would you offer something like this…after…after our conversation this morning?"

"We hardly spoke." His gaze dropped to the buttons at her throat. "You did more staring than talking."

He tilted his head and she wasn't sure if he was being sincere, or about to crack a smile. The dimple in his cheek gave it away.

She tried to stop the flow of heat that rose straight to her face. Why did he love to tease the way he did?

"But it felt different between us. Pleasant almost. Didn't you feel it?"

He unlocked the front door and waited as she brushed by him in her pleated navy skirt. His eyes were unreadable as he followed the movement of her waistline, tucked beneath a wide black belt.

Wasn't he going to answer her?

Hadn't he felt the smoldering affection between them, when he was naked and she the watchful wife? She'd thought of nothing *but* in the church. Even now, as he glanced down at her, she wondered what he'd feel like, pressed up against her if *she* was naked.

The cabin air seemed suddenly hot.

Perhaps a proper lady shouldn't think this way. Wife or not, maybe these thoughts of them being together in the physical sense were something that a decent woman wasn't supposed to have.

But then she recalled the talk her mother gave her, and grew easy on herself. Her mother hadn't thought it unnatural.

Flustered by her strong physical attraction to him, Milly stepped away from his tall torso, but he yanked her back. Her flesh caught fire. His fingers dug into her upper arm. His touch confused her. She liked the way his grip felt, enjoyed his possessive hold, even as she struggled to be free.

"I felt it," he murmured, finally answering. "This morning, I felt every beat of your heart. But if we decide to do anything about it before you fully think this through, we won't be able to get an annulment."

"Why do you keep saying that word? Annulment. Would it please you to be rid of me?"

It hurt her to think how much he wanted to push her away.

He leaned in to her face, and with a resulting shock of surprise that ran clear through to her toes, he kissed her neck.

"That's how much I want to push you away."

Her pulse pounded at her throat where his lips breathed against her flesh.

With expert agility, he unbuttoned the top of her blouse. His cool fingers seared her hot skin.

Another button. Another one.

He kissed her ear, her cheek, the side of her lips, and then murmured. "You'll have to learn to breathe while we do this."

She let out a lungful of air in one big giggle. And then grew so very serious and silent when he pressed his forehead into her own. His lips came down on her mouth and she responded by reaching up on tiptoe and wrapping her arms around his neck.

He pulled her against his body, chest to chest and thigh to thigh. She quivered beneath his mouth, reveling in the warm feel of his lips, the stirring of sensuality in her limbs.

Reaching up, he trailed his fingers down her opened blouse, above the corset, along the top of her breasts till she felt as though every cell in her would explode.

With a hunger she'd never known possible in a man, he pressed her to the sofa, he on his knees on the fur rugs by the fire, unbuttoning the rest of her blouse and clawing it off her shoulders. Stroking. Kissing. Murmuring.

The coals in the fireplace were still red from this morning. With a brief kiss on her shoulder, he turned and planted two more logs on the fire. They ignited immediately, and when he swung back to her, it was her turn to unbutton him.

His shirt came off, exposing a broad chest with a slight matting of hair, firm muscles and curvy planes of brown skin.

She kissed his shoulder blade and went lower down his chest. "Oh...Milly...."

His hands slid up her corset and he undid the crisscrossing ribbons. Her corset fell open and he gazed for a stunned moment at her naked breasts.

What was he thinking? Did she look odd in some way? Perhaps ridiculously sprawled on the sofa...

She wiggled to straighten herself, but he clenched her arm and stopped her. "Don't move. I've never seen anything so incredibly beautiful."

Milly inhaled, adoring the way he looked at her. His eyes trailed down to her nipples. When he leaned over and suckled one, the feeling went straight through to her thighs. A bolt of sexuality she'd never felt before.

More. She wanted more.

A sharp bang on the door made her jump.

His hands on her stilled. He moved in front of her, to guard her as if by instinct, at the same time they both pivoted to see who it was.

There was a panel of muted glass at the top of the door that revealed hats and bonnets. Seemed to be a silhouette of her cousin Genevieve, her husband Luke and her parents on the porch.

"Oh, no," Milly whispered.

Weston groaned and tore his hands off her. She snatched the folds of her corset against her breasts.

It wasn't that she was going to open the door. She wasn't ready to speak to her father. She wanted time alone with Weston to talk and be intimate. Why couldn't her family and friends just leave them alone? They'd each been newlyweds at one point, didn't they understand how it must feel?

Besides, she was a mess. Her corset was askew, her hair ripped out of its bun, her blouse thrown across the room. She had no intention of presenting herself in such an intimate display.

With the private spell between them broken, Milly sat on the sofa, Weston on the floor before her, staring between the crackling fire and the door. After two more unanswered knocks, her family must've decided she and Weston weren't home, and finally turned away.

Milly had been surrounded by everyone she once held in the highest of affections, but was somehow lonelier than she ever thought possible.

"I'll make it up to them at the festivities tonight," Milly told Weston five hours later as they prepared for their outing. Their uninvited visitors had put a stop to their lovemaking, before they had a chance to get started and Milly felt surprisingly disappointed. She yanked the brush through her air, enjoying the massage of bristles against her scalp. "I can certainly say hello to my mother. She didn't have anything to do with this situation. She deserves my respect."

Weston grumbled, frustrated by the interruption, but resolved to stand by his wife. "Suppose…suppose you come and get me when you decide to speak to her."

"Truly? You'll say howdy? Oh, Weston, I do appreciate your effort."

"If someone else behaved poorly—" said Weston, and she knew very well he was referring to her father "—it doesn't mean we have to. Let's say we start all over this evening."

"In what way?"

"Between us. Husband and wife."

She smiled, buoyed by his efforts. Their marriage didn't have to be so horrible. At one time last summer, she'd been so riveted by Weston she wasn't able to take her sights off him. She'd thought he was the most handsome man she'd ever met. Skilled and capable with horses and livestock. Tender in the way he spoke and cared for animals. That was the Weston she'd fallen for. That was the Weston standing at her side.

They left the house and ambled down by the river.

Everyone was there. Rose. Cora. Her parents by the riverbank, talking to the musicians.

What should she say to her father? Pretend as though nothing odd had occurred? Thank him for forcing the marriage? Certainly she was not going to lash out.

Weston got sidetracked by someone calling for his veterinary advice. There was an ill-tempered mare chomping at the bit by the river's edge, pulling a wagon filled with kegs of ale.

"Somethin' might be wrong with her, Weston. Could you come have a look?"

"Sure thing," Weston replied. "When did you first notice it?" His voice drifted off as he saluted Milly in good spirits and went to do his calling.

Rose walked by. "How are you?" She sniffed the cool Yukon air.

Milly threw her arm around her friend, determined to patch things up. "Feeling better, thank you. If you'd like to drop by tomorrow at the dress shop with Cora, I'll bring my plaid dress. We can do a fitting right there."

"You mean it?"

"Absolutely."

A horse whinnied behind them. It didn't sound right. Screechy somehow. Milly glanced over at Weston. He was holding it by its bridle, stroking its shoulder and trying to calm it. Milly turned back the other way and glanced at her folks. They hadn't spotted her yet. She felt such a pang of regret at how terribly she'd treated her mother. First by ignoring her in church, then at her own door. Rose must have noticed the sorrow in Milly's expression.

"Why don't I go grab Cora," said Rose, "and we'll come with you to say hello to your folks."

"Oh, Rose. You always seem to know when something's troubling me."

Rose slipped her arm through Milly's, giving her courage. "You promise to tell us how this happened?"

"I promise," Milly whispered. "It came as a surprise to me, too."

She finally admitted it to one of her dearest friends. Instead of laughter or retribution, Rose hugged her.

Milly looked over her shoulder again, searching for her husband. He was releasing the mare from the wagon of ale. "I promised I'd get Weston when it was time to talk to my folks."

But the horse he was trying to settle wouldn't. It reared, as if ready to bolt.

Weston warned the crowd, "Stay clear! Out of the way!"

Terror shot up Milly's spine. What was wrong with the mare? Why didn't Weston get out of its range?

The crowd parted, the horse reared again, the owner tried to swing up onto its back.

Weston hollered, "No! Get off! She's headed to the fields, let her go!"

Too late. The owner released the reins, but the mare changed directions, straight into the crowd.

Women screamed, children fled and men shoved people out of the way.

Rose stood in the path, mouth agape. Milly pulled her sharply as the mare thundered by, but Rose was knocked to the ground at the hard tug.

Milly extended her hand to help her friend to her feet. "Sorry. Are you all right?"

"Yes, but…"

Milly looked up in time to see the horrible events unfold.

The runaway horse charged straight for Milly's parents. She watched in fear as her father rushed to aid her mother, but was trampled then himself.

Chapter Ten

⚜

Weston raced to help Theodore in the panicked crowd. Weston had kept his eye on the horse's hooves during the entire commotion, knowing how important it was to see exactly where and how hard they'd strike. The mare had stomped Theodore once on his ankle, once in the chest.

Milly was quick to run and situated closer to her father than Weston. She reached him first.

Abigail fell to her knees above her husband's gray head, her faded dress ballooning around her, her face skewed with alarm.

"Theodore," she called. Her heavy shoulders shook.

Her husband gasped for air, his mouth blue when Weston arrived. Milly, pale and petrified, cradled her father's face.

Weston knelt on the soft grass on the other side of Milly. He spoke for her sake as much as to comfort Theodore. "No bleeding from the ears or nose or mouth."

She and her father looked up, uncertain what it meant.

"No head injury, Theodore," Weston reassured the gasping man. The old eyes looked clear and equally dilated, too. But hell, when Weston tore open the shirt, buttons flying, it was obvious his bottom ribs on the left side were crushed. No wonder he couldn't breathe.

"Easy," said Weston, straightening his head so he could assess the damage. "Easy."

The chest rose and fell evenly on inhalation. Evenly on exhalation. Symmetrical.

"No punctured lungs." Thank God. That would've been the worst crisis.

Internal bleeding was likely beneath the crushed rib cage, but there wasn't much they could do about that.

Weston tugged off his jacket and used it to prop the old man's head and shoulders. Gravity would help him expand his lungs. It worked immediately.

Theodore still rasped when he inhaled, but the blueness around his lips and nostrils turned to a pale pink. Hallelujah.

He struggled to rise. What was he doing?

Weston placed his hand on his father-in-law's warm shoulders. "You got a five-hundred-pound blow to the chest, Theodore. It's important you lie still. Till we have a look at everything."

"Pa, I'm sorry," Milly whispered. "I turned my back on you and I'm sorry."

The weathered eyes rotated toward his daughter, but he was unable to speak.

"Nothing to upset him now," Weston said as gently as he could to his shattered wife. "Calm. He needs to remain calm."

She swept her hand across the wrinkled old brow and her gaze found her mother's.

Abigail's head was bowed and she was sobbing quietly behind Theodore. Milly, stroking her father's head, reached out and grasped her mother's hand. No words were necessary as mother and daughter clung together.

Weston took note of the boot strangely twisted on Theodore's left foot. Its unnatural angle indicated the ankle was likely broken. It must hurt like bloody hell.

If Weston removed the boot, he had nothing to splint the fracture with, and would likely cause more trauma. The boot itself provided a splint and would have to do till they got him to the hospital.

"Any doctors here?" Weston called.

It took the crowd a few seconds of looking and murmuring to respond, no.

Five minutes later when Theodore's breathing had stabilized, although he was still struggling, Weston and three other men circled him. On the count of three, they lifted him gently into the back of a straw-filled wagon.

Another Mountie in the crowd had captured the runaway mare. "Should we put her down?" the constable whispered into Weston's ear. "The mare's nearly killed him."

Weston shook his head. "Not till I have a look at her. Take her to the outpost. Let her go free in the corral. I'll be there as soon as I can."

"But she might do it again." The constable placed his hand on his holstered gun. "I should take her behind the woods and—"

"*No.* Do as I say. There's no such thing as a bad horse. Just bad circumstance."

And with that, Weston and his team tore off for the hospital, Milly and Abigail in the back of the wagon praying for Theodore.

Milly watched helplessly as her father faded into unconsciousness. Transferring him from the ground into the back of the wagon had taxed him. His lips grew into that pasty blue color again, he rattled with every breath, and his hands grew cold.

Everything seemed to go so slowly from there.

The horses dragged their way to the hospital, it took numerous shouts to get the attendants, Dr. Elizabeth Hunter arrived to examine him and he was lifted again by Weston and three others and placed inside the log cabin marked with the big painted sign, Dawson City Hospital For Men And Women.

He didn't open his eyes the next day or the next.

Weston stayed with Milly the first day, bringing water, whispering words of strength and comfort. At night, he urged her to come home and rest, and when she did, he wrapped his arms around her on the walk. But when they entered the cabin, he left her alone. Perhaps he thought he shouldn't pressure her to sleep at his side, but in fact, it seemed to widen the lonely gap between them.

Back at the hospital, her mother, sleeping beside her father in a rocking chair the entire three days, refused to leave his side.

"Come home with me," Milly begged her.

"We spent every day of thirty years together. I'm not leavin' him."

"Please…let me take you home. I'll stay with you while you get some proper sleep."

"Not until I know he's gonna pull through."

Elizabeth, the same kind doctor who'd helped Milly through an illness of her own last year on the ship from Vancouver, couldn't tell them much on the good side. Weston dropped in on his lunch hour and listened.

"He's suffered some internal injuries." Elizabeth's blond braid fell over her shoulder as she pressed a gentle hand to his pale forehead.

"Such as?" Milly's mother asked.

Weston folded his arms across his chest and tucked his hands underneath them. They'd barely spoken for the last two days. He came when he could to be with Milly, but he was needed in his duties with the runaway mare, and there wasn't much he could do here.

He could comfort me, she thought. He could be here anyway, to help me with my mother and talk to me about the future.

Yet, Weston was so withdrawn in his own thoughts, she wondered if and when they'd ever be able to call themselves a wedded couple.

Mr. Slayton visited every day. Didn't say much, either. He showed up at the front desk, removed his hat, peered down at Milly and nodded, past the row of eight beds where strangers in various stages of recovery or illness lay looking up at the ceiling. Some of the men were recovering from a bad bout of stomach sickness, one fella had a broken arm, another had lumps all over his body.

Milly was polite to all, but focused on the thin, unconscious man with the white ponytail.

On the fourth day, Weston arrived in the late afternoon.

"How's he doing? Any word?"

She shook her head and pulled him aside. "You've been avoiding talk of the horse. What happened to her?"

"The mare's sick, Milly. She was running a burning fever at the time of the accident. Her leg was cut and infected with sores. I've been wrapping it with poultices."

"It didn't work?"

"It did." He furrowed his brow and lowered his voice. "I just can't put her down, Milly. She was ill, not demented."

"And now she's getting better." Milly understood, but worried how others would take it. "Better not tell my mother."

"Would you like me to stay?"

She lowered her lashes. "You have your work."

Weston sighed, went over and whispered something to her exhausted and sobbing mother, giving her a comforting rub on the shoulder, but not to Milly. Why was he afraid to come near her? He didn't put up any resistance when she said he needn't stay, but the sorrow building in her throat belied her words.

She wanted Weston to stay at her side like her mother was staying at her father's.

Later that afternoon, Slayton stopped by with a basket of dried fruit for the entire ward, and a kind word to her.

"You're a lovely daughter," he told her. It was as though he knew what she needed.

She'd been a horrible daughter, in truth. She'd held a grudge against her father—intending in her heart to hold it against him forever—and had treated her mother miserably.

"Don't forget about me," said Mr. Slayton. "My offer still stands. You might need me more if something should happen to your pa."

Filled with sorrow, Milly turned away. She couldn't lose her father.

Just then, Weston slid inside the doors in full red uniform.

"Brought some pastries the cook just baked. He sends his good wishes."

Weston took one look at Slayton standing in the corner, the smile left his face, he tipped the wide brim of his brown Stetson and left without saying another word.

What right had either man to assume she owed them something?

Slayton left.

Milly sat at her father's side and wiped his face with a sooth-ing cloth.

"Pa, wake up."

He didn't stir.

She was so sorry for the last time she'd been this close to him. On the porch that night after her wedding ceremony and trudging out to meet Weston with her luggage, she hadn't even answered her father when he'd whispered words of good luck.

Maybe he'd done what he thought he needed to do. All her life he'd protected her from harm, provided a loving home filled with good food and hard work.

And laughter, mostly.

Now she might never get the opportunity to tell him how she felt. At this very moment, he might be slipping away....

And then there was Mr. Slayton, pursuing her at every turn, Weston troubled by the horse, her mother half out of her mind with grief and Milly's marriage...well, that seemed to be in name only.

There was no intimacy, no shared feelings of love or belong-ing between her and Weston, and worse yet, might never be.

Chapter Eleven

$\iff$

Alone again two days later on Saturday morning, Milly rose early to go to market. Weston had already left for work. The bed-sheets were gone from the sofa and neatly folded on the corner table. This couldn't go on, she thought with a sadness that dipped straight to her heart.

She put on her wide straw hat, tied the velvet sash beneath her chin and headed out the door.

At the market, another steamboat had arrived and she hurried to buy the necessary foods before leaving for the hospital. She bought coffee beans, a jar of molasses and one tin of salmon, but rushed past baskets of wrinkled apples.

Something made her stop. She picked up a creased red one, and stared at the glossy skin. Had it only been a week that she was last here, announcing her marriage to her friends Rose and Cora, watching in alarm as the men had fought in this very spot?

How much her life had changed.

When she'd asked for Mr. Slayton's help to stop the fistfight between James and Weston, the miner had stepped back and bit into an apple. Later in the week, when she'd hurried past Weston to the bedroom, thinking she'd lock him out for the second night, he'd also been eating one of these apples.

Weston. Perhaps it was *she* who could learn something from

observing the devotion her mother had for her father. All this time, Milly had been waiting for Weston to come to her, but maybe marriage meant something more.

"A dozen apples, please," she said to the friendly vendor, bustling with the excitement of a new thought.

She knew what she had to do.

Basket in hand, Milly wrapped her shawl around her shoulders and barreled down the boardwalk toward the newest building in Dawson. It was a two-story structure, built of the finest logs and skilled craftsmanship gold could buy.

"Mornin'," folks said as she hurried past. "Any word on your father?"

"No, but thank you for asking."

"Milly!" Rose hollered from across the street, black hair swaying beneath her bonnet. She was about to enter the bank with her mother. "Any word?"

"Afraid not!"

Three more people nabbed Milly on her way to the building, but she wouldn't be diverted from her task.

His three bodyguards were standing at the entrance. The sign above their heavy shoulders read Slayton Holdings.

"Mornin', Miss Thornbottom," the widest one said as he held open the door. She nodded, well aware he was using her maiden name.

"Where's your boss?" she asked.

"Up the stairs, ma'am. Office to your left."

Dirk Slayton must've been expecting her, for his men couldn't remove their hats fast enough as she passed them in the hall, all seeming to know her and expecting her arrival. She swirled her long blue skirts behind her and raced up the stairs at a clip.

When she knocked on his door and entered, Mr. Slayton looked up from a map he was studying, leaned his immense body back in his chair and smiled real slow.

"Well, well, well."

He nudged the other gentleman in the room with him to leave.

Milly recognized him as a government official from the Land Claims Department.

The businessman tidied up and whizzed past her at the doorway.

When she and Mr. Slayton were alone, she felt no threat. He'd groped her last week at the Ball, but she realized now how ineffective he was. And she felt strangely protected by Weston, even though he wasn't here.

"I knew you'd come, Milly." Mr. Slayton flagged her in to take a seat. "Do make yourself comfortable."

Good gracious. It was true. He really did keep a bowl of gold nuggets on his desk, as though they were a bowl of candies. She planted her heavy basket on the rug by her feet. When she sat in the plush chair across from him, he raised the bowl toward her, offering some sparkling clumps.

She stifled a smile. Half from embarrassment at being offered something this extravagant, and half from a childish shiver of delight.

She picked out a particularly shiny piece, more gold than ore. Yet he kept the bowl raised, urging her to take another.

"Thank you, one'll do fine." She leaned in and whispered. "Am I really to keep this? Or is there another bowl at the bottom of the stairs where I'm to return it on my way out?"

He bellowed with laughter. "You're the first person who's ever asked me that."

"Can't be the first one who thought it."

"It's all yours, darlin'. One of my men fills up the bowl every Monday mornin'."

She gasped at the notion. "How utterly insane."

"I suppose."

"Don't you still find it mad? How rich you are?"

"Yeah. I suppose."

He didn't, though. She could see from the dimming expression on his wide face that he was accustomed to his wealth; that it came without surprise; that he likely never really looked at that bowl anymore.

How sad that he had to offer riches as enticement to visitors.

Like a child trying to buy friends. Suddenly the heavy gold nugget sitting on her lap seemed more a reminder of his cheerless situation than her possible future.

"So. You decided to come see me." His smile was gracious.

"Yes, I have."

The giant gazed at her so hard it made her flush with heat. He pointed his finger at her for effect. "You're going to look mighty fine in a dress shop all your own."

She fidgeted uncomfortably. "His breathing is the same, but he hasn't reopened his eyes."

"Oh, your father. Yes, yes, your father."

He hadn't asked and she was terribly disappointed.

"Forgive me." The wrinkles around his nose deepened. "I was too distracted thinking of your new dress shop, and how many panes of glass we'll use in the windows."

There he went again. Trying to buy friendship with money.

She curled her fingers into her skirt. "I do appreciate the vision you have for me. But my cousin Genevieve will be having her baby soon. She's asked me to look after *her* shop while she tends to her child."

"Let her hire someone."

"What you don't understand, sir, is that a stranger is not the same as family."

His grin faded. "You're saying you'd like to run two shops at the same time?"

"Mr. Slayton…what I'm saying is I don't wish to marry you. I never did."

He stammered. "But—but you'd be wealthier than your wildest imagination."

"Shiny rocks."

"I know for a fact you were forced into your marriage."

"It doesn't seem to be a secret, does it?" She straightened her spine, blouse crackling with starch. "No matter how it came to be, the point is that I am married to Weston." She rose and placed the nugget back into his bowl.

He stared glumly at her fingers as she did, her announcement finally sinking in.

"No one's ever put one back before. Keep it."

"No, thank you. I'd rather take the path no one else has. And now, I have someone else to see. Good day, Mr. Slayton."

"Have you seen Milly?" Weston hollered to her cousin, Genevieve, who was coming out of the mercantile with packages.

"She's opening the dress shop in an hour. I'll put on a pot of coffee if you'd like to—"

"This can't wait!" Weston tore off.

She wasn't at the market, wasn't at the bakery and definitely wasn't at the hospital.

"Rose!" he hollered as she exited the bank. "Have you seen Milly?"

Rose glanced nervously across the street at the two-story log building with the sign, Slayton Holdings.

"Don't tell me…"

"I'm not telling you anything, Weston, I really don't know—"

But he was already lunging across the dirt street, dodging a team of oxen and two miners heaving picks and swinging empty pails.

Hell, why'd she have to do this and now of all times?

At the etched glass doors, Slayton's bodyguards stepped in front of his path. With a scowl, Weston barged right past them.

"Hey!" shouted one. "You're not welcome here!"

"I don't give a damn." Weston had a few things to say to his wife.

She was coming down the stairs, swirling her skirts, hanging on to a basket of fresh foodstuff. Slayton stood at the top of the stairs watching her leave. The smirk on his face as he watched her behind made Weston flinch. Son of a bitch.

But this whole thing wasn't between him and Slayton. It never had been. It wasn't between Weston and her father, either. It had started and needed to finish between him and Milly.

She was startled to see him. Her eyes flashed. "How did you know…how to…where to…"

Weston raised his jaw and glared over her big straw hat, ready to defy Slayton, but the man was gone. Coward.

"It's your father," Weston said to her as gently as he could.

Her hand came up to her face. Her jaw slackened. "Oh, please don't say…"

"He's awake, Milly. He came to twenty minutes ago."

The flush of excitement that rushed up her cheeks was enough to make any man come to life. Weston grabbed her basket to lighten her load, then her hand—yes, held it tight in plain sight for all the world to see his affections—and walked his wife out the door, down the street and to the hospital.

"Pa!" she cried upon seeing the old man sitting up in bed, eating a bowl of vegetable soup. Abigail was smiling proudly, her round body squeezed beside him in the tight bed.

Theodore's eyes glistened with warmth at his daughter. Their reunion was a sight to behold.

Lots of hugging and laughing and tears.

"Honey, I'm sorry," the old guy said when the initial shock had worn off.

She insisted, "It's me who—"

Theodore waved a hand in the air, begging her to stop. He looked at Weston standing at the foot of the bed, arms crossed and urged him to come closer.

Weston moved in beside Milly, sliding his palm against her waist.

"I might have been wrong to force you two," Theodore said to them. "Maybe I should've waited to calm down before makin' such a huge decision."

Milly twisted her lips in concentration and lowered her head.

Her father cupped her chin and lifted her gaze to his. "I'm sorry."

Milly took a moment to absorb things, then bowed her face to her father's ear and whispered something Weston couldn't make out. They both nodded and looked up at Weston, making him wonder what it was.

An hour later when Theodore was fast asleep and Weston and

Milly had walked Abigail home for the first time in five days, they headed to the tiny log cabin they called their own.

"What'd you tell your father?" Weston asked when they entered the house. He placed her basket of food on the counter and turned to face his young wife.

"That you are the best man I could have married."

His jaw tightened. "You said that?"

"Yes, I did."

"You mean it?"

"With all my heart."

"Milly, I've been a fool. I kept you at bay as if you were the one who forced this on me. The things I said—" he cringed as the words *dream marriage* came to mind "—I'm sorry." Ashamed, he turned and removed his jacket, grasping for a way to express his sentiments.

The heels of her boots clicked on the plank floor as she came toward him. He felt her warm hand on his.

"It's true, you were awful."

He jolted at her words. When he looked up, she was smiling slightly and he knew it was her way of making light of a difficult situation.

"But so was I. I think I had a lot to learn real fast this week. That marriage, our marriage, if it's to last as long as my ma and pa's, is something to cherish."

He traced the sinews of her hand, loving the warm feel of her next to him, the pretty turn of her cheeks, the scent of her hair.

"Weston, I thought I didn't know you. I thought because we'd never talked much this past year, we couldn't possibly know much about each other. But I've realized that it's more about what a person does than what they say, that defines who they are."

She shivered in the chill. He sighed with wonder and led her to the parlor, sat her on the sofa and turned to light the fire while she continued.

"You're good with animals, Weston. The way you took the sick mare and turned her health around was astounding."

He turned on his knees on the fox fur rug toward her.

"The fact that you couldn't—*wouldn't*—put down the mare was when it struck me. Your love of life. And especially the way you took care of my father when the horse trampled—"

Her voice was shaky. She broke off for a breath of air. "He was the man who forced your hand in marriage, yet you did everything humanly possible to save his life."

Weston had never thought otherwise. "I would have done it for anyone."

"You see, that's what I discovered about you, Weston. One of the things I adore about you."

She stared into the burning fire. "Last summer I followed you around like a little schoolgirl and I apolo—"

"No," he said. "Don't apologize. I loved your company."

"But you said—"

"It wasn't you that turned me away. I'm not very proud to say, but it was your father."

"He ordered you to stay away from me?"

"No, not at all. He…he made it difficult to pursue you. Very protective."

She sighed in frustration.

"He loves you very much."

"I know that now."

"And you know what I discovered about you?" he asked gently, moving on his knees to press against her legs at the sofa. "I discovered a woman with much more patience than I will ever have. With the ability to think calmly in the midst of madness. You handled James, you handled Slayton, you handled Rose and Cora and your parents, too. At times when my fist and my anger were doing the talking for me."

She smiled at him in that captivating way that aroused him. The curve of her full lips, the blade of her cheeks, the sparkle in her brown eyes. His focus lowered to her stiff white blouse. All those buttons that he would enjoy undoing.

"Let's try this again, shall we?" he asked. "I, Weston Williams, would love to have the honor of marrying you, Milly Thornbottom. Would you be my wife?"

Her smile grew wider. Her skin glowed. "My answer's yes. Would always be yes. I got my dream marriage after all."

With an exclamation of approval, he scooped her off the sofa. She yelped. "What are you doing?"

"Taking you where you belong." He headed to the bedroom and tossed her to the mattress. When he fell onto it beside her, he pressed his face against the pillow and inhaled. "Mmm... smells fresh and inviting."

She giggled.

"What is it?"

"My mother would be proud."

"Huh?"

"Nothing. Come here and kiss me."

He did, pressing his mouth along hers. She parted her lips and he was lost in the sensual bond. The kiss was extraordinary, gentle at first, nipping at his senses, then deepening into an urgency where neither held back. He caressed her face, her neck, ran his hands along her rib cage and slid her blouse from its skirt. All the while moving his mouth along hers, sliding his tongue along her upper lip and growing hard the instant she met his tongue with her own.

They took their time, for this was their first. There were no interruptions, no knocks on the door, no duties outside the home, no market to go to, just the two of them alone to unpeel clothing, and revel for hours in the splendor of a lover's touch.

Epilogue

"Milly?" Weston clamped a warm hand around her naked ribs and nudged her, two weeks later in the morning sun.

"Hmm?" she answered, groggy from another night of passion.

She felt his warm kiss on her shoulder and opened her eyes. She was facing the window and its streaming sunshine. He was spooned behind her on the bed, his naked body and all its delicious curves and planes tucked into her backside.

He ran a hand along her buttock and she smiled.

"I love you, Milly."

Her heart tripped. Her throat clamped. It was the first time he'd said it.

Rolling in the sheets to face him, she stared up into big blue eyes that held the depth of the ocean.

"I love you," he repeated, kissing her softly on the mouth.

She responded with all the feeling that'd been building for the last year, it seemed. When their lips parted, she stroked his strong, bristly jaw. His dark blond hair swept the top ridge of his wide, naked shoulders.

"I think I've always loved you, Weston. And I'm proud and lucky to be your wife."

He moaned softly and ran a finger along her cheek, down her throat, her breastbone and across to a nipple. It stirred a warm rush of desire and longing in her limbs.

"I'll never be able to get enough of you, Milly."

And then, with amusement, he ripped the sheet off her to stare at her body.

She basked in the attention, the overwhelming joy she felt for how things had turned out. And then marveled at her own lack of inhibition when it came to loving Weston.

She, in turn, ripped the sheet off his body, admiring the view. Sitting up and rolling on top of him, she pressed his naked arms above his head, her bare breasts dangling above him. His mischievous gaze lowered from her eyes downward, while she, quite frankly, did the same.

She loved the way his shoulders moved, the bulk of his biceps, the rich hue of his skin. His abdomen was as flat as a board, matted slightly with dark blond hair that trailed to his private area. She adored looking at that, too, the size of his erection and the smooth, silky skin she knew she could have at any time she pleased.

He kicked his thighs up behind her, surprising her with his deftness, for he maneuvered her to sit on top of his lap.

With no hands to guide him, he slid his body along her damp center, then slipped inside of her, laughing at her gasp of pleasure. He completely filled her.

"I do admire your skills," she said, lowering her head to bite the side of his mouth.

"I aim to please."

He slid his arms out from beneath her grasp, and placed a hand on each side of her hips. She closed her eyes and began a slow and steady rhythm, up and down. When she felt his hands on her breasts, a thrill like no other pulsed through her body.

"My beautiful wife," he whispered, and she seared this moment in her mind to remember forever.

Gentle Weston brought her to the brink, taught her about love and intimacy and showed her that a man was never stronger than when he displayed the softness of his inner side.

He revealed it today, and the following month, and the year after that, through the birth of their three children and for the many loving decades to come.

* * * * *

SPRINGVILLE WIFE
Charlene Sands

Dear Reader,

I was thrilled to be a part of the *Western Weddings* anthology! The story formulated in my head faster than my fingers could hit the keyboard, and Grace, Caleb and little Opal's story was born.

I hope you enjoy this heartwarming tale of two people whose destinies bring them together in Springville, Texas. Caleb, the young scamp who teased and tormented Grace as a child is a handsome rancher now, raising his young niece. Grace, the newly widowed schoolmarm, hasn't the heart for romance. But when fate lends a hand, along with young Opal's assistance, their lives entangle, and well-kept secrets are revealed.

Sit down, relax and stay awhile as I welcome you to Springville!

Charlene

Chapter One

Springville, Texas
1888

Grace Lander dusted off her sapphire-blue traveling suit as she stepped down from the stagecoach. She hadn't journeyed by stage since the horrendous robbery that claimed her husband's life one year ago. Shivers of the fear she'd lived with during her stage ride from the rail station in Fort Worth slowly ebbed and she found herself taking her first easy breath. Yet, the painful memory and the guilt she felt over Harrison's untimely death were always with her.

But she was here in Springville now, her childhood home, and hoping to carve out a new life as a schoolmarm to a full brood of eager children.

"You made it, deary!" Her spry, rosy-cheeked aunt came rushing forth, a silly violet-feathered hat bobbing on her head.

"Aunt Enid, it's good to see you." She embraced the aunt she hadn't seen since her visit to Boston some six years ago—her favorite aunt, if Grace were being truly honest.

"It's about time you came back to your only livin' kin."

"Only kin? Aunt Enid, you know darn well, Aunt Flo and Auntie Roberta are still alive."

"Alive, deary, but not *livin'*."

Grace chuckled and relief washed over her. She put aside any doubts she'd had about her return to Springville. Her aunt Enid, who ran the Springville Boardinghouse, would be sure to keep Grace on her toes.

With somber eyes, Aunt Enid grasped her hands and squeezed gently. "Are you ready to start *your* living again, honey?"

The connection and the love flowing between them warmed her through and through. She gazed down the street to see familiar shops: McKenzie's Dry Goods, Springville Bank and Trust, Shorty's Longhorn Saloon, the marshal's office and Spring's Diner. Not too much had changed in thirteen years. Grace found great comfort in the small, thriving town where she'd grown up. Springville was different than Boston, in ways too abundant to name. Even the May sky seemed clearer, the air crisper and the sunshine brighter.

Was she ready to start living again?

On a shaky breath, Grace nodded. "I think so, Aunt Enid. I'm ready."

"Good." She released her hands and looked over at the young depot operator. "Chuckie, send over Miss Lander's bags to the boardinghouse as soon as you can, boy. There'll be a warmed slice of cherry pie waiting for you."

"Yes, ma'am!"

Aunt Enid's wide smile took twenty years off her aged face. "Ready to settle in?"

"I am, but I'm eager to visit the schoolhouse. To see if it's how I remembered it. It's all that's kept me sane these past few months."

Her aunt nodded in understanding. "Then go on." She winked. "You know where it is."

"Won't you come along?"

"No, deary. You go revisit those memories by yourself. I think you'll like what you see."

Grace kissed her aunt's cheek. "Thank you, Aunt Enid. I'll be along soon."

Grace picked up her satin skirt and walked briskly toward the opposite end of town where the schoolhouse stood, the light brown paint appearing fresh and new, though the white of the window frames was slightly faded. She approached the school slowly as good memories flooded in. She'd gone to school here until her family moved away when she was twelve: Her father's venture into ranching had proved unsuccessful and they'd left town to move in with their family to the east.

But Grace always believed herself a small-town girl. And she'd loved learning. School meant getting away from grueling chores at the failing ranch. It meant being acknowledged and encouraged by schoolmaster Mr. Mobley for her thirst for knowledge. And presently, she hoped it meant a way to forget the heartache that plagued her daily.

"Oh, Harrison," she uttered, standing just outside the school gate. "I'm so sorry."

She entered the schoolyard and closed the gate behind her. Stepping on overgrown bluebonnets lacing the path to the schoolhouse, she made a mental list of work she'd have to do on the grounds. But most importantly, she'd start the school up again. Mr. Mobley's sudden death had left the town unprepared and the children hadn't had instruction in over three months.

When she reached the front door, she tried the latch. The door didn't budge. She walked over to the side window and peered inside, glad to find the desks in order, set up in rows of four just like when she attended school. A side bookshelf contained *McGuffey Readers* and the potbellied stove that billowed smoke on cold winter days still claimed the back corner of the room. The black chalkboard centred the front wall and Grace's mind flooded with all those days she'd stay after class to help Mr. Mobley wipe it clean. One impudent classmate had labeled her "teacher's pet," but she'd only held her head up high, proud of the title.

A deep voice from behind the schoolhouse broke into her thoughts. "Tarnation! Damn it! Get away from me, you dang little pests!"

Curious, Grace raced around to the back of the building toward the commotion. She bumped a ladder and brown paint rained down in big, clumpy droplets, just missing her head. "Oh!"

She looked up and another "oh" fell silently from her lips. A man stood on the ladder she'd just bumped, his chest bare, broad and bronzed, a black Stetson covering his head as a swarm of bees circled around him. His denims hugged his body below a very trim waist and a narrow line of dark hairs arrowed down beyond his thick leather belt.

Grace squeezed her eyes shut and turned her back on him, but the image remained in her head. Lordy, he was a fine-looking man. Her heart pumped hard against her chest at the sight.

Immediate remorse set in. She'd been a widow for a year now, and blamed herself for Harrison's death. She had no business bearing such lusty thoughts.

"Sorry for the intrusion," she said softly, opening her eyes. She was the new schoolmarm. She shouldn't behave like a foolish, smitten girl of fifteen.

The man stepped down from the ladder, setting the paint can and brush onto the ground. When he lifted up, she caught another glimpse of his muscled chest. "Suppose I should thank you. I was about to be eaten up by them bees."

"Those bees," she corrected automatically. Her face flamed with heat, not so much from the ill-timed correction but by the vision he made.

He studied her for a long moment, his gaze raking her over from head to toe without apology. "By God. You're Gracie. Little Gracie Greene. Would've never guessed except for that uppity tone you take."

Grace eyed him with caution now. She was certain she'd just been insulted. "Yes, I'm Gracie. I go by Grace Lander now. And you are?"

His quick smirk rekindled a vivid childhood memory. One she'd rather forget. Grace suppressed the urge to crinkle her nose when she recalled her own personal school tormenter. He'd bully her every single day while in class or outside for recess.

They chorused both at the same time.

"Caleb Matlock."

* * *

Caleb cocked a grin her way.

Gracie Greene.

He'd known she'd been hired on in Springville as the new schoolteacher, but he surely hadn't expected her to look so dang blasted inspiring. The gangly awkward girl he'd teased and tormented in school had grown into a beautiful, auburn-haired, amber-eyed woman with pale skin and tiny nose freckles. He assessed her female form and liked what he saw, as well. "Gracie, Gracie, green like a frog and just as jumpy."

She rolled her eyes without granting a smile. Caleb smiled enough for them both, recalling his daily taunt.

"I haven't thought about your silly prose in years."

Caleb suspected differently. She'd been easy to goad and he'd been unmerciful back then. "You never called them prose back then, Gracie." Caleb reached for his shirt sitting on the fence. He put his arms through the sleeves and began buttoning. "Truth is, you retaliated pretty darn good. Let's see," he said, staring deep into her pretty eyes. "As I recall, you called me a big oaf, ugly as a longhorn, smelly as a skunk, stupid as—"

"I don't recall any such thing." Her eyes flitting to his bare chest for a second, before she turned five shades of red when he noticed.

His groin twitched. He hadn't been so instantly taken by a woman since courting Felicia Holmes eight years back. He'd asked Felicia to marry him and she'd agreed, then she ran away with a traveling tinker the day of their nuptials. Since then, Caleb didn't have much use for Springville females, Opal, being the exception.

Caleb shrugged off Grace's denials. "No matter. Just glad you're here."

"You are?"

"The school's been closed for months. Me and some of the others took up getting it ready again."

She glanced at the work he'd done. The back of the building he'd painted was almost finished. "Thank you for that. Except for cleaning up the yard, it doesn't look like you've left much for me to do."

"That was the intent," he said, staring at her. Damn, there wasn't any one thing about her he didn't enjoy looking at. Nothing had surprised him more. Little Gracie Greene had developed into a striking woman.

"What?" she asked, her expression filled with question.

"It's you, Gracie. You're all grown-up."

She smiled a little, just enough to shape her mouth prettily. "That's what happens with time."

He shook his head. "Usually time only wears on a person. But you, you've become a beautiful woman."

Grace turned away from him. Stark memories of the horrid stagecoach holdup brought tears to her eyes.

"She's too beautiful to leave behind, Pa. I'm taking her for myself. And no one's gonna stop me."

Grace would never forget her desperate panic that day or the clawing way Gray Bullock held her and groped at her body. She fought him off the best she could, crying for Harrison's help.

"Get your hands off my wife!"

Her husband rushed toward her, armed with only righteous fury and had been gunned down right before her eyes, trying to protect her.

There'd been three other women on that stagecoach, but she'd been the one singled out. She'd been the one widowed that day. The passengers had been saved when a band of gypsy wagons came down the road, scaring off the bandits who'd left her behind and Harrison dead on the ground at her feet.

And since then, there were times when she looked at her image in the mirror and hated the reflection staring back at her. She wasn't one who wanted undue attention cast upon her, yet since her husband's death, she'd had three proposals of marriage. All nice men who had promised to care for her, yet she'd seen that same lust in their eyes as that bandit and she knew she wouldn't marry again. She'd lost her beloved husband that day, but she'd also lost the unborn baby she carried and any chance to be with child ever again. So Caleb's compliment to her beauty meant little to her. It was only a painful reminder of the saddest day in her life.

"Grace?"

She inhaled deep in her chest and blinking tears away, she turned back to him. "I plan on starting classes the first of next week," she said, straightening her spine. "That'll give me the rest of the week to work on the weeds."

"If you need help with that—"

"No," she cut him off quickly. "I want to do it myself."

"Okay, I'll tell Opal."

"Opal?"

"My niece. She's my brother's child. I've raised her since she was a babe. Just so you're not confused, she calls me her pa."

"Oh, I see. And Opal wanted to help?"

He grinned. "She's excited to start school again."

"I'm glad of that. And you can be sure I'll give her plenty of chores to do once school commences."

Caleb nodded. "If you need anything else," he began, fastening up the last of his shirt buttons. "For the school, I mean," he said with a grin. "I'm three miles out, at the Bar M Ranch."

"Thank you, but I'll be just fine on my own." She tilted her chin up while she admonished herself for taking that one last glimpse of his chest. "Are you through here?"

Caleb hesitated a moment. Then he closed the paint can and wiped the brush clean. He set them inside a small shed and laid the ladder down next to it. "Seems I am. For today. But I'll be back." He tipped his hat and smiled. His expression brightened in much the same way it had when he spoke of his niece, Opal. "To finish what I started."

Grace ignored that chest-thumping feeling she got watching Caleb Matlock saunter away in long, confident strides.

He was halfway off the grounds when he turned clear around. "You need the key to open the school. You'll find that at the marshal's office."

He kept walking backward until she acknowledged him.

"All…right. Thank…you."

Then on a nod, he hopped the school fence and was gone.

"Oh my." Grace put her hand to her chest and leaned her shoulder against the newly painted wall. She shoved away the moment she realized what she'd done.

"Darn you, Caleb Matlock!"

Caleb always managed to get her all jumbled up and now she'd spend her first day home, washing paint stains out of her blue satin riding suit!

"Did you see anything interesting at the school, deary?" Aunt Enid unfolded clothes from Grace's trunk in the pretty yellow-curtained, nicely furnished room that would now become her new home. Grace worked with her as they put some clothes up in a smooth burl-wood armoire and arranged her perfumes and soaps and other such essentials on the dresser before a tall, framed mirror.

"You knew Caleb Matlock would be there, didn't you?"

Aunt Enid's eyes crinkled and she smiled. "He's been working at the school, getting it ready. That man's been on his own for some years now. Raising little Opal all by himself."

"That's commendable." She offered no other compliment. No need to give Aunt Enid false impressions. Grace had her chance at happiness with a wonderful man. She wasn't interested in involving herself with anything but her students and their needs. "I'll look forward to meeting his niece."

"Caleb's a good man, Grace."

Grace scoffed. She had no such thoughts. Why even today, he'd managed to get her flustered enough to nearly destroy her traveling suit.

Aunt Enid hadn't asked any questions when Grace walked in minutes ago, paint-stained. But she'd insisted Grace change her clothes immediately and her aunt worked on that garment until she got every lick of paint out.

"When I knew him, he was a bully and tormented me no end." Grace set the silver-handled hairbrush and comb Harrison had given her down onto her small night table next to a blue-bubbled glass lamp.

"Did he kiss you?"

"Aunt Enid! Of course not! Why would you ask me a thing like that?"

"Paint stains."

Goodness, her aunt surely was astute. The older woman had an uncanny ability to see far too much. Even though Grace was ashamed of her momentary weakness with Caleb Matlock, she had no intention of ever letting that man close enough to kiss her.

"I just lost my balance, Aunt Enid. And knocked into the painted wall, is all."

"Pity." Her aunt's eyes lit with a faraway look. "If only I was a younger woman."

"I surely don't intend to have Caleb or any man, for that matter, ever kiss me. You know where my heart lies."

"I know *how* a heart can lie to you. Fool you into thinking you're through and washed up as a woman."

"I'll have a full life in Springville, teaching my students. That's what I came here for. If I'd wanted a man, I could have remarried back east. But that's not what I want anymore," she said softly.

Aunt Enid helped her put the last of her clothes into the armoire then turned to give her a warm smile. Taking her hands in a firm, loving grasp, she said with utmost sincerity, "Deary, let me give you a bit of advice. If Caleb Matlock ever wanted to kiss me, I wouldn't give him my cheek, if you know what I mean."

Grace tossed her head back and laughed heartily. "Oh, Aunt Enid, I'm so glad I'm here."

Aunt Enid patted her hands. "I'm glad of it, too. Now, you rest up a bit. Dinner is at five every night."

"I'll come down to help you."

"No, not today. You lay your head down and get some sleep. Dream good dreams, Grace."

And minutes later, Grace laid her head down on the soft goose-down bed and closed her eyes, but instead of her beloved

Harrison's face appearing, as it always had in the past, another face came to mind.

Caleb Matlock.

Grace squeezed her eyes shut even tighter and fought off the image of him, up on that ladder, fighting off bees and looking tastier than honey.

Chapter Two

Grace set the last of the washed dishes up on a drain board after having breakfast with Aunt Enid and five of her boarders. Some of the men were stopping over on their way to Fort Worth or Austin and others were cattlemen eager to have a warm bed and square meals instead of eating hard tack on hard ground, but all were there temporarily.

Grace wiped her hands on an old calico print dress. Much to her aunt's displeasure, she'd insisted on helping with the cleanup. "Breakfast was delicious, Aunt Enid."

"Oh, pooh! It's just flapjacks and a slab of bacon. With some muffins thrown in."

"Those were the best walnut cranberry muffins I've ever tasted. No wonder you're never lacking boarders."

"I've been blessed in that regard, deary. Now, here," she said, handing Grace a checkered-cloth-covered basket. "Take this on over to the school. I put muffins inside along with a jug of lemonade. And don't you be working too hard in the hot sun pulling weeds."

"I have my bonnet. I'm just terribly excited to get started. I'll be home late in the afternoon."

Grace kissed her aunt's cheek and dashed out of the house and down the steps. She felt like a schoolgirl today instead of the *teacher,* filled with the excitement she recalled making her way to school on the first day of class.

She reached the schoolhouse quickly, her breaths coming in fast puffs from her brisk walk. She stopped right outside the gate to assess the work she'd have to do today. She figured she'd have to start on the path that led directly to the front steps first, before she attempted weeding the back where the children would play for their recess time. Luckily a swing still hung from a tall mesquite tree, the seat appearing in good shape. No need for repairs there.

Grace entered the grounds and walked right up to the front door. She took out the key Marshal Tupper had delivered to her last night and opened the door, stepping inside. Familiar scents assailed her instantly, of dusty chalk and blackboards, the pine of wood desks and the smell of musky books in bookcases that needed wiping down. Grace set her basket atop a student's desk, then walked to the front and turned, picturing herself in front of her students, teaching her lessons in the very same classroom where she'd grown to love reading and learning about the world. Her job would be to bring that same excitement to her students.

This would be her life now and she hoped to enjoy every minute of it.

Once outside again, she hunkered down closest to the steps and began pulling at weeds that had intermixed with bluebonnets, all looking like spidery webs. She had visions of planting a colorful garden, keeping the bluebonnets healthy and the weeds down.

Half an hour later, deep in thought and fully immersed in her chore, a shadow moved over her, blocking out the morning sun. Grace looked up to a child's smiling face. "Hello, Mrs. Lander."

"Why, hello." She smiled back.

"I'm Opal Matlock," the child said. "Papa's coming, too, soon's he gets supplies he needs. I ran on ahead."

"It's nice to meet you, Opal." Grace wiped her hands on her dress then put out a hand in greeting. Opal's blue eyes widened with joy when she took her hand, hers so small and vulnerable. Grace thought of the tiny baby she'd lost, the quick flash something she had learned to live with during those momentary reminders. But she had to move on, to forget, and embrace her new life as schoolteacher. And this young girl with the blondest of hair braided in two long lengths helped her remember that, as well.

"Papa's gonna paint the last walls today."

"I see."

The girl glanced longingly at the weeds Grace had piled up so far, her bright smile fading some. Clearly the child really wanted to help.

"Opal, I see you've met Mrs. Lander."

Grace looked up to find Caleb approaching. "Yes, Papa. Only just now." Then Opal glanced back at Grace. "My daddy says not to disturb you."

"Oh, heavens, Opal. You're not disturbing me." Grace narrowed her eyes on Caleb as he entered the gate.

He tipped his hat. "Mrs. Lander."

"Good morning," she said, banking down at her annoyance. After all, yesterday she had led him to believe she'd wanted to do the work all by herself. And now, Grace felt the fool for disappointing such an adorable child.

"I'll be finishing up today on the school. Opal just wanted to meet you." Caleb put a hand on Opal's shoulder, a loving, protective gesture that Grace couldn't miss. "She'll be running along soon."

"Oh, there's no need for her to rush off."

Opal looked at Grace, then faced her father. "Can I stay, Papa?"

Caleb smiled. "Sure thing, Turnip. You can watch me paint."

The little girl put her head down and nodded.

Caleb glanced at Grace, his dark eyes meeting hers.

"Or, you can help me with some chores," Grace offered immediately. "And I've brought along Aunt Enid's muffins and lemonade for later. After we get the path cleared, we'll stop and take a break. Would you like that, Opal?"

"Yes, ma'am!" The child's eyes lit with joy and when Grace glanced at Caleb with satisfaction and a note of thanks evident on his face, Grace was struck with another bout of chest pounding.

She bent again and took up the task at hand. "Well, we've all got work to do. Let's get to it."

This time, it was Caleb who responded with a deep, resounding, "Yes, ma'am."

Grace twisted her lips and yanked at a stubborn weed with all her might, wishing it Caleb Matlock's head. Once she lifted it from the earth, Grace sat on her bottom, staring at the weed, fully satisfied, until she heard that same voice coming from behind.

"Can't wait for them muffins, Mrs. Lander."

Grace turned and looked up. "*Those* muffins," she corrected out of habit, staring into Caleb's dark, gleaming eyes.

He grinned.

Then walked off.

And she realized he'd just taunted her, once again.

"I'll have to thank your aunt Enid personally for these delicious muffins," Caleb said, sitting on the steps of the school, taking a hearty bite. He'd finished painting at the same time Grace and Opal decided to take a break from weeding. "Opal, you like these here muffins, don't you?"

Little Opal sat between the two adults on the steps, finishing off her second muffin and taking a long sip of lemonade. "Yessir! Mrs. Lander said I could come over one day to watch Mrs. Greene bake them up. Then I'd know how to make them, too."

Caleb glanced at Grace, who refused to meet his eyes. With dirt smudges on her cheeks and that long hair tied in a braid going down her back, wearing an old print dress, she still made a pretty picture. "That so? Well, that's really nice of her to offer."

"Uh-huh. Pa, can I swing now? Just for a little bit while you and Mrs. Lander finish up resting."

Caleb released a quick chuckle. "Go on, Turnip. Have yourself a little swing."

Opal raced away, her smile staying on his mind long after she'd gone.

"She's very helpful," Grace said, looking out at the piles of weeds she and Opal had pulled up together. "I expect she's a good student."

"The very best," Caleb said, leaning back and stretching his legs out. Without Opal as a buffer, he could look his fill and speak his mind to Grace. "When school was in session, we'd spend time reading at night after all the chores were done. Opal likes school. She doesn't mind her studies and she isn't a complainer."

"Unlike you, who hated school," Grace said without hesitation.

Caleb shook his head. "I wasn't much for studies, I'll admit. I had better things to do."

"Like trying to lift girls' skirts and tug at their braids and call them silly names."

"Nah, I didn't do that to just any girl," he said, leaning on his elbow and shifting his body toward her. He rested his head on his hand and looked into her eyes. "Just you."

When he thought she'd rise and begin working again, she surprised him by leaning her back against the wood post to face him, tucking her dress over her ankles.

"Why me, Caleb? How'd I get so lucky?"

There was no malice in her question, just plain out-and-out curiosity. Caleb thought on that a bit then spoke the truth. "I guess because I trusted you."

She raised her eyebrows, making tiny lines appear on her forehead. "You trusted me?" She shook her head. "I don't understand."

He sat up now and lifted a shoulder in a shrug. "I knew you could take it. You didn't go running to the teacher. Only time I got in trouble was when Mr. Mobley caught me in the act. Even back then, you had my respect, Gracie."

She scoffed at that. Then she laughed. "Because I allowed you to mistreat me? Some would think me a fool."

"I didn't. You were what made coming to school bearable. Like I said, I wasn't a good student. I'd rather be working the ranch with my pa."

"And now the ranch is yours alone?"

"Yes, ma'am. It's mine…and Opal's."

Grace smiled, her eyes glowing with warmth. "Well, you may not have been any kind of student, but I can tell you're a good father, Caleb."

Her comment did his heart good. One thing he prided himself on was Opal. He didn't always get it right, but he'd go to his grave trying.

Right then, Caleb had the urge to kiss Grace Lander into oblivion. All he had to do was lean over and touch his lips to hers and they'd be on their way. God, he hadn't wanted to hold a woman in such a long time and now Grace was making up for all that, just sitting there, giving him a compliment and making his heart work like a busy water pump.

But there was time for that, he figured. No sense rushing it. She'd probably slap his face silly for even thinking it. Instead he snuck his hand into the basket and came up with the last muffin. Grasping it, he rose then bent down to tug on her braid. "I like you, too, little Gracie Greene."

He left her sitting against that post with her mouth gaping open and walked off before she had a chance to argue the point.

On Monday morning Grace had opened the schoolhouse door to fourteen students, eight girls and six boys, ranging in age from six to fourteen years old. Back in Boston, the schools had enough students and enough space to accommodate different grades, but here in Springville, Grace had one room, so her lesson plans varied accordingly. She enjoyed the challenge of differing age ranges. Of course, she knew there were more children in the vicinity and she'd have to make personal appeals to their parents to get their children back into school. Mr. Mobley left very accurate records. She'd studied them carefully and had a good idea who was a good student and who wasn't and more importantly, which children hadn't shown up for their first day of class.

Opal Matlock was always waiting to help her after school, unlike the others, who'd run off as soon as Grace dismissed the class.

"Can I help wipe down the desks?" the bright-eyed child asked.

"Opal, you did that yesterday," Grace replied kindly. "I don't think I've ever seen such sparkling desks before."

Opal beamed.

"You've been such a great help this week, that we're all caught up." Opal was clearly in line for "teacher's pet," reminding Grace of herself more than a decade ago. Opal had swept the floors, cleaned the blackboard, straightened the books and helped Grace plant a row of flowers by the front steps.

"Yes, ma'am," Opal said, keeping vigilant eyes on Grace's face.

"Thank you." Grace didn't want to shoo her away, but she was certain the child had other things to attend to, like helping her father at the ranch, or playing with her friends. "And I want to commend you on your studies. You turned in your lessons and you're reading is coming along very nicely."

"Papa reads to me, then I read to him. We take turns."

Grace still had a bit of trouble visualizing Caleb sitting patiently with Opal, listening to her read. The image of him up on that ladder, swatting at bees, shirtless, with the sun gleaming onto his chest, constantly plagued her. She'd had a dickens of a time relating that handsome, overconfident man with the one Opal described.

But no matter, she'd not seen or heard from him all week. Several of the townsfolk had come to the school on Monday morning to meet her while others had stopped by the boardinghouse. She felt welcome now and was beginning to adjust to her new life as she settled into a daily routine.

But even though she'd come home to Aunt Enid and a houseful of boarders in the afternoons, at night when she turned down the lamp, Grace felt an overpowering sense of loneliness.

Looking into Opal's eyes, she was once again reminded of the child she would have had, if that stagecoach robbery hadn't also robbed her of her husband and unborn child. Grace's life would have turned out so differently. They'd been on their way to the Harrison's family home in Virginia for a visit when they'd been ambushed.

"Opal, maybe I'll see you at church services on Sunday," Grace said, as she walked Opal to the door.

"Yes, ma'am. Only the church burned clear down to the ground last month. So we don't got us a real church anymore."

"We *don't have*," she corrected gently, then went on, "It's a good thing no one was hurt in the fire." Aunt Enid had relayed the goings-on in the community so Grace knew the church was now a row of rickety wood benches placed under a tree, nearby where the pretty steeple church once sat.

"Papa's gonna help build us a new one."

"He is?"

Opal bobbed her head up and down. "He says he's tired of attending church in the very hot sun. All the ladies get the shade of the oak, while the men suffer listening to Reverend O'Connell's long sermons, sweating like pigs."

A laugh escaped Grace's throat and when she gazed into Opal's eyes, she saw a measure of mischief there before she put her hand to her mouth. "Papa says I shouldn't always go repeating things he says."

Grace laid a hand on Opal's shoulder walking her down the front steps, trying to hide her complete amusement. "It's okay this time. I won't tell if you don't. Now, you be careful walking home, Opal."

"Okay," Opal said, skipping to the front gate. Then she turned to look solemnly into Grace's eyes. "Mrs. Lander?"

"Yes?"

"You like my papa, right?"

Taken completely by surprise, Grace stuttered, "Well, uh, yes. He's—" Grace held her tongue, fearing she'd say something altogether inappropriate and finally finished with "—a fine man."

Opal beamed again right before she closed the gate. "I, uh, like all my students' families," Grace offered, far too late. The little girl was on her way, skipping happily home.

"I look forward to seeing Lenny at school Monday morning!" Grace called out, waving farewell to Mr. Roland Strovenski as she turned Aunt Enid's borrowed buggy off their property, heading for the last house on her list. The Strovenskis had been difficult to convince, but Grace had managed to argue her point that eleven-year-old Lenny deserved an education. Being one of the poorest families in the community, Grace used diplomacy explaining that though he was needed on their homestead to help with chores, Lenny's future would hold more promise with the learning he'd receive in school.

"The crops don't grow themselves, Mrs. Lander," the tall Polish farmer had argued. "Last I looked, they need tending each day."

Seeing hope in the boy's eyes, Grace offered them a compromise of sorts. Lenny would attend school three days a week, but he'd be responsible to do the full weeks' lessons. Grace figured some education was better than none at all and she'd stay after school if necessary to help Lenny catch up. Reluctantly the proud farmer agreed. And Lenny seemed pleased as punch. Clearly he was a child who looked forward to coming to school.

Feeling somewhat satisfied, Grace headed toward the Sawyer homestead, the last stop before returning to town. Mr. Romeo, Aunt Enid's aging gelding *clip-clopped* along at a slow, uninspired pace. Grace couldn't complain or lay fault with the faithful steed; he wasn't used to being out all day. Most days, he either grazed in the small yard behind the boardinghouse or slept his time away in the barn.

But when he stopped dead in his tracks on the road, Grace began to worry. "Romeo! Romeo!"

The horse hung his head.

"Romeo, get going." She slapped at the reins.

The horse turned his head to look at her with unblinking eyes, before turning back around.

Grace set the reins down and bounded from the buggy. She came face-to-face with Mr. Romeo. "What is it?"

The horse stared straight ahead, refusing to budge.

Exasperated, Grace took hold of his harness and tugged. "Let's go, Romeo!"

Grace didn't have the power to move the stubborn gelding. He'd simply given up.

She stood by his side for the next ten minutes, watching him, coaxing him, trying to get him to move to no avail. Then, fully confounded, Grace grabbed her cape and hat from the buggy, along with her traveling bag to set upon the road, heading toward town.

She kept turning around hoping something had changed until she could no longer see the buggy in her sights.

Just when her legs began to stiffen from walking along the deserted road for more than an hour in bright sunshine, she heard pounding hooves coming from behind. Fear quaked her insides, and she held her breath, recalling a similar sound when robbers had waylaid her stagecoach. The memory flashed before her eyes and she reacted quickly. She raced off the road to conceal herself behind a tree. Peeking out, she saw a wagon clamoring down the road with two familiar faces.

Grace released her breath and relief washed over her. She stepped onto the road as the wagon slowed its approach.

"Whoa! Hold up!" Caleb Matlock reined in his team and pulled his wagon to a halt.

As soon as he'd seen her, he bounded off his seat and walked toward her, his eyes filled with concern. "We spotted the buggy on the road with no rider. Thought someone was in trouble."

Grace held back her gush of gratitude. "No trouble, really. Romeo refused to budge. I don't know what got into him. So I left him with Juliet and started walking."

"Juliet? We didn't see anyone else around."

Grace flushed and looked over at Opal, sitting on the wagon seat, looking mighty confused. Grace shook her head. "Sorry, it's Aunt Enid. She's fascinated with the works of William Shakespeare. She named her buggy Juliet."

"The *buggy?*" Caleb's mouth twisted, holding back a witty retort, she assumed. He still had the devil in him, even when he was on his best behavior. "Well, let's get you up on the wagon. We'll go back and check on the gelding, see what's wrong with him."

"Thank you," she said, and Caleb took the bag out of her grasp, put a hand to her lower back and guided her to his wagon. Oddly his touch felt comforting.

"Hello, Opal," Grace said.

"Mrs. Lander, are you all right? We saw you hide behind that tree."

Grace's face flamed. She closed her eyes briefly blotting out that terrible incident and her embarrassment that she'd been seen hiding. She doubted it was the time or place to explain to Opal something so complex. Even she couldn't fully explain it. She hadn't felt that same terror since the robbery or such relief that they'd come along when they did.

"I'm fine. Really. I appreciate your concern."

Caleb didn't say a word. And the next thing she knew, he was holding her waist, his hands firm and in control, splaying around her. He peered into her eyes as he lifted her up without any effort at all and set her carefully onto the wagon. Speechless for a moment, and tingling from where his hands had wrapped around her, she watched him walk around the wagon and climb on up.

Opal jumped into the back of the wagon, leaving Grace sitting next to Caleb, his strong thigh brushing her skirt. She swallowed a lungful of air and looked straight ahead, ignoring that heart-thumping feeling she got whenever Caleb was near.

Chapter Three

❦

"He's just being stubborn," Caleb said, stroking Romeo along his nose. "And I think you wore him out. This old boy isn't up to pulling a buggy around all day."

"You mean Juliet, Papa," Opal said with a giggle.

Caleb smiled wryly.

"I didn't know. Aunt Enid never mentioned his age. When we started out this morning, he seemed fine." Grace stroked the horse along the nose, too, concerned that she'd done the animal harm.

Caleb turned to her. "He'll be good as new with some rest. My place isn't far from here. We'll take him in. Let him rest up a bit."

"Papa, Mrs. Lander can stay for supper!" Opal tugged at her father's pant legs. "Can she, Papa? Can she?"

"Oh, no, I wouldn't think of it. You've done enough already." Grace spoke up immediately, unwilling to burden Caleb any more than she had already.

"Wouldn't be any bother, Grace."

Caleb's voice, so low and deep, sent a fresh batch of shivers up and down her spine. Lordy, he looked so handsome, standing in the late-afternoon sun, his hat casting a shadow over his eyes making the strong line of his jaw appear even more pronounced. It still fascinated her how a man could be so dang appealing, with powerful

arms and long, lean legs, a stance that spoke of confidence and arrogance, a grin that could melt any girl's heart and then appear so
darn vulnerable when he hugged his daughter to his chest.

Grace could find herself in deep trouble with Caleb Matlock.
The kind of trouble she no longer wanted. She'd had her one true
love and was paying the price for his death.

"Mrs. Lander, I know how to cook up chicken stew. Papa
taught me."

Grace's heart went out to Opal. How could she disappoint her?
She bent down to look into Opal's hopeful eyes and knew she had
to refuse the invitation. No sense getting too close to father and
child. "Opal, I can't stay for supper. My aunt would worry over
me. I told her I'd be home this afternoon."

"But Papa could—"

"Don't argue, Turnip. You have Mrs. Lander's answer." Caleb's
voice was even and steady.

Opal put her head down. "Okay."

Grace lifted up to peer into Caleb's eyes, hoping he found
apology in hers, but she was met with a quick, cool look before
he turned his attention toward the buggy.

"We'll tie up old Romeo here to the back of our wagon and
drive Mrs. Lander into town."

"Will he go?" Grace asked, her head spinning and her heart
sinking fast.

"He'll have no choice. We'll get you home before sunset. Your
aunt Enid won't have a thing to worry about."

Caleb lifted her back up on the wagon, his eyes meeting hers
once again as he held her firm. Once she settled in, he set about
tying up Romeo and the buggy to the back of the wagon, then he
climbed up to sit next to her.

Poor little Opal didn't say a word from the back.

"I'm sorry to have ruined your plans today. Obviously you
were on your way somewhere. I don't know how to thank you."

Caleb picked up the reins and the team took off toward town.

"I won't have a lick of trouble thinking up a way," he said,
darting a quick glance her way.

And the old, mischievous Caleb Matlock was back.

It did her heart good.

The next day, Grace sat with Aunt Enid under a giant oak, while Reverend O'Connell gave his sermon on the beneficial attributes of Christian generosity, warming the congregation up for the fund-raiser that would secure the cash needed to build the new church from the ground up. The plans were already in motion and the whole community seemed intent on having this church built before the intense heat of summer. As it was now, Grace felt little qualms of guilt sitting comfortably on a bench completely blocked from the Texas sun while the men stood outside the area of shade for nearly an hour.

Caleb's comment came to mind about *sweating like pigs,* and Grace found herself covering her giggles with a cough. She glanced at Opal, who sat with some of her classmates on a bench seat on the opposite end of the rows. Their eyes met and Opal waved, smiling, and Grace returned the smile, feeling an odd tugging in her heart.

Grace, you should have stayed for supper yesterday.

Opal's hope-filled eyes flashed in her mind and then the child's disappointment afterward. It was for the best that she didn't get too friendly with the child or the father, Grace assured herself.

"That little one needs a mother," Aunt Enid leaned over to whisper. "It's a shame she never knew her ma."

"It's a wonder Caleb hasn't married," Grace said absently, thinking of his hands on her waist and the deep piercing look in his eyes yesterday. Surely the handsome bachelor would have met a woman to settle down with by now.

Reverend O'Connell dismissed the congregation with a prayer and a reminder of the festival next week. When Grace began to stand, Aunt Enid pulled at her sleeve and she lowered back down.

"Let me tell you about Caleb," her aunt began and ten minutes later, Grace knew all about Caleb's courtship and heartbreak at the church altar. "He's had his hands full with Opal and the ranch, but that doesn't mean that he hasn't had a wagonload of women wanting a piece of that pie. Any woman he glances at twice—should take notice," Aunt Enid said with a nod.

"We've all had our heartaches," Grace said, warding off any ideas Aunt Enid might have about the two of them. "I, for one, am grateful not to have to make any such decision again."

Aunt Enid scowled and shook her head, but thankfully this time, she refrained from disagreeing.

After exchanging a few pleasantries with some of the families on the church grounds, Grace politely refused individual offers of a buggy ride and a picnic from three of Springville's bachelors and widowers. Lordy, she'd had enough of buggy rides yesterday with Romeo and Juliet.

She spotted Caleb instantly, his back against the old oak, one boot heel pressed against the bark of the tree, smoking a cheroot, his dark, piercing gaze on her. A warm batch of trembles flowed inside her and she stood still, returning his stare. When Opal ran up to him with two of her little friends, Caleb tipped his hat her way, then returned his attention to his child.

Grace picked up her skirts and headed toward the boarding-house. She had lessons to plan, a meal to help Aunt Enid prepare and much to her dismay, one very troubling man to get off her mind.

"Why can't we invite Mrs. Lander to supper, Papa?" Opal asked as she set two plates on the table. "If she tells her aunt Enid, then there'd be no cause for her worry, right?"

Caleb knew this was coming. Opal had taken a fancy to her new schoolteacher. He couldn't rightly blame her, but he wasn't going to give Opal false hope. It'd been just the two of them for seven years. Up until this point, Opal hadn't any complaints but as Enid Greene never failed to mention lately, the child was growing up and needed female companionship.

Caleb let go a labored sigh. "I'm not saying we won't, Turnip."

"When can we then?" Opal pressed, her blue eyes wide with anticipation.

Some days Caleb wondered if he was cut out to be her father. He didn't always have the right words and he wasn't ever sure he'd given her what she needed but there was love flowing between them and that counted for something.

Of course, her real father hadn't the decency to show up in seven years, ever since he left Springville behind. Each year Caleb had gotten a letter saying he was coming to see his daughter. After the first four years of excuses, Caleb realized Martin was blowing smoke and had no real intention of ever coming back. From then on, Caleb had kept the letters private, vowing to protect Opal from disappointment.

"When can she come to supper, Papa?" Opal repeated.

"Someday."

"That's what grown-ups say when they mean *never*, Papa. Someday isn't ever coming."

Opal set out the forks and one knife, while Caleb stirred the pot of meat and beans. "Opal, when have I gone back on my word?"

Opal put her head down. "Not ever, Papa. But—"

"Listen, Turnip. Mrs. Lander is nice enough and all, but she's got the school to run and she helps her aunt at the boardinghouse. She's got responsibilities."

"You don't like her?"

"I like her just fine," he said, remembering the feel of her tiny waist in his hands, the lush fullness of her body as he helped her up onto his wagon. With those pretty, tawny eyes and fiery lengths of auburn hair, there wasn't much not to like about Grace Lander. "She's a widow and she's still sad over the loss of her husband."

Opal turned big eyes his way. "That's why we should cheer her up, Papa. She told me she liked you, too."

"When'd she say that?"

"When I asked her after class on Friday."

Good God, Caleb thought. It was bad enough the new school-marm had entered his dreams. He'd been lightning struck when he first saw her and there'd been a sizzle of awareness between them, even if Grace was too proud and stubborn to admit it, but now Opal pushed at him, too, wanting to include Grace into their lives. And it was true that Grace could use some cheering up. She was too young and intelligent to waste her life away in that schoolhouse. But word around town from the menfolk was that already the new young widow had refused more offers than a horse has flies.

Caleb dished up the meal and sat. "Eat, Opal," he said, "and no more talk about Mrs. Lander tonight."

Opal settled down and ate quietly.

"After supper, I'll read you that Little Women book you love so much."

Opal only shrugged her shoulders and Caleb knew he'd sacrificed his night to read his daughter a story about four young women and their delicate sensibilities.

The second week of school didn't go as smoothly as the first. Grace figured the children had been on their best behavior that first week, but after realizing what was expected of them some of the older children did their work grudgingly at best. She'd had a few disciplinary problems as well, nothing too serious, but the child who had surprised her most of all was Opal.

She'd been acting up, speaking out of turn, giggling or talking to her classmates when Grace was teaching and not answering questions when asked. She hadn't stayed after school to help with the chalkboard or with sweeping. By the fourth day Grace decided to get to the bottom of her bad behavior. She made her stay after class.

Grace sat behind her desk, Opal facing her. "Now, what seems to be the problem, Opal? You're not doing your assignments."

"I turned them all in, Mrs. Lander," Opal said, her expression earnest.

"Yes, but they're incomplete. You've only done half of your arithmetic problems and you haven't volunteered to read in class this week. Aside from that, I've had to reprimand you five times for causing a ruckus. You're laughing and giggling and talking while I'm speaking. And today, you fell asleep at your desk."

"Yes, ma'am." Opal hung her head.

"Do you have an explanation for your behavior?"

Opal's bright eyes lifted to her. "Well, I, uh…I'm doing chores at home until late at night. I guess I'm a little tired." Opal yawned, then yawned again.

"Will you promise to get more sleep tonight?"

She shrugged. "I suppose."

"And will you promise to complete your assignments?"

Opal's large eyes rolled to one side, contemplating. "I'll try, Mrs. Lander."

"See that you do," Grace said, baffled by her behavior. "I know you're capable of much more. You're a very intelligent girl."

"Yes, ma'am," Opal said, clamping her lips closed, refusing to say more.

"Okay, then." Grace blew out a breath. "I'll see you tomorrow."

Opal turned to leave and was halfway down the aisle before Grace stopped her when a thought struck. "Opal, is there anything else bothering you? Is there something wrong at home?"

Opal thought on that a minute, then shook her head, before running off.

Leaving Grace to ponder her behavior all the more.

But by Friday, Grace was beyond pondering. Opal had done something reminiscent of the sneaky, calculating Caleb Matlock back at a time when they'd attended school together. Little Opal had deliberately taken Susie Hilgard's lunch sack and hidden the contents inside of Benjamin McKinley's sack. Susie had come crying to Grace that her lunch bag was empty and she'd exclaimed loudly when she saw Ben pull out the lunch her mama had made for her.

About then three other students pointed fingers, not at Ben as the culprit, but at Opal.

Grace could barely contain her disbelief. She'd never thought the child capable of such hurtful behavior, until Opal confessed it was her doing.

Once Susie's lunch was returned to her and Ben was exonerated from the deed, Grace knew she'd have to make a visit to the

Matlock ranch to speak with Caleb. She'd keep her own suspicions at bay until she spoke directly to Opal's father.

Although, she'd rather do just about anything but, including having a one-sided conversation with Hamlet, Aunt Enid's pet parakeet.

Chapter Four

⚜

Caleb finished mucking out the stalls in the barn and set his shovel against the wall. Wiping sweat from his brow, he cursed the late-morning sun that brought on a sizzling swell of heat that one might mistake for summer. He removed his shirt and tossed it atop a stack of hay, before picking up a pitchfork, ready to lay down a fresh bed of straw for his horses.

He wasn't into his task more than five minutes when he heard a female voice calling out his name. "Mr. Matlock? Caleb, are you here?"

Caleb stabbed the pitchfork into the haystack and walked around the barn to the front of his yard. If he'd been plied with liquor then dunked in the water barrel he wouldn't have been more surprised, seeing prim little Gracie Greene-Lander waiting behind his front door.

He liked looking at her on his property, seeing her thick hair loosen out her pins and her backside fitting into that simple pink-and-white calico that refused to hide her womanly form.

When she knocked again, Caleb sauntered up. "Mornin', Grace."

"Oh," she said whirling around. Her bright, amber gaze met his instantly, before traveling down the length of him. He'd like to think there was admiration in that quick, measured look. His body reacted in kind—a twitching in his groin never failed whenever Grace Lander was around. "I'm terribly sorry to bother you."

"No bother." He glanced at the horse attached to the buggy her aunt had named Juliet.

Grace's face colored to a rosy hue. "I had to borrow a horse from the livery. Mr. Cochran was very nice to allow me the use of the mare."

Robert Cochran? The miserly liveryman hadn't a charitable bone in his body. Stood to reason, he was smitten with Grace. "Nice isn't the word," Caleb muttered. "What brings you out here, Grace?"

Grace glanced at his bare chest again and swallowed. Caleb didn't mind one bit causing Grace a little trouble. She'd been on his mind since the moment she returned to Springville.

She cleared her throat and glanced around. "Is Opal here?"

"Not at the moment. She's taking some eggs to our neighbors down the road. Do you want to speak with her…or me?"

"You, actually. It's good that she's not here. This is a professional call, Caleb. I need to discuss Opal's behavior with you."

Puzzled, Caleb walked over to face her. "Opal's *behavior?*"

Grace glanced once more at his chest, and then all prissylike she lifted her chin. "Yes, her behavior. Could you put on…I mean, can we speak in private once you've dressed?"

Caleb grinned. He liked seeing her discomfort. He pushed open the front door and let her slide by him. "Have a seat inside. I'll clean up. Won't take a minute. Pour us some lemonade, if you don't mind."

Caleb walked over to the water barrel and dunked his face in, then splashed water over his dusty chest and shoulders. He grabbed his shirt and put it on as he strode back to the house, wondering what Opal had done to bring her schoolteacher out to the ranch. Whatever it was, he might just be grateful. He liked the notion of Grace Lander in his house, maybe a bit too much.

Grace stood by the kitchen table and handed him a glass as he entered. He stared into her eyes, took a sip and continued to study her.

"You have a nice home, Caleb."

"You've been here before."

She thought a moment. "Yes, I guess I have. Many years ago."

"We were kids, full of mischief."

"*You* were full of mischief. And I'm afraid that Opal might have picked up some of your unruly behavior."

"Opal? Hard to believe." He slid out a chair and gestured for her to sit. When she took a seat, he sat across from her. "What's she done?"

"She isn't turning in complete assignments and she doesn't care to participate in class. She claims she's tired. That she had a good deal of chores to do, but I'm not sure I believe that."

"Opal's always had chores. But she never has more than a girl her age could handle. And she loves school. She always has."

Grace fidgeted with the pins in her hair, trying to tidy it up. Nerves, he figured. Caleb reached clear over the table and pulled the pins out, letting her hair fall naturally. "Better."

"Caleb!" She came partly out of her seat and reached for him, but he snatched his hands away, keeping the pins firmly in his grasp. "Let me have them."

"You're not in school today, Grace. Leave your hair be."

"No!"

"It looks pretty that way."

She sat back and sighed. His gaze flew directly to her breasts heaving up and down.

"You haven't changed much. Still a rascal."

Maybe he hadn't changed all that much. But she had. Anyone who'd known her could see how much Grace had transformed from the awkward little redheaded child to the tempting fiery-haired beauty she was now. He liked teasing her then, and liked it even more now.

"I've been called worse things. Some of them, by you." He grinned.

Grace smoothed her long locks with her fingers, then set her expression like stone. "Opal played a mean trick on Susie yesterday. She made the girl cry. And most importantly, she tried to lay the blame on a boy. It was quite a day. I came over here to speak rationally with you. Do you think you can manage that?"

Caleb stopped grinning once he heard the sincere concern in Grace's voice. "Tell me everything."

A few minutes later after getting all the details, he stood to pace the floor in front of Grace. "That's not like Opal."

"I know. This all started..." she began, biting at her lower lip, hesitating. "Well, I have my suspicions."

"What?" Caleb wasn't sure what Opal was up to. She'd always been a good girl, though she had a mind of her own. Sometimes, Caleb wondered about his fathering skills. He'd been thrown into the role as father to the young babe and hadn't really expected an instant family. Yet, now he wouldn't want it any other way.

"This all started the day you rescued me on the road. After that, Opal began acting out in class."

Caleb was beginning to suspect Opal's intentions. "And she's been after me to invite you for supper every day. She's been wanting to get you to the ranch."

Grace stood up and faced Caleb. "She's succeeded, hasn't she?"

"Sonofabitch," he whispered, as realization dawned.

Grace wasn't offended by his use of profanity. She simply nodded with a knowing gleam in her eyes.

Caleb had to admire Opal for her craftiness. When he was younger, he might just have tried the same such scheme, but he had to put a stop to it. Opal had never caused a ruckus in school before and he wouldn't allow her to continue. His fathering instincts took hold and he nodded right back to Grace. "I'll speak with her. Straighten this out."

"I hoped you'd say that. She's a very bright girl—"

"Too bright for her own good sometimes."

"Every young child wants a mother," Grace said, her compassion coming through.

"But they don't go picking out one for themselves, now do they?" Caleb said, then explained, "Opal's mother died birthing her. She's never had a female in her life. Hannah would've been a good mother, had she lived. I'm the only kin Opal's really got now. Except for Martin."

"It's hard to imagine a father leaving his only child behind."

"Martin's selfish. I think he was glad when Hannah couldn't conceive a child right away. Took her four years and finally Opal came along."

"Has Opal ever met him?"

Caleb shook his head. "No. He makes threats. Every year he sends a letter or wire saying he's coming to get her, but he never shows up. Now, he'd have to walk over my grave to take her from me."

Grace's eyes shone differently when she looked at him now. And her smile appeared unguarded, genuine. Caleb got a raw, achy feeling in his gut. "You're here now. Want to stay for supper?"

She shook her head. "I can't."

"Or won't?"

"You know we'd be playing right into Opal's hands if I stayed. Besides, you need time to speak with her." Grace walked over to stand right in front of him. "I know you'll be kind with her."

Then she reached out and swept her hand over his and his heart tripped over itself breathing in her sweet female scent, feeling her soft caress.

"I'll be going now," she said and she sashayed out the door.

When Caleb looked down, he found his palm empty of the pins he'd stolen from her hair. He laughed at her smooth, clever trick. Then he whipped around and followed her outside. The least he could do to thank her for making the trip out to his ranch was to splay his hands around her waist and hold on to her a little longer than necessary when he helped her up onto the buggy.

His way of letting her know that though Opal's method wasn't fitting, Caleb might just approve of the notion behind it.

"Are you planning on working at the church fund-raiser on Sunday?" Aunt Enid asked as she prepared the evening meal for her boarders. Grace always lent a hand, making up a side dish or setting the table, although her aunt never asked for any help. Grace had come to realize her aunt thrived on running the boardinghouse and enjoyed every ounce of effort she put into it.

"Yes, I'm looking forward to it. Betty O'Connell is doing the coordinating and she's asked me to crochet bookmarkers to sell that day. I've set aside the rest of the week to work on them."

Grace smashed boiled potatoes in a bowl and added a bit of cream to make them light and fluffy. While she whipped, Aunt Enid prepared batter-dipped chicken on the stove, making Grace's stomach grumble. "But I still plan on helping you with your pies."

"Thank you, deary, but ten pies ain't much to get excited over."

"You make the best pies in the country, Aunt Enid. People will be getting excited over them and they'll sell that day before noontime."

"Pooh!" Aunt Enid waved off her comment. "But I tell you what'll sell best of all—the kissing booth. If you'd volunteered for that, there'd be a string of men lining up that would wrap clean around the entire town."

Grace let go a chuckle. "I wasn't asked to be a part of that." She would've declined the offer anyway.

"Reverend O'Connell's wife has too much respect for your widowhood to ask. Which means that the men folk will be puckering up for Josephine Moore, the thirty-two-year-old spinster. That gal hasn't held a man's interest in over a decade. Seems to me the only way she can get a kiss is for a charitable cause."

Aunt Enid always spoke her mind and Grace was becoming accustomed to some of her *uncharitable* thoughts, but no one had a better heart or a more giving nature. "Now, Aunt Enid, I think Josephine will do just fine. She'll raise money for the new church and have a bit of excitement, as well."

Aunt Enid eyed her carefully. "Not much excitement selling bookmarkers, deary. You ought to start living again."

"I am. I'm enjoying my position as schoolteacher. The children have been good this week."

"You saying Caleb's little one isn't getting into trouble anymore?"

Grace shrugged. "No, she's been good this week. And very helpful."

She didn't know exactly what Caleb had said to her, but Opal was back to being a good student who completed her assignments and helped after school. Grace had been greatly relieved. She'd even seen little Opal apologize to Susie and Benjamin, without an ounce of coaxing.

It almost seemed too perfect.

Aunt Enid smiled. "That Caleb, he sure has a lot to offer. Good fathering ain't that easy to come by."

Grace whipped the potatoes a bit harder in the bowl. "I'm sure he's…he's…" Grace couldn't get the image of him out of her head—pulling the pins from her hair the other day and the silly fight that had occurred afterward. How free she'd felt in that moment, enjoying their slight banter. And how nervous she'd gotten when he cast a hungry look her way, watching her hair tumble onto her shoulders. He was a rake and a teaser, but he was also a good father and a generous man.

She was thinking less and less about Harrison lately. And that worried her, causing her even more guilt.

"He's what, deary?" Aunt Enid waited on her response.

Grace shrugged. "He's doing a fine job with Opal, that's all I was going to say."

Her aunt blinked, then a spark entered her eyes. Grace had seen that look right before an unruly student would get himself in a bucketful of trouble.

On Aunt Enid, that look doubled in magnitude and Grace could only hope she wouldn't act upon whatever that flicker in her eyes had meant.

Sunday arrived and the whole town was buzzing with fund-raiser festivities. Even Reverend O'Connell's sermon seemed more energetic than usual. And when the service about charitable giving was over and done with, Caleb caught a glimpse of Opal laughing with her school friends behind a shade tree.

Thankfully his daughter's unruly behavior in school had been remedied in time for the fund-raiser. Opal was no fool, and he'd hinted that unless she caught up on her lessons, neither of them would have time to attend the fund-raiser today. Opal was a good-natured girl, but at times, she displayed a stubborn streak that reminded him of himself when he was her age. After that one talk, Opal had changed her ways and was back to being studious in class and responsible at doing her home assignments.

Caleb looked out at the clearing, beyond where the new church would be raised, seeing two long rows of wooden booths and tables decorated with colorful ribbons and banners facing each other with a wide berth in between. The congregation, which consisted of nearly everyone in town, was making its way over to the grounds.

Reverend O'Connell set up a ticket booth and was in charge of collecting the cash and giving out tickets. He posted a long list of items available on Grace Lander's school chalkboard, writing in the entry fees for apple-bobbing, dart-throwing, relay races and other games. It was all in good fun, folks donating their wares and other folks buying their goods with the tickets they purchased at Reverend O'Connell's booth. When all was said and done, it all evened out monetarily, he supposed.

Caleb built a sturdy cedar chest to contribute to the Trading Post, the biggest booth on the grounds that was a mock general goods store. Opal contributed half a dozen hand-stitched lace hankies and he was real proud of her efforts.

Caleb hadn't seen the entire town come together like this since Lucinda Rose Runyon's one hundredth birthday celebration. The eccentric widow had been married for seventy years, a milestone at that, and had outlived poor old Renfred by thirteen years.

Just as he was unloading the cedar chest from his wagon, Opal came running up. "How many tickets did you get, Papa? How many?"

Caleb hoisted the chest and began walking to the Trading Post. "Let's see. I think I got five tickets." Opal's face fell with disappointment. Then he shook his head. "Nope, not five. Make that ten."

Her face lit a little. "Ten?"

Caleb stopped halfway to the Trading Post and set down the chest, pulling out the tickets he'd purchased from his pocket. He held them in one big wad. "I guess, not ten, either. Why, it looks like I got more than two dozen tickets here in my hand."

Opal blinked with wide eyes. "Can I have some, Papa? Susie and Anna are waiting for me at the apple-bobbing barrel. Then we want a taste of Mrs. Greene's peach pie."

"Apples and peaches?"

Opal kept her eyes on the tickets in his hand and nodded. "Uh, huh."

Caleb handed her all the tickets. "There you go. Have fun, Turnip."

"Thanks, Papa." She leaped into his arms and hugged him tight, then she took on a thoughtful expression. "But you don't have to give me all of them."

"Sure I do. Just save us a few for supper later. I'm thinking I want some of that fried chicken from Clara over at the Spring Diner's booth. Maybe a cold lemonade, too. Fair deal?"

Opal grinned. "Fair deal," she said, eyes twinkling before she raced off to meet her friends.

Caleb set up his cedar chest at the Trading Post booth, then wandered over to view some of the other wares being traded for tickets. When he came upon a booth filled with books, periodicals and crocheted bookmarkers, he stopped to say hello to Betty O'Connell.

"Have a good turnout here, Betty. We should get that new church built before you know it."

Betty smiled warmly. "We're very grateful to everyone who contributed. The reverend doesn't need much in the way of frivolities to preach the gospel. He'd do it out in the blessed sun or underneath the nighttime stars, so long as he got his message across. But honestly, Caleb, we're real excited. The town of Springville deserves this."

Caleb agreed. He looked down at the table filled with a dozen colorful crocheted bookmarkers. He lifted one up and examined it. "You think Opal might like this one?"

Betty peered at it. "I don't know for sure." Then she called over her shoulder. "Grace, can you come over here for a moment, dear?" Betty looked back at Caleb and twitched her nose. "She'd know better than me. I've been trying to get her to come out from sitting under that tree. She insisted on crocheting instead of enjoying the day."

"Betty, how can I help—" She stopped midsentence when she saw Caleb. "Oh, hello."

She acknowledged him with a quick smile. Looking into her pretty golden-brown eyes made his skin prickle with awareness, like when he was out on the range, knowing the storm clouds were going to erupt and he couldn't do a damn thing about it.

But run like hell.

Caleb planted his boots and stood his ground. "Afternoon, Grace."

"Grace dear, I think I need to spell myself. Would you mind helping Mr. Matlock? He's looking at your pretty bookmarkers for Opal."

Grace bobbed her head without hesitation. "Of course, Betty. You take all the time you need."

"Thank you, dear," she said, then she peered at Caleb, her gaze darting back and forth between the two of them. "I will. You and Caleb…have yourself a nice talk now."

Grace stared after her, her face coloring like blooming roses.

He laughed and shook his head.

When their eyes met again, Grace grinned, too. Seemed everyone in this town set about to matchmaking.

He cleared his throat and gestured to the bookmarker he held in his hand. "You think Opal would like this one?"

Grace gave the bookmarker serious attention before taking it from his hand, her fingers accidentally brushing his. The spark between them was undeniable. Caleb flinched inside, but Grace couldn't much hide her reaction. She blinked and stuttered. "Oh, uh, I think…Opal is partial to pink." She lifted up a more colorful bookmark and handed it to him.

Caleb deliberately slid his fingers over hers to take it from her.

"Right, pink. I'll take it, but I'll have to come back for it later. Opal's got all the tickets."

Grace looked so beautiful standing there in the open booth, the spring sunshine putting ten shades of reds and golds in her hair. He was partial to pink himself now, seeing Grace wearing that color today in her Sunday dress.

"And how did she get all the tickets?" she asked, attempting to ignore the second brush of their fingers.

"I gave them to her."

Grace lifted her lips in a hint of a smile. "I'll wrap it up. You can come by later and settle up."

"I'll do that."

She made herself busy wrapping the bookmarker, while Caleb watched her slender, delicate hands working the paper and tying up the gift in a bow. "I'm glad Opal's come around in school. She's back to being helpful and studious."

"She's a good girl," Caleb said in agreement.

"And I'm glad she's over whatever was in her head...about... well, you know."

Caleb stared into her eyes. "You and me?"

Grace nodded then put her head down and set about straightening the items on the table.

"Yeah, foolish thing for a girl to hope for a mama."

Grace snapped her head up. "I didn't mean that she—"

"I'll come by later for the bookmarker," he said, cutting Grace off when he noticed Enid Greene hunkered in a huddle with Opal just beyond the Bake Sale booth.

Both females were nodding with their heads down, wearing mischievous expressions.

Whatever those two were talking about...couldn't be good.

Chapter Five

After Grace spelled Betty O'Connell in the booth, she met up with her aunt Enid for a bite to eat. They sat at one of the long wooden tables in the clearing, sharing bench space with two other families. "I told you, your pies would sell out first thing."

Grace was glad of it. And her aunt Enid beamed at the compliment. "Weren't much competition, deary. Mine were the only pies. Beatrice Archibald's molasses cookies sold well, and Chester Mueller's niece sold half a dozen prune strudels."

"Well, you helped raise quite a bit for the new church with those pies."

"Hmmmmph, I suppose. We all do our part. But lookee over there, Grace. Josephine's had to close down the kissing booth."

Grace noticed that Josephine no longer stood behind the table, giving kisses on the cheek. The line of men she'd seen there just a few minutes ago had disappeared.

"It's too bad. It was a puny line, but a steady moneymaker," Aunt Enid said.

"Maybe she'll be back."

With a shake of her head, her aunt replied, "She won't be back. I heard someone say her beloved cat, Speckles, got out again. They saw her chasing a rabbit two miles from town. Hard to miss that cat, she's got more colors on her back than a rainbow."

Aunt Enid cast her a thoughtful look. "You finished eating, Grace?"

Grace still couldn't get accustomed to Aunt Enid's swift changes in conversation. "Why, yes. I think so."

Aunt Enid took her plate and stacked it on top of hers. "You know, someone should fill in for Josephine."

Grace shook her head, fully aware now where Aunt Enid's conversation was heading.

"The reverend and Betty O'Connell sure have worked hard setting up this fund-raiser. Be a darn shame if we don't get all the cash we need today."

Grace smiled and continued to shake her head.

"Why I bet, a young, unattached pretty female could raise twenty dollars or more, just for a few minutes of her time."

"Aunt Enid." Grace's warning went on deaf ears.

"I bet the reverend would be very appreciative."

Grace slowed her head shaking.

"The entire town would be grateful."

Grace closed her eyes.

"And poor Josephine won't feel she failed to do her part today."

Grace sighed.

"All that money for just a few minutes of time."

"Okay! I'll do it." Grace rose from the table. "I sure wouldn't want to disappoint Reverend O'Connell and the *entire* town now, would I?"

"That's a girl! Come on, I'll walk you over there."

If it weren't for such a charitable cause, Grace would have died of mortification. Aunt Enid made it her personal mission to tap every male in the vicinity on the shoulder, announcing that the new schoolteacher, Grace Lander, was now available for kisses at the kissing booth.

Available for kisses.

Though, Grace had to admit, the kissing really wasn't so bad. The men who approached her were sweet natured and very respectful. They'd hand her a ticket, then she'd give them a little peck on the cheek. And she noted a few of the single gentlemen returned to the back of the line several times, showing a more than charitable interest, asking to court her, but Grace politely turned them down.

The one man who hadn't stood in her line was Caleb Matlock. She didn't exactly know how she felt about that, except the thought of putting her lips to his cheek made her stomach queasy.

Thankfully the line had diminished to just a few hangers-on. The festivities were coming to an end. She noted people dispersing and booths being shut down as the sun lowered behind the tall trees.

After the last man in line left, Grace began counting the tickets.

"There's got to be at least a hundred tickets there, if there's a one."

Grace looked up into Caleb's handsome face. The brim of his hat partially covered his eyes, so she couldn't tell whether or not he was teasing her. "One hundred and two to be exact."

He pushed his hat back on his head enough for her to see the sincere look in his eyes. "You more than tripled what Josephine would have collected."

"We don't know that."

"Yes, we do. But you're too kindhearted to say."

His unexpected compliment warmed her heart.

Just then, little Opal peeked out from behind him. Grace had been so distracted by Caleb she hadn't noticed her. "You've got tickets left, Papa. And all the other booths have closed down."

"I know, Turnip. I'm going to give them to Mrs. Lander."

Opal's eyes nearly bulged out of her head. "You can't *give* them to her. It's the kissing booth. She's supposed to kiss you."

"Opal, settle down," he said. "I owe Mrs. Lander two tickets for the bookmarker. Did you thank her for making it up so pretty?"

Opal put her head down. "No, sir."

"Well?"

Opal turned her big, disappointed eyes on her. "Thank you, Mrs. Lander."

"It was my pleasure, Opal."

"You closing up now?" he asked.

Grace looked around. Everyone else was on their way home, except the reverend and his wife and Aunt Enid, who sat with them, counting up the cash. "Yes. I'm officially closed. I just have to get these tickets over to them."

"Add these to your count," he said, setting the remaining tickets down. "Opal will take them over to the reverend."

Grace gathered them up. "I'd appreciate that, Opal."

"Yes, ma'am." She held out her palms, but Grace got the feeling the young girl was surrendering to defeat instead. "Here you go." Grace put the batch of tickets in both her hands.

"I'll meet up with you at the wagon, Turnip."

"But, Papa, you gave Mrs. Lander five extra tickets."

"Go on, Opal. Now."

"Yes, Papa."

Both of them watched her saunter off at a pace a snail wouldn't envy.

"You know she's right. She saved up those tickets for this kissing booth."

"She wanted…oh," Grace said, the truth just dawning on her. "You don't think she had anything to do with Josephine's cat running off."

Caleb removed his hat to scratch his head. "I don't think even Opal could come up with that one *on her own*."

Grace closed her eyes. It had to be. "Aunt Enid."

Caleb set his hat back on his head and grinned.

"I'm sorry. Those tickets could have been put to good use today."

"They will be," he said. He leaned over the table to whisper softly, "You owe me."

Grace's nerves tingled, her body growing warm from the intimate tone he took. "What do I owe you?"

Caleb sauntered around the table to face her. "Five kisses."

A thrilling gasp escaped her throat.

"But I'll settle for just the one."

Grace figured she'd gotten off easy. Though her stomach tightened at the notion, she leaned toward him, ready to pay up and brush a kiss onto his cheek. But he pulled back and looked deep into her eyes for an instant, a devilish grin taking shape, before he wrapped his arms around her. Holding her firmly, he pressed closer, her gown rustling against his trousers now. She blocked out every sane and rational thought in her head, when she realized his intentions. She closed her eyes.

Then he kissed her. His lips came down on hers in a powerful way, strong and demanding, but oh, so gentle and she fell into his kiss, the taste and texture of him, enough to make her swoon.

His stubble scraped her cheek. His belt buckle rubbed at her belly. His thighs spread hers apart slightly. She stirred restlessly, breathing in his male scent, relishing his arms around her, her heart pounding wildly. Grace hadn't felt this alive and vital and female in more than a year.

No, she amended immediately—she hadn't ever felt like this before.

"Sweet, Grace," tumbled out of his mouth as he cupped her face in his hands.

Grace let go a moan of pleasure as he covered her lips again, tasting her and expertly loving her mouth. His breath stole all of hers. She sighed deeply and kissed him back with impatience and urgency that left her in desperate need of oxygen.

Caleb broke away from her with deep regret in his eyes, telling her silently if they were truly alone, he'd never have stopped. "That was worth more than a thousand tickets," he said softly, backing up and tipping his hat in that lazy way of his that drove her crazy.

Grace put her trembling fingers to her lips and watched him walk off, heading to his wagon where Opal would meet him.

"Oh, Aunt Enid," she muttered, her emotions in turmoil, "what have you done?"

"No harm was done, deary," Aunt Enid said for the tenth time this week.

Grace looked up from grading school papers, giving her aunt a look of utter annoyance. She'd already had this argument with her and she'd just as soon let the whole incident drop. But Aunt

Enid wanted not only her forgiveness, which she'd finally managed to give yesterday, but she wanted Grace to acknowledge the benefit of her little scheme. "Yes, harm was done. You involved Opal in your plan. That little girl has hopes…and that's just not fair."

"Opal didn't lie deliberately," Aunt Enid went on to explain once again. "She repeated to Josephine what I'd told her to say, was all. She didn't know it wasn't exactly true."

Grace shook her head vehemently. It didn't matter how many times Aunt Enid explained, Grace still couldn't abide her deception. "That's not the point."

"Caleb's a good man."

"I didn't say he wasn't."

"You liked kissing him."

"I didn't kiss him…he kissed me."

"And you didn't exactly push him away."

Grace rose from her seat, exasperated. "Aunt Enid! Stop!"

"If you're worried about what we saw, the reverend and Betty and me, we were busy counting up the money, Grace."

Thankfully. She believed that her aunt hadn't seen Caleb's kiss. His back was to her at the time and Aunt Enid's eyesight from long distances wasn't all that wonderful. If she had seen the potency of that kiss, her aunt would surely be measuring her for a wedding dress.

Grace had a hard time blocking the kiss out of her mind. She'd find herself drifting off in the classroom and stumbling over her daily instruction, when thoughts of Caleb entered her mind. But the evenings were the worst. When she dimmed her lamplight and got into bed, her mind was free and open. Though, she felt like a prisoner to those thoughts, she'd relive every second, every sensation, every heart-stopping moment of being in Caleb's arms, kissing him for all she was worth.

And enjoying every moment of it.

Grace couldn't make Aunt Enid see the futility of what she'd done, the damage she'd inflicted. And now, just six days later, Grace would have to face Caleb for the first time since the church fund-raiser.

"Are you gonna help your old aunt bring along this food for the men?"

"I shouldn't," Grace said with little regret. But her aunt really did need a hand in delivering the lunchtime meal she'd cooked for the volunteers framing the new church.

"Ah, deary, I've never known you to pout and fuss so."

Her aunt hadn't seen her after Harrison died, when Grace had lain across his grave refusing to move until her brother-in-law picked her up bodily and dragged her away. She'd lost her husband and her unborn child within those few horrible days.

Her grief had been unbearable.

Yes, Grace had pouted and fussed. There were times when she plain didn't want to live anymore. Those days were gone, but the blame and guilt she felt soaked deep into her soul like a fresh coat of paint on dry wood.

Grace stacked up her graded papers and rose from her seat in the kitchen. Setting the schoolwork aside, she began packing up the platters of cold ham, biscuits and fresh peaches, fitting them into a large straw basket. "You know I'll help you," she said, "but don't you even think about trying anything this afternoon with Caleb Matlock, you hear?"

Aunt Enid pursed her lips and hesitated as if thinking that very thing.

"I need your promise, Aunt Enid."

She waved her arm in the air, "Oh, I don't know what the fuss is all about. I promise."

"Good." Grace covered one basket with a yellow gingham cloth.

Her aunt began arranging foodstuffs into the second basket, muttering, "Elmer Honeywell's pretty young niece visiting from down San Antonio way invited Caleb and Opal to supper the other day. They met last week at the fund-raiser. Rumor has it she's looking for a husband."

Grace froze from the searing jolt to her system. "Well, that's not my concern," she managed. Then blurted, "How pretty?"

"Pretty enough, I suppose."

Her aunt lifted one basket and gestured for Grace to pick up the other. "We'd best be going."

Grace rallied quickly, but the thought of Caleb being entertained by Elmer Honeywell's pretty young niece settled in her stomach like a ten-pound sack of potatoes.

Before they reached the clearing, the sound of men busy at work resounded in her ears. It was a beautiful day, full of sunshine, the grass lush and crisp under her boots and the subtle scent of wild-flowers flavoring the air.

The hammering got louder as they approached and once they reached the clearing they peered at the skeletal beginnings of the new church. "It's going to be grand," Grace said, visualizing the church down to the very last detail.

"Springville's a growing town," Aunt Enid said. "And the men have growing appetites. I believe they're ready for a break. I'll let them know there's a meal waiting for them."

Aunt Enid walked off while Grace set out the table covers on the ground in the shade of a cottonwood. When she turned around she saw Aunt Enid leading more than half a dozen men her way, looking mighty hungry.

And beyond that, she noticed Caleb leaning against a newly constructed post, drinking lemonade and speaking to a young female with glossy dark hair. He wore no shirt. Daylight glistened on his sun-bronzed skin, his chest broad and powerfully built. She remembered seeing him that way once, when he'd been swatting at bees up on that ladder when she'd first come to town. The image was never far from her mind.

Jealousy crept inside her gut. Her heart plummeted and beat with dread.

Yet, Caleb Matlock had no place in her life. She'd had her one true love. She couldn't love like that again, but most importantly, she didn't want to. The pain of losing that love had almost destroyed her and her guilt ate at her every day.

Caleb reached for his shirt and moved away from the girl, heading to the shade of the trees. He slipped his arms into the sleeves as he strode forward, a true sight to behold, but Grace wouldn't be caught watching him. She put her head down and made herself busy.

"That'd be Miss Lorena Honeywell from San Antonio," Aunt Enid said quietly and not so matter-of-factly as she began handing out the plates of food. Then she whispered, "She's set her sights on Caleb, that's for sure."

Grace was either too proud or too cowardly to stay any longer. She wasn't ready to face Caleb yet. And she certainly wasn't ready to see Miss Lorena Honeywell fawn all over him. "Aunt Enid, everything's set for now. And I have papers to grade at home. I'll come back later to help you clean up and carry the baskets home."

Aunt Enid shook her head. "Never knew you to be a coward, deary."

And there, Grace had her answer—she was a coward because she dashed off before she had to look Caleb directly in the eyes.

Chapter Six

Heavens, Aunt Enid didn't have to invite Caleb to supper, Grace thought selfishly when her aunt had trudged home with three men who'd volunteered their services at the church raising today.

"This wasn't my doing," Aunt Enid said in her own defense, as she and Grace peeled potatoes for a spicy beef stew in the kitchen. "It's only fitting that I help Betty out. She doesn't have a big place and I have three empty rooms upstairs right now. Those men worked very hard today and it'd be a pity to send them home so late when they'd planned on coming back by sunup tomorrow. A hearty meal and a comfortable place to sleep isn't much for all they're doing, but it's sure a good way to thank them."

Grace couldn't argue the point. Feeling a little ashamed of herself for her less than charitable thoughts, she wiped her brow and sighed. "You have a good heart, Aunt Enid. I don't blame you for asking half the volunteers to supper. I'm sure Betty appreciated you offering the help, too, it's just that," she said, lowering her voice, "I really didn't plan on seeing Caleb today."

"Landsakes, Grace. Then don't look out the window."

Of course, Grace immediately peered out the kitchen window. It was Caleb's turn to wash up at the water barrel. Grace held her breath, seeing him shirtless again, splaying his fingers into dark, wet hair and combing it back. The sun was setting now and the last of fading light cast him in a glow that had Grace whipping around quickly. "Oh, my."

"I told you not to look." Her aunt grinned before picking up a stack of plates to bring to the dining table.

"That's one time I really should've listened," Grace muttered, giving the stew a good, vigorous stir.

Caleb couldn't take his eyes off Grace during the entire meal. She wore a creamy-colored blouse with lace and frills tucked into a skirt that reminded him of rich, brown earth. Her hair was tied up in a knot at the back of her head except for the few fiery tresses escaping to graze her cheeks.

She refused to look at him.

She didn't like feeling things for him. She'd used her grief and widowhood as a shield to keep all suitors away. And Caleb would have honored that. He would've given her the time she needed. He would have let her be.

Until he kissed her.

That one kiss told a different story.

She'd kissed him back wholeheartedly and the combination of sweet innocence and hot passion nearly dropped him to his knees.

"The meal was real good, ladies," Caleb said, finishing off every bite on his plate and taking a sip of coffee.

"Thank you, Caleb," Enid said. "You send Opal over one day, and I'll teach her how to fix up a stew like this."

"I'm sure she'd appreciate that, Enid." Though he'd have to think real hard before letting Enid and Opal together for any stretch of time.

Grace pursed her lips and he'd figured she was thinking the same, although he couldn't fault Opal entirely since it was Enid Greene's conspiracy that put his daughter in the middle of all this. He'd had a talk with Opal about butting into adults' business. You can't force two people together like that, he'd said. Both parties have to be willing.

But Mrs. Lander likes you.

Caleb hadn't argued that point with Opal.

She was right.

It was high time he did something about it.

"Where's your Turnip, today?" Gabe Wendell, owner of a chicken farm to the north, asked, "My little one, Annie Beth, is sure tickled to see her when you all stop by."

"Yeah, I was wondering the same, Caleb," Junior Adler, one of Caleb's neighbors asked. "That girl's by your side, usually."

"She's helping out at the Hilgards overnight. Mrs. Hilgard delivered a baby girl this week and Opal couldn't wait to go over to Susie's to lend a hand. She's hankering for a brother or sister of her own."

Grace lifted her gaze to his quickly, then lowered her eyes to stare at her plate.

"That so?" Gabe said. "You just send Opal over to my house when she's lonely. I promise, it'll cure her of wanting brothers and sisters when she sees the ruckus the six of mine cause."

Enid waved him off. "Gabe, you wouldn't trade a one of them. They're good kids."

"Maybe I should send them over here one day, Enid," he said with a playful wink. "And let you see for yourself."

"Be my privilege," Enid said, then rose to bring in dessert. Grace followed her into the kitchen. Caleb had barely gotten two words out of Grace all day. She sure was a stubborn one. But he'd be damned to let her ignore him the way she had today. One way or another, he was going to speak with Grace tonight, and then he was going to kiss her again.

After dessert, Caleb excused himself and went outside to check on Romeo in the small barn Enid had built for her boarders' animals, as well as her own.

By the time he'd finished checking the gelding and smoking a cheroot, the spring air had cooled down considerably, but Caleb only felt heat from rising anger. He walked into the back door of the house to find all the lamps out downstairs. That was just fine with him. He'd have some dang privacy when he knocked on Grace's door. He made his way toward the staircase, but stopped short when he heard the front door open then close.

He followed the sound.

And found Grace alone on the front porch, standing against the post and looking out at a sky filled with bright stars. In the distance, a coyote howled, the sound a faint echo in the quiet night.

"Can't sleep?" he asked, startling her.

She whirled around. "Oh, I thought everyone had gone to bed."

"They have. Except you and me." He stared into eyes so sad, it pulled at him in ten different ways. "I was checking on Romeo, gave him a good brushing down. Had a thorn wedged in his shoe. Got that out, now he's fit to run a race."

Grace's face brightened for a second. "That'd be a sight." She almost smiled. "I'm sure Aunt Enid would appreciate you caring for him," she said politely enough to frustrate Caleb all the more.

He drew breath into his lungs. He didn't want to talk to her about horses. He kept his voice quiet. "Grace."

"I should get to bed," she whispered. She moved to pass him, but he blocked her from the door, denying her escape.

"If you do, I'll only come up there and get you." She opened her mouth, but no words came out. Caleb had a mind to kiss her pretty mouth shut.

"Why would you do that?"

"Because you refuse to talk to me," he said, "and that's no way for friends to act."

Grace searched his eyes. "Are we friends?"

With a quick nod, he said, "I thought so."

Grace gave up the idea of going inside for a moment and took a seat on the porch steps. Caleb sat next to her.

"It's impossible, you know."

"Nothing's impossible, darlin'."

Grace wrapped her arms around her middle. Then shivered. "I can be your friend, Caleb. But nothing more."

Caleb slid his arm around her shoulder and brought her up close, warming her. He took in a breath of her hair. "You always smell so pretty, Grace."

"You always feel so good, Caleb," she whispered and leaned

her head on his shoulder. He held her tight and rubbed her arm, up and down.

"There, you see. Friends. So what's got you so sad tonight?"

"It's nothing."

"You're thinking about your husband?"

She nodded. "Yes. No. Oh, Caleb…why'd you have to kiss me?"

Now that was a silly question. He'd wanted to kiss her since the day he looked down from that ladder and saw little Gracie Greene, all grown-up, looking up at him with those pretty eyes. "Because I had to. You owed me my five tickets' worth."

Grace peered up from his chest to meet his eyes. He grinned. He liked having her all tucked up beside him.

"You shouldn't have collected."

"I'm not sorry. You shouldn't be, either."

"Why?" she asked, her face inches from his.

"Because I'm about to do it again."

Caleb curved his hand around her delicate jawline and brought his lips down to hers in a soft brush. When she didn't pull back, he set his mouth on her with added pressure, encouraged by her willing surrender. He angled her head to deepen the kiss and stroked her lips until she opened for him. He pressed his tongue to hers and the sweet taste and her tiny moan of delight would have knocked him to the ground if he hadn't been sitting already.

A hot jolt of desire ran through him. He continued to kiss her, stroking her with soft, slow, deliberate thrusts until her breath came up short in little puffs. Raw, painful need warred with his attempt not to frighten her.

She'd been scarred and she wasn't ready to allow him into her heart or mind, yet he itched to touch her naked skin, his body begging for completion.

He brought his hands to her shoulders and squeezed just once, before breaking off the kiss. He looked into her eyes, soft, dewy and dazed with desire.

"Go on up to bed now, Grace," he said, his voice a low rasp.

She blinked and her face flamed with color. "Oh, Caleb."

"Shush, now. Go, Grace."

When she hesitated, he whispered, "Before I take you right here on the porch steps."

It did his heart good to see the debate in her expression for a moment and a thoughtful gleam in her eyes before she bounded up and walked into the house.

Three days later, Caleb pounded at a fence post, securing it good and tight into the earth, his hands gloved and wrestling with the barbed wire that kept his cattle in and rustlers and any other threat out. But those threats he could handle. He could deal with lawbreakers or diseases that might plague his herd.

It was the threat sitting in his pocket, the words scrolled on Martin's letter, that could destroy him and the life he'd etched out for himself and Opal.

Martin was coming to town. He wanted Opal. This time Caleb knew he meant business. He'd spelled out the exact date and time he'd arrive to pick up his daughter—three days from today. Be sure to have her packed up and ready, he'd written.

Martin had always made threats.

But he'd never named dates and times.

His brother was to be married. The wealthy woman couldn't bear children and Caleb was sure Martin, who'd never once shown any interest in Opal, was using her as a pawn to secure a wealthy, barren wife.

"Over my dead body," Caleb spouted, whipping at the barbed wire so hard, it ripped a hole clear through his leather glove, slashing at his hand.

Caleb bled, but the slight gash of blood dripping from his hand was nothing compared to the bleeding in his heart. He'd fight for his daughter with everything he had to prevent Martin from taking her.

Opal had a good life here. Springville was her home and Martin was a stranger to her. Martin knew nothing about parenting a child. He knew nothing about Opal and he'd never made any attempt to get to know her. He'd dropped her off one day when

Opal was a babe, wrapped in a blanket and said as offhandedly as if he'd asked Caleb to care for his horse, "You'll take care of her for me, won't you? It's only temporary."

Caleb had looked into the rosy cherub face of his niece and his heart melted on the spot. He'd taken Opal off Martin's hands and had thanked God every day for his good fortune.

It hadn't been easy. Caleb had a ranch to run. He'd had to ask for help from his neighbors at times. He'd had to trade off favors, so that Opal would have someone tend her while Caleb worked the ranch. But it had all worked out. And once Opal was old enough to attend school, Caleb found ways to tend the ranch during those hours, relying on his hired hands for the rest.

Opal had taken to ranch life. She'd been good with chores, but she sure had a streak of mischief in her that kept Caleb on his toes. They were a family, he and Opal, and Martin threatened to disrupt their home.

He mounted his mare and took off, riding hard, checking fences, herding cattle and thinking of nothing but Opal, the young child he loved with his whole heart. He worked with a vengeance, repairing downed fence posts, straightening wire and shooing young strays back to their mamas.

Half-baked from the afternoon sun, he finally rode up to the house, angrier than he'd ever been in his life and fighting a foul mood that could seep over into his evening time with Opal if he couldn't find a way to ease it out of his system.

He dismounted and led his mare to the barn, just as a wagon pulled up to house.

"Caleb," Grace called out, reining in Romeo and Juliet, with Opal lying across her lap. "Thank God, you're home."

Chapter Seven

Caleb rushed over to the wagon with concern deep in his dark eyes. "Opal?"

Grace patted Opal's hair tenderly, keeping her down on her lap while she explained. "There was an accident in the schoolyard. Opal was trying to catch a stray kitten and she followed her up a tree. She'd almost had a hand on the kitten when the tree branch broke and Opal fell. It wasn't too hard a fall," Grace assured Caleb. "But she bumped her head. And now she's feeling dizzy."

"Papa," she said, lifting up from Grace's lap to reach for her father.

"It's okay, Turnip."

Caleb stepped up onto the wagon and took Opal in his arms.

"I took her to the doctor, but he was out of his office. I thought it best to drive her home."

"Glad you did."

Opal snuggled into her father's arms and he kissed the top of her head. "We're going to take you inside the house now, honey. And check out that head."

"There's a bump," Grace warned.

"I figured," he said before carrying Opal down from the wagon. He waited for Grace to step down, making sure she had her footing before turning and entering his house.

Grace followed, her worry over a hurt and dazed Opal more considerable than she'd imagined. Grace had reacted instantly when Opal fell and the feelings she had for this little girl had come rushing forth.

Little blue-eyed, blond, precocious Opal had somehow wedged her way inside Grace's heart. She admired the child's strength of character and her determination, albeit not always prudent, to see things through. She'd lost her mother at birth and had been abandoned by her real father. By all rights she could have become bitter and insecure, yet with Caleb's affection, Opal had become a sweet-natured, giving child.

Caleb placed Opal on her bed and then took a seat next to her. Grace stood by his side, and even through her worry, the sights and smells of a little girl's room brought her comfort and…despair for what she would never have.

There were drawings on the wall of the ranch with horses, drawn obscurely but enough for Grace to make them out, and pictures of a man and young girl standing in front of a house with the words *Bar M* scrolled across the top. Hairbrushes and combs and ribbons littered the dressing table and two crocheted dolls, one pink, one robin-blue, rested on a small rocking chair.

"Okay, Turnip, let Papa see if it's a pea or a walnut."

Opal smiled, still clutching her father's side. Caleb searched with nimble fingers feeling for a bump. When he reached the tender spot, he probed and nodded. "No squirrels will come knocking on your door, Turnip."

Opal giggled and he kissed her forehead. "But there's a little lump there. Are you sore anywhere else?"

"No, Papa. Just my head."

"Still dizzy?"

She thought about if for a moment then shook her head. "No. Just tired."

To Grace's great relief, the color had come back to Opal's face.

Caleb removed Opal's shoes and set a light blanket over her on the bed. "You rest now, honey. I'll come check on you in a few minutes."

He rose from the bed and looked into Grace's eyes, his appearing troubled and something else...something more. "Appreciate you bringing her home."

A lump formed in Grace's throat. She'd never heard that subdued tone from Caleb. She lifted her lips in a quick smile, then focused on Opal, bending down to brush a few wisps of hair from her forehead.

"Mrs. Lander?" Opal reached for her hand.

"Yes, Opal."

"Will you stay awhile?"

"Oh...I...yes. Of course I'll stay."

Opal nodded then closed her eyes. "Thank you."

Grace sat by Opal's side, holding her hand until her breaths rose uniformly in a peaceful sleep. Caleb had long since left the room, leaving her alone with the child.

This is the closest I'll ever come to being a mother.

Grace believed she would have made a good mother had she been given the chance. She fought her tears and took a second to compose herself from those disheartening thoughts before entering the kitchen. Caleb sat at the table, his head in his hands, his eyes downcast.

When he noticed her, he rose from his seat. "How's Opal?"

"Sleeping."

Caleb walked toward her bedroom door and peeked inside, then returned.

"She'll be fine," Grace assured him. "I see this all the time at school."

"It's not the bump on her head that worries me. She's tough. I raised her that way." Caleb paced back and forth, muttering an oath. "Damn it. *I* raised her. *I* took care of her when she was sick. I *love* her."

Grace stood to approach him, seeing the desperation on his expression. "Caleb? What is it?"

He pulled a crumpled letter from his pocket and handed it to her. "This."

Grace read the entire letter and her stomach clenched at

Martin Matlock's heartless words. *"Pack her up. Have her ready. I'm taking her to meet my fiancée. She's always wanted a child of her own."*

Martin would come for Opal in three days. The unfairness of it all shook Grace to the core and she could only commiserate with Caleb's pain right now. He would lose his child. Grace knew something of terrible loss and the injury to one's soul caused by the devastation. She didn't want to see Opal torn away from the only father she'd known by an unprincipled man. "Oh, Caleb."

"He'd have to kill me first."

Grace believed that Caleb meant it and that worried her, though she'd always admired his unqualified devotion to his daughter.

"Maybe it's an idle threat." Grace put a light of hope in her voice. "You said he'd threatened to come for her many times."

Caleb looked out the kitchen window to the barn, the corrals, the ranch he'd built for his child, and shook his head. "He means it this time. You read the letter. He's getting married. To a widow with no children. The woman wants Opal. And Martin is willing to ruin his daughter's life to see that end. He'd use her that way to get what he wants."

Grace went to him. She put her hand on his sleeve tenderly and when he turned to her, anguish, frustration and fury all raged in his eyes. "I can't lose her."

The pain she witnessed touched the deepest part of her. She'd fallen in love with Opal almost from the first day, but now, seeing Caleb so torn up inside, broke loose the bricks of denial she'd carefully put up. Little by little, he'd chipped away at her defenses, leaving her open and vulnerable and powerless.

She was in love with Caleb.

Both father and daughter owned her heart.

Grace wouldn't think about the frightening implications of that love right now.

Caleb needed her.

She moved to face him, then lifted up and brushed a soft, healing kiss to his lips. "I'll help you, Caleb. Any way I can."

He pulled her into his arms and held her tight, his body trembling with untold despair. She wove her fingers through his thick, dark hair, curling around the locks and showing him without benefit of words that she cared deeply.

He shifted enough to peer into her eyes. Grace couldn't hide her feelings—the way she looked at him now revealing her true emotions. He put his hands on her waist and clamped her to him, pressing their hips together, tightening his hold on her. "Grace."

It was plea from deep in his heart.

I love you, Caleb. But it's hopeless.

He crushed his lips to hers then and those thoughts scattered like falling leaves in a windstorm. All she could do now was feel.

He backed her up against the wall and continued kissing her, his passion reckless and out of control, but Grace understood what he was going through. She'd felt that same overwhelming sense of heartache once.

And now...she felt it again, for him.

He streamed kisses all along her face, chin and throat, then back up to her mouth, parting her lips and driving his tongue deep inside. Grace could barely catch her breath from the intense driving force. He angled his body, his legs pressing hers, his thighs tight against her and his manhood thick and full against her belly.

Everything female below her waist responded. She moved to feel more of him, clutching at his back, shoulders, holding him tight, offering everything she had to give.

It went beyond physical, emotions churned and feelings poured out in their locked embrace.

Caleb ran his thumbs over her breasts, circling the tips that jutted out from her arousal. A jolt of heat raced through her body from the delicious sensation.

"I need you, Grace," he ground out, his voice a rasp of desire and pain.

"I'm here, Caleb," she whispered. But she knew she couldn't give him what he really wanted. She couldn't be the woman he needed. Not for any length of real time.

But today, she couldn't bear to deny his request.

"Papa?"

Opal's tiny voice carried in the kitchen like a booming clap of thunder. Caleb put his head down, bumping foreheads with her.

Grace blinked, then gently shoved Caleb away and immediately missed his heat.

When they both looked toward the voice, Opal stood in the kitchen threshold. She darted a gaze from her father to Grace and smiled. "I feel better."

Caleb strode over to her. "That's good, Turnip." He lifted her up into his arms and turned to Grace.

Opal's eyes beamed. "You stayed."

"Yes…I did."

"Papa looks glad, too."

Caleb cleared his throat and Grace prayed Opal couldn't see the heat rising on her face.

"I *am* glad. Mrs. Lander is having supper with us, tonight." He glanced at her silently, daring her to refuse his offer.

Grace didn't want to give Opal false hope, but she also couldn't turn down Caleb today. She felt he needed her right now even more than Opal did. "Yes, I'm staying for supper," she said, watching Opal's big eyes brighten all the more.

Caleb set her down.

"Your papa will cook and you and I will go over your lessons for today," Grace announced with some semblance of composure.

He grinned. "Bossy."

Grace strode toward Opal, taking her hand and peering deep into Caleb's eyes for a long moment. There was a measure of happiness there now and it did Grace's heart good to see him that way.

If only for tonight.

It felt right having Grace at the Bar M, sitting down to supper and talking with them like she belonged there. The meal wasn't much—just smoked ham and beans—but Grace insisted on making biscuits and they were just about the best-tasting ones he'd ever had. She puttered around in the kitchen afterward, too, helping with the cleanup and every so often their bodies would brush.

Caleb wanted to grab her again and hold her close. Kiss her pretty mouth. Touch her skin. But Opal had keen eyes and it wouldn't do much good for her to see that. He was grateful his daughter hadn't seen him kiss Grace earlier, pressed against that wall.

Grace finished wiping her hands on a cloth and folded it neatly onto the counter. She stacked the dried dinner plates and placed them into the cupboard. "I should be going," she said on a sigh. "It'll be dark soon."

"Do you havta go, Mrs. Lander?"

Grace shot him a quick glance, then nodded to Opal with soft eyes. "I do. It's time for you to get to bed."

"It's not bedtime yet, Papa. Is it?"

"Just about, Turnip."

Caleb didn't want the evening to end with Grace, either, and he surely wouldn't allow her to drive home in the dark with that fickle gelding at the lead. Romeo and Juliet had themselves a tragic end, hadn't they?

"We'll drive Mrs. Lander back to town."

"No, that's—" Grace stopped in midsentence, then cast those soft, beautiful eyes his way. "All right. That'd be very nice," she finished.

Opal jumped for joy. "Yippee!"

Grace let go a chuckle.

Caleb smiled, but the biting sting of Martin's intentions remained fixed in his mind, the letter searing a hole in his pocket.

"Opal, get a wrap for you and for Mrs. Lander. It's bound to be a little chilly on the drive."

"Okay," she said, taking off for her room.

Grace faced him now, a somber look in her eyes. "Are you going to tell her?"

"Nope."

"Caleb," she said quietly, seeming to choose her words carefully, "don't you think Opal has a right to know what's happening?"

"What's right and what's fair is for Opal to stay with me, Grace."

"I know," she said, "but what if—"

"This one's for you, Mrs. Lander," Opal said, bounding into the room full of energy. She handed Grace a cream crocheted shawl, oblivious to the conversation. She stared at the shawl in Grace's hand for a long moment. "It was my mama's."

"Oh." Grace's throat tightened. She swallowed and managed, "It's…lovely."

"My mama was very *lovely*. Right, Papa?"

Caleb drew in a deep breath and nodded. "Hannah was pretty. Just like you, Turnip."

He poked her nose and she giggled.

"She had long, blond hair and blue eyes, just like me."

Grace's lips curved up at Opal's viewpoint. "Just like you."

"Papa thinks you're pretty, too, Mrs. Lander."

Caleb raised his brows and stared at Grace. Normally seeing her discomfort would tickle him, but today, he only wanted to keep her close. "Mrs. Lander is beautiful on the outside and on the inside."

Opal crinkled her nose in confusion. She darted glances from him to Grace. "Does that mean she's nice?"

"It does," he said. "So long as you do your lessons on time." He winked then announced, "It's time we got going."

And after he tied his horse to the back of Enid's wagon, he helped Grace up onto the seat. Opal went in next and the three of them took off for Springville, the wagon bumping along the road. For the first time that he could recall, he wished the three-mile trip into town took a little longer.

The sun had almost laid to rest, shooting red-gold flames of color up, fighting for its last breath as darkness loomed. Silence settled on the land, the last vestiges of the day giving way to a peaceful night. But Caleb knew no peace right now, his mind ever churning with uncharitable thoughts of his brother.

He clicked the reins and old Romeo continued on the trek to town, as if the old gelding knew better than to mess with Caleb. Opal and Grace played a spelling game, their cheerful banter easing the ache in his heart some.

"Spell *wildflower*," Grace said to Opal.

"That's a hard one, Mrs. Lander!"

"It is. But I'll help you. First sound out *wild*."

"W...i...l...d."

"Good. Now try *flower*."

"Not the sack we bake biscuits with, Turnip," Caleb added.

"I know that!" Opal grinned. "I know it's a flower, like the ones we plant in the garden."

"That's right, Opal. Try it."

Opal thought for a few seconds. *"F...l...o..."* She looked to Grace for assistance.

With Grace's help, Opal sounded out the entire word and spelled it correctly. "I did it!" She leaped into Grace's arms and the two females in his life hugged tight with happy smiles on their faces. Grace looked over Opal's head at him, and seeing her hold his daughter in her arms with joy in her eyes only confirmed what he'd known all along.

Those two females were his future. And he'd be damned to lose either one of them.

Chapter Eight

Grace sat at her desk in the front of her class, staring at Opal as Lenny read from *McGuffey's Reader*. For the past two days, she couldn't take her eyes off of her. Opal, the child with no mother and a worthless father, had found a loving home with her uncle Caleb. Little did she know that in just one day, all that she'd known here in Springville could be taken away from her.

Martin had the law on his side. He was Opal's father and Caleb would have a difficult time proving that she didn't belong with her own flesh and blood.

A sense of impending dread stole over Grace. She'd had trouble sleeping. She'd had trouble eating. This time was reminiscent of when she'd lost her husband and child; the sorrow and misery claiming her daily life had touched everything in it.

If Grace were to compare, Harrison's death had come suddenly and harshly and a ruthless man had almost kidnapped her. They'd been surprised by the attack. They'd had no forewarning. One minute they were speaking of pleasantries with passengers on the stagecoach, the next, they were being dragged out of the coach at gunpoint and robbed. The shock of that horrible day still lingered, haunting her memories.

With Caleb, the shock was looming, the horrible day would arrive and he would anticipate it with apprehension, gearing up for the worst. His anger and fierce sense of parental protectiveness could cause him to do something foolish. Something rash. Something dangerous.

Grace couldn't stand to think about it, yet all she did was think and think and think.

"Mrs. Lander? Mrs. Lander?"

Students' voices broke into her thoughts. Lenny had finished the pages she'd asked him to read.

"Very well done, Lenny," she said, then noted many sets of eyes staring at her in disbelief. In truth, she hadn't heard Lenny at all and now she admonished herself for not paying attention. Judging by the faces peering at her with confusion, it was obvious Lenny hadn't read well at all. "You gave it a nice attempt," she finished. And appeased the majority of students who'd appeared relieved that justice was done.

"Mrs. Lander," Susie spoke up, "it's past time to go home."

Grace glanced at the clock on the wall donated by Mr. McKenzie from the Dry Goods store. "Oh, I suppose it is. Clean up your desks, children."

Shuffling sounds resonated in her ears as the children took up their papers and straightened their desks, wiping down their individual chalkboards. The fresh scents of spring filtered in and birds chirped outside, the sky was clear blue today, but Grace hadn't noticed until this very moment.

"Mrs. Lander, are you all right?" Opal stood at the door with a perplexed expression on her face.

Grace walked over to the girl and put her arm around her shoulders. "I'm fine, Opal." They walked outside and down the steps of the schoolhouse.

"It's just that you look like my papa does. He's always staring at me lately, then looking out the window. Like you do."

Grace's brows rose, but she shouldn't be surprised. Opal was certainly an observant child. Grace could only guess how upset Caleb was about this, when she could barely contain her distressed thoughts. "Oh, really? Maybe he's just thinking about how much he loves you."

She shrugged, unconvinced. "I guess." Opal wore a yellow eyelet dress with puffy sleeves, her long hair fashioned in one braid down her back tied with a thin ribbon bow. She appeared especially bright and cheerful today.

Grace lifted Opal's chin to meet her eyes. "Your papa loves you very much, Opal. Always know that."

The little girl nodded.

Then Grace bent to place a kiss on the top of her head. "I'm glad your bump is better," she said in way of an excuse to kiss the child.

"Thank you," Opal said.

"You'd best be going. Don't want your father worrying over you. It's late as it is."

"Yes, ma'am," she said, and once she was out of the gate, she began skipping home.

"You gonna tell me why you've been lookin' sadder than a rabbit in an empty lettuce patch, deary?" Aunt Enid brought over a tray with two cups of tea and molasses cookies and sat next to her on the parlor sofa. She set the tray between them, a precarious notion, but one Grace couldn't miss. Her aunt was willing to risk her velvet-cushioned settee for answers. "Why, for the past few days, you've come home from school looking like the world's gonna end. Are you feeling all right, Grace?"

"I'm fine, Aunt Enid. Truly." Grace had deliberately kept Caleb's secret from her aunt. Not that she wasn't good-hearted and well-intended, but Aunt Enid was known to gossip and the last thing Grace wanted was for Opal to hear about this from someone other than Caleb.

"No, you're not. You're not yourself. Tell your aunt what's got you so turned around."

"Okay, I'm a bit upset, but it's not for me to say, Aunt Enid. I shouldn't tell you anything else."

Her aunt laid a comforting hand on Grace's knee, like she'd done when she was a child. "There's nothing you can't tell me."

Grace shook her head, willing to protect Opal at all costs. "Not this."

Aunt Enid bobbed her head up and down resolutely. "It's Caleb, isn't it?"

She'd let her believe it was a romantic dilemma and nothing else. "Maybe."

"I saw you three coming up the road the other night with Romeo and Juliet. Why, you looked like a family, all cozy together on that bench seat. Opal's face was clearly beaming."

Grace drew a breath and sighed.

"He's a good man, that Caleb."

"I agree, Aunt Enid. You don't have to keep persuading me that he's a decent man. I've seen him…with Opal."

Tears welled in her eyes at the mention of Opal and painful thoughts of what tomorrow would bring rushed in.

"Something's happened, hasn't it?" Aunt Enid leaned in closer and wouldn't let the subject drop.

Grace nodded. "Yes, but if I tell you, you can't say a word." Grace sniffed and took a handkerchief from her pocket to wipe her nose gently. "You have to promise."

Aunt Enid sat back. "Deary, I've kept some secrets that would make the padres in the church confessionals stand up and take notice. I promise."

"Okay," she said, willing to believe her aunt and slightly relieved to unburden herself. After all, tomorrow, one way or another, the truth would surely come out. "It's about Martin Matlock. He's coming to town tomorrow to get Opal. Caleb got a letter from him this week and he's getting married. The woman wants a child. They're planning on taking Opal away from Caleb."

Grace kept her voice steady, but she was broken inside, just thinking about Opal being forced away from her home.

"You're sure it's real this time?" her aunt asked. "Martin's made threats before."

Grace nodded slowly. "Caleb's certain of it. This time, Martin has something to gain by taking Opal. A wealthy wife."

"I see." Aunt Enid pursed her lips and thought for a moment, then she took hold of Grace's hand and squeezed. "Grace, dear. There's nothing really to worry about."

"Aunt Enid! You can't possibly think Opal would be better off with Martin."

"Heavens, no."

"Then how can you say I shouldn't be worried?"

Her aunt's light brown eyes crinkled at the corners when she smiled, her face open and sincere. "Because Caleb Matlock is Opal's true father."

The next day, Grace rose from her bed, helped Aunt Enid make breakfast for her boarders then walked to the schoolhouse, just like it was any other ordinary day. But today wasn't ordinary. Today, the truth of Caleb's paternity gave cause for hope. Aunt Enid had explained the situation in great detail and though Grace had been well-schooled in literary accounts, both fact and fiction, she would have never guessed this outcome. If Aunt Enid was correct, and Grace believed her tale wholeheartedly, then Opal was Caleb's flesh and blood and he'd never known it. He'd never known he'd conceived a child.

And today, Grace agreed to go along with her aunt's plan to secure Opal into her true father's life forever.

Grace went about her daily routine, teaching vocabulary, having students do addition and subtraction on the chalkboard, spending time with them in the schoolyard during lunch and just before dismissing them, she gave them each a turn at reading.

During the day, she'd kept a watchful eye on Opal as she did every day since her fall from the tree. The little girl had exuberance and enough energy for the entire class, which gladdened Grace's heart. If all went well, Opal would never know what a monumental day it would turn out to be.

As the little girl gathered up her books and readied to go home, Grace waited for the rest of her students to leave. "Opal," she said. "I have a surprise for you. Aunt Enid is making her spicy Spanish stew today and she's invited you over so she can teach you. Would you like to do that?"

Her eyes widened with delight. "Oh, boy! Does Papa know? I havta always tell him when I'm gonna be home late."

Grace assured her, "I have to visit your papa today. I'll make sure to tell him first thing. Aunt Enid will see you home a little later. Would that be all right?"

"Yes, ma'am!" Her blue eyes filled with excitement.

"Good." Grace hugged Opal to her, the love she felt for this little girl searing straight through her. "You run along now to the boardinghouse. Aunt Enid is waiting for you."

Grace had to face Caleb now and reveal the truth, speaking of intimate things that would solve his problems with Martin.

She decided to walk the distance to the Bar M Ranch, leaving Aunt Enid with Romeo and Juliet to take Opal home later on. She didn't mind the three-mile trek. It gave her a chance to sort through her thoughts and formulate the right words to say to Caleb. He'd be relieved, but his other reactions might surely need a gentle touch.

The sun hid behind graying clouds, which made her walk more enjoyable. There was a bite to the air, the Texas spring weather always unpredictable. With her shawl wrapped loosely around her shoulders, she continued on, noting the colorful wildflowers along the road. Bluebonnets were always among them, their clear sky hues contrasting with the golden-yellows and fiery-pinks lifting up across the flapjack-flat plains.

Tumbleweeds drifted by, big spiderlike branches twisted together in almost perfect circles rolling along as slight breezes shifted into stronger winds. With her shawl tightly wrapped around her now, she entered the gates of the Bar M.

And found Caleb in front of his house, arguing with another man.

Caleb barely contained his fury. Martin had never been on time for anything in his life, yet here he stood, prompt and pompous, ready to take Opal off his ranch.

"Be reasonable, Caleb. She's my daughter. I'm offering her a good life. Great schools, everything she'd ever want. She'll have the best of everything."

Martin wore fine clothing; a black suit coat and vest, his boots

polished to a mirror finish and a belt buckle and tie clasp made of
pure silver. He'd obviously had the best of everything. Bought and
paid for by a rich woman.

"She has a good life here. She won't want to go with you.
You're a stranger to her. And I'm sure as hell not turning her
over to you."

"She's mine, Caleb." Martin's sigh of impatience annoyed him
to no end. He walked right up to Caleb, staring him down. "You
have no right to her."

"You're using her!"

"That's a lie!"

"You haven't seen her since you dropped her on my doorstep
seven years ago." Caleb's teeth gnashed and his jaw tightened.
"You don't even know what she looks like."

"I'll get to know her. We'll have plenty of time from now on."

"Like hell! She's my daughter now. I raised her and you're
gonna have to kill me before I let you have her."

Martin pursed his lips and shook his head. "I have the law on
my side, you know. I've already spoken with a legal representative."

Caleb's hands tightened into fists. "You bastard."

"Come on, Caleb," he said with a pathetic whine of desperation in his voice. "It's been rough on me these past years. I've
been broke and hardly scraped by. My luck just about ran out
until I met Regina. I've got a chance now. *A real chance.* For the
first time in my life. Regina wants a child. She'll love Opal."

"Not good enough!"

"You've always been stubborn!" Martin's face reddened in
frustration and he shoved Caleb hard.

Caleb fell backward, then righted himself, his rage boiling
over. He threw a punch that landed in Martin's gut.

Martin grunted and slipped back. "If that's how it's gonna be."
He tossed his jacket and lunged at Caleb, missing his chest. The
punch landed on his shoulder.

"I said you'd have to kill me first."

He tangled with his brother and they both went tumbling to the
ground, fists swinging. Caleb took a punch to his groin, which

would have doubled him over if rage hadn't been running through his veins—Martin always fought dirty. Then he connected with Martin's jaw, the sharp swipe making him groan.

In the background, Caleb heard a stern female voice calling out, "Stop! Stop!" but he was too intent on saving Opal to really comprehend. "This won't solve anything!"

Caleb took a blow to his chest. He landed one right back.

Both of them grunted.

The female's scolding grew louder. Caleb recognized Grace's voice, just as Martin caught him off guard with another strike to the chest. Caleb shoved hard and managed to roll over and pin Martin down, his fists high in the air ready to descend when a shot rang out.

The booming sound of Caleb's rifle startled both of them. They froze.

And looked toward Grace.

"Get up!" she said, standing over them. "Both of you!"

She pointed his rifle and Caleb rose quickly, speaking in a calming voice, "Grace, put that thing down."

Martin lifted up, straightening slowly, his shirt and vest a mass of dirt and blood.

Grace continued to point the rifle. "You don't think I know how to use it?"

Slowly, with caution, Caleb shook his head. "Shows you how much you know," she said, quietly assessing him. Then to his relief, she lowered the rifle. "I hate that you made me resort to this," she said, shaking now. "Both of you. You should be ashamed of yourself, fighting like schoolchildren!"

"Grace, honey. You know the situation."

She softened her eyes toward him and another round of relief swamped him. He walked over to her and took the rifle out of her hand. "You grabbed this from the house?"

"Well, what was I to do? Neither one of you stubborn mules would stop when I called to you."

Martin mopped up blood on his face with a handkerchief he'd removed from his pocket. "Gracie Greene?"

"Martin," Grace said, casting him a blistering look that the devil himself would envy.

And Caleb had never been more proud, or more in love with Grace than at that very moment.

Chapter Nine

The bleak, turbulent sky matched all their moods right now, each angry individually for the impossible situation at hand. Grace shivered and tightened her wrap, glaring at Martin and wondering where her charity of spirit had gone.

But she had news to deliver and it would settle matters. "Can we go into the house and speak rationally? I have something to say that will clear everything up."

"Martin is not welcome in my house," Caleb said firmly.

Martin drew a breath, his nostrils flaring, like a bull ready to charge. "Everything's clear from where I stand. I'm taking Opal to Denver."

Caleb cursed under his breath. When he opened his mouth to argue, Grace interrupted, "No, you're not taking Opal out of Springville. I have news that will shock you, Martin, but it's the truth. You're not Opal's father."

Martin laughed scornfully. "Just because Caleb raised her doesn't mean that he's—"

"He's her real, flesh and blood father."

Caleb looked skeptical at best, but there was a glint of hope in his eyes, as well. "What are you saying, Grace?" he asked.

"If both of you will listen, I'll tell you something Aunt Enid has kept secret for Opal's sake. And for Hannah's."

"Hannah? What does my dead wife have to do with this?" Martin asked, his tone belligerent.

Grace looked into Caleb's dark eyes. She took his hand. "When you were left heartbroken at the altar almost eight years ago, you went on a drinking spree, from what I understand. It lasted days."

Caleb nodded. "I did."

"Well, it seems that Martin and Hannah had been having trouble conceiving a child. They'd tried for many years and Hannah was desperate for a baby. It had become an obsession with her. At times, she'd been frantic over it. Martin wouldn't allow her to see the doctor or get any help in the matter. He didn't want anyone knowing."

Caleb's eyes went wide. Grace ignored Martin's heavy sigh of impatience. "She came to you that night, sneaking in the dark. She knew you wouldn't know her since you'd consumed a lot of liquor. She'd used a saloon girl's name, pretending to comfort you in your hour of need. And…"

Grace gulped. She'd gone over this in her mind all last night and today, rehearsing the words. She hated thinking of Caleb making love to a woman and having to describe the scene, the impact of the truth hitting her hard. The only consolation in that truth was Opal, the beautiful child conceived from that night. Her emotions running raw, she continued, "She conceived a child that night with you. And she pretended it was Martin's."

"That's a damn lie!" Martin faced Grace, fury reddening his face, his eyes closing to narrowed slits.

Caleb shook his head. "I barely remember anything after I got home that night."

"You're making this all up!" Martin accused, taking a step toward Grace.

Caleb shielded her with his body, warning Martin off.

But Grace stepped up, unafraid now to reveal to Martin the entire truth. "No, Aunt Enid was there when Hannah died. She confessed it all to ease her conscience once she realized she was dying. Dr. Stewart knows the truth, too. She made them both promise to keep the secret."

She turned to Caleb. "When Martin left Opal on your doorstep, Aunt Enid figured Opal was where she should be. She didn't want to bring shame onto Opal or her mama. She figured you and Opal were meant to be together, and Martin," Grace said, directing her attention to him, "you never showed any interest in Opal. You abandoned her early on. So there was no need for the truth to come out. Until now."

Caleb's face brightened. "It's the truth then? Opal is my daughter?"

"She is, Caleb," Grace offered, gladdened to be the one to give him this news. "You're Opal's father."

"I don't believe it!" Martin howled, pacing back and forth, his voice competing with thunder booming off in the distance.

"It's the truth. Dr. Stewart has a record of it. Both Aunt Enid and the doctor were witness to Hannah's deathbed confession."

"We'll just see about that," Martin said, grabbing up his coat. He mounted his horse and looked down at Caleb. "This isn't over."

"It is, Martin. Unless you want the entire town to know you couldn't father a child. That you were duped by your wife and played for a fool. Go back to your fiancée in Denver and work it out, Martin. Leave Springville for good. And no one will ever have to know the truth."

"Is that a threat?"

"It's plain fact."

Martin hissed several oaths then rode off in a rush, hanging on to his hat, heading in the direction of Springville.

"What will he do?" Grace asked.

They looked off in the distance, as Martin's form became a dark speck against the landscape. "He'll seek out Doc Stewart. I've never seen a man so desperate."

"But he'll learn the truth and have to leave you and Opal alone."

"Yeah." Caleb nodded, then turned to her, his face open with relief and joy. "Opal is mine!"

He picked Grace up in his arms and swung her around just as thunder boomed again, the threatening sound louder this time. Grace laughed, throwing her head back, so happy for Caleb and Opal.

When he set her down, noises of spooked animals from inside the barn caught their attention. Caleb glanced up at the clouded sky. "There's bound to be a downpour. I'd best settle the livestock."

Grace smiled. "I'll go with you."

Caleb took her hand and they raced to the barn just as the sky opened up, bringing down sheets of rain upon them. Once inside, Caleb guided Grace to a haystack where she took a seat while he calmed his horses and checked on the milk cow.

Not five minutes later, the big wide barn door slammed shut. Must have been a powerful wind to shut that heavy door, Grace thought, walking over to take a peek outside. But when she tried to open the door, it didn't budge.

Grace pulled and tugged, her attempts futile. "Caleb?"

He came to stand behind her and she glanced back at him. "The door's stuck."

Then a voice from the other side of the barn door rang out, battling against the storm. "Sorry, Mrs. Lander."

"Opal?"

"It's me, Mrs. Lander."

"Opal, the door is stuck. I need you to open it."

There was silence on the other end for a few seconds. "No, ma'am. The door's not stuck. Not stuck at all."

Caleb laughed.

"Opal, you open this door right this minute."

"Sorry, Mrs. Lander. You and Papa need to be in there. Together. That's how I figure it."

Grace couldn't believe Opal's intent. She whirled around to face Caleb. "Do something! She's locked us in!"

Caleb took his hat off and scratched his head. "That girl's got a lot of *me* in her. I've always known. Gotta give her credit for this one."

Grace's mouth fell open.

"You're not going to demand that she open this door?"

Caleb leaned against the post lazily and smiled. "Well, now, I sorta like the idea of being stuck in the barn with you, Gracie."

Grace rolled her eyes. Then she turned back around. "Opal, you're in big trouble if you don't open this door."

"Don't try and scare the girl now, Grace." Aunt Enid's voice competed with the rain and wind. "Wasn't all her idea. I'd like some of the credit."

"Aunt Enid! Ohh, I can't believe you've done this!" Grace rapped on the door with all her might. "Open this door. Or I swear—"

"Ain't polite to go swearing now, honey. I'll be taking Opal inside the house now. The rain's coming down in buckets! You all have yourself a cozy evening."

"Aunt Enid!" Grace stomped her feet.

"Caleb?" her aunt called out.

Caleb perked up and walked to the door. "I'm here."

"Don't you worry over Opal. I'll take good care of her tonight."

"Obliged, Enid."

"You ain't mad about any of this, are you?"

He focused on Grace and shook his head. "You did the right thing, Enid."

With that, Grace threw her arms up in the air then strode over to slump down in a thick patch of dry straw.

Caleb whistled as he fed the horses, supplying them with grain and a few carrots in their stalls, while Grace paced back and forth by the barn door, gritting her teeth both from cold shudders running down her body and frustration at being locked in the barn. The storm had mellowed some and patches of dim light cast its way into the barn from a tiny window up in the hayloft.

When Caleb returned to her, he began unbuttoning his shirt. Grace's stomach plummeted, seeing him undressing casual as you please, right in front of her. "What are you doing?"

"I'm soaked. Gonna set my shirt to drying. It'll be dark soon."

He grazed his eyes over her wet, pink-flowered calico dress and arched a brow. She'd discarded her shawl minutes ago, as the saturated material only added to her shivering, and now Caleb was looking too much like a wolf stalking a chicken coop.

"Don't even think it," she warned, but the thought of shedding her clothes and letting go of all her fears and doubts to be close to him caused her heart to flutter wildly like butterfly wings.

Caleb set his gray cotton shirt over a hook that held a bridle. His chest bared now, his belt sitting low on his hips, he sauntered over to her in a slow, easy stride that erupted goose bumps on her arms. He smelled like fresh spring rain and solid earth. He raked his gaze over her and the shivers she felt turned to a quickening heat that melted her clear down to her toes.

"I'm only thinking how lucky I am."

Grace swallowed. "Why is th-that?"

"Because now I have all night to convince you to marry me."

Grace blinked several times, absorbing those impossible words. She breathed out slowly, a quiet sigh of deep regret, her heart breaking from the truth of her next words. "I can't marry you."

Caleb only smiled and came closer, within a breath of her. He reached out and lifted her chin, his thumb caressing her cheek, his eyes dark as midnight now, holding her captive. "When I kiss you, anything seems possible."

"I know." In those moments, Grace, too, felt that they could conquer all that kept them apart. But she couldn't subject Caleb to a life without children. He'd said it himself—Opal wanted brothers and sisters. Lots of them, and that's the one thing that Grace couldn't give to either of them.

She'd known guilt in her life. But she couldn't live with knowing that she'd be depriving the two people she loved with her whole heart the family that they deserved.

It would be the height of selfishness.

"Grace, marry me."

"I can't."

"Would you rather I ask Elmer Honeywell's niece?"

"No!" Then she caught herself.

Caleb was grinning. He'd taunted her and she'd fallen right into his trap. She whirled around to hide her jealousy and exasperation.

Caleb came up behind her to wrap his arms around her waist, pulling her in so that his chest pressed against her back. He set his head on her shoulder and spoke in a low rasp of a whisper. "I love you, Gracie Greene. I don't want any other woman. You've got to know that. You're strong and smart and so beautiful it makes me dizzy inside."

"Caleb, please...don't."

She heard the smile in his voice. "Don't what? *Love you?* I do, with all my heart, darlin'."

Grace silently ached from his passionate declaration. She remained quiet, unable to say the words he needed to hear.

"You love me, Grace. I know you do. You tell me every time I kiss you."

She spun around to look at him, holding back tears. "I can't love you. It would be too painful for both of us."

Caleb held on to her waist and peered deep into her eyes, his gaze confident and so hopeful her heart shattered. "Why?"

"Oh, Caleb. Those men...they took so much from me that day."

And Grace cried now, spilling out her heart, as well, explaining to Caleb about the stagecoach robbery and the day her life had changed forever.

She sobbed bitterly, the tears and words flowing freely. "That awful man tried to take me away with him and Harrison died protecting me. They shot him right in front of me."

Caleb hugged her tight, placing her head onto his chest and stroking her hair. "It's okay, honey, get it out. All of it. I'm here and you're safe now."

Grace pressed her body to his, sobbing and trying to explain, but soon her words died down and all that was left was the comfortable haven of his arms.

"Caleb?"

"Hmm?" His murmur resonated against her body and she felt as if her very skin absorbed every sound he made.

"I love you."

He spoke quietly, in a serious tone, "I'm glad to hear it."

"But I can't possibly marry you."

Caleb lifted her chin and gazed into eyes swollen from tears. "You keep saying that."

She sniffed away the last of her tears. "I know."

"But I *don't know*. Tell me why you think you can't marry me?"

Grace bolstered her resolve. She'd come to Springville to start a new life as a schoolteacher. She'd expected to find fulfillment with a classroom full of students and Aunt Enid's lively boarding-house antics. She'd never expected to fall in love again. She had trouble formulating the words to explain to Caleb, because once she did, he would be lost to her forever. "I…" she said on a deep breath, "I can't bear children. I lost my baby after that stage robbery. I lost…everything important in my life that day. I can't give you a child, Caleb. I know Opal wants brothers and sisters."

Caleb kissed her soundly then, his lips a soft, sweet, loving caress. "I'm sorry for your loss, honey."

She put her head down. "Now you know the truth."

Grace moved to step away from him, but he wouldn't let her go. Darkness had descended into the barn, but she couldn't mistake the confident look on his face or the gleaming twinkle in his dark eyes.

"Grace, Opal's more than enough child for the both of us to handle. Lord knows, she's got enough of me in her to keep the two of us busy for a long time. I know she loves you the way I do. And if given a choice she'd trade having a brother and sister any day to have you for her mother."

"Really?" Grace felt a smattering of hope.

"Really." He nodded and kissed her again briefly and her heart opened up, her love flowing out like the rush of a thundering river. "As for me, I've got all the family I need. You, me and Opal—it's more than any man can ask for in his lifetime."

Grace looked up and witnessed the truth in his eyes, the sincerity in his tone.

"Grace Lander," Caleb said, with a hitch in his voice, "will you be my wife and mother to my daughter?"

She let go her doubts and fears, banishing them now forever and knowing that with Caleb and Opal's help, she could look forward to a future that held so much promise.

"Yes, Caleb. Oh, yes! I'll marry you."

Caleb took her into his arms and kissed her until her body quaked and her breaths quickened. "Come, lay with me. Let me hold you in my arms all night."

And Caleb covered a wool blanket over a thick batch of straw and together they lay down, holding on to each other and waiting for the new day to begin.

Morning dawned with sunshine pushing through the remaining clouds. Streams of light entered the barn. Grace woke up, staring into Caleb's gleaming eyes. The night had been wonderful, filled with excitement and plans for the future with anticipation for the wedding night to come. Caleb hadn't pressed her last night though resisting temptation had never been Caleb's strong suit and she loved him all the more for it.

"Good morning," she said quietly, reaching to outline his strong jaw with her finger. Touching him and knowing that she'd have that right every day of her life brought her such contentment.

"Mornin', honey." He took her into his arms and kissed her silly until her heart spun like a windmill on a breezy day. He looked her up and down leisurely, possessively, with hunger in his eyes, making every bone in her body liquefy. On a groan, he said, "We're getting married at the end of the week or I'm bound to go crazy. Sooner, if it's possible."

"I hope it's possible, too."

He shook his head and laughed, raking a hand through his hair. "No more than I do, sweetheart."

There was a clatter of noise outside the barn and then a full stream of light poured in as the door was opened.

Caleb helped Grace up and cast her an encouraging nod. She nodded back and they walked over to meet Opal, who stood in the wide-open doorway with sunshine beaming behind her, casting her in the glow of early-morning light. The child appeared angelic, but for the fear in her eyes as they approached.

"Am I in trouble, Papa?"

"Well, now," he said, squatting down to look directly at her. "I suppose I should be angry with you, Turnip. But as it turned out, instead of getting punished, you're getting a mother. And I'm getting me a wife. How's that sound?"

Opal's bright blue eyes rounded and she looked up at Grace. "I'm getting a mother?"

Grace bent down next to Caleb. "That's right, Opal. I love you and your papa very much. I'm going to marry him. Would you like that?"

Opal's face lit up. "It's what I've been praying for, Mrs. Lander."

Grace blinked back tears. "So have I, Opal, but I didn't even know it until I met you and your father." Then she smiled. "You don't have to call me Mrs. Lander anymore."

"Can I call you *Mama?*"

Grace glanced at Caleb, her heart in her throat. "Yes, call me…Mama."

Opal's brilliant smile rivaled the sun. "Wait until Susie hears about this!"

Caleb grinned. "I'm pretty happy myself."

He took them both into his embrace and the three of them huddled together in a circle of love. One day Opal would know the true story of her paternity, but right now all that mattered was that they'd be together and enjoying life on the Bar M.

They were a family.

Grace found the true measure of happiness now, brought on by one precocious, adorable girl and the potent, earth-pounding power of Caleb's kiss.

* * * * *

THOROUGHBRED LEGACY
*The stakes are high when it comes to love,
horse racing, family secrets
and broken promises.*

*A new exciting Harlequin continuity
series coming soon!*
Led by New York Times *bestselling
author Elizabeth Bevarly*
FLIRTING WITH TROUBLE

Here's a preview!

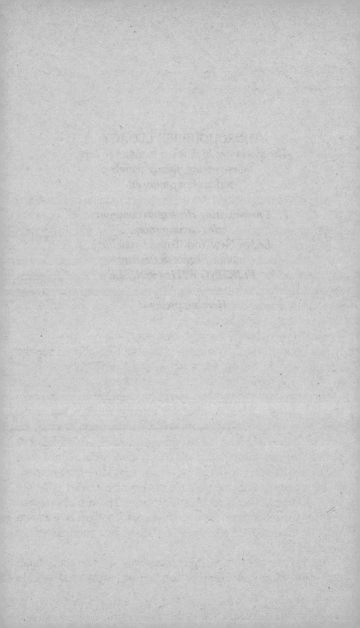

THE DOOR CLOSED behind them, throwing them into darkness and leaving them utterly alone. And the next thing Daniel knew, he heard himself saying, "Marnie, I'm sorry about the way things turned out in Del Mar."

She said nothing at first, only strode across the room and stared out the window beside him. Although he couldn't see her well in the darkness—he still hadn't switched on a light...but then, neither had she—he imagined her expression was a little preoccupied, a little anxious, a little confused.

Finally, very softly, she said, "Are you?"

He nodded, then, worried she wouldn't be able to see the gesture, added, "Yeah. I am. I should have said goodbye to you."

"Yes, you should have."

Actually, he thought, there were a lot of things he should have done in Del Mar. He'd had *a lot* riding on the Pacific Classic, and even more on his entry, Little Joe, but after meeting Marnie, the Pacific Classic had been the last thing on Daniel's mind. His loss at Del Mar had pretty much ended his career before it had even begun, and he'd had to start all over again, rebuilding from nothing.

He simply had not then and did not now have room in his life for a woman as potent as Marnie Roberts. He was a horseman first and foremost. From the time he was a schoolboy, he'd known what he wanted to do with his life—be the best possible trainer he could be.

He had to make sure Marnie understood—and he understood, too—why things had ended the way they had eight years ago. He just wished he could find the words to do that. Hell, he wished he could find the *thoughts* to do that.

"You made me forget things, Marnie, things that I really needed to remember. And that scared the hell out of me. Little Joe should have won the Classic. He was by far the best horse entered in that race. But I didn't give him the attention he needed and deserved that week, because all I could think about was you. Hell, when I woke up that morning all I wanted to do was lie there and look at you, and then wake you up and make love to you again. If I hadn't left when I did—the way I did— I might still be lying there in that bed with you, thinking about nothing else."

"And would that be so terrible?" she asked.

"Of course not," he told her. "But that wasn't why I was in Del Mar," he repeated. "I was in Del Mar to win a race. That was my job. And my work was the most important thing to me."

She said nothing for a moment, only studied his face in the darkness as if looking for the answer to a very important question. Finally she asked, "And what's the most important thing to you now, Daniel?"

Wasn't the answer to that obvious? "My work," he answered automatically.

She nodded slowly. "Of course," she said softly. "That is, after all, what you do best."

Her comment, too, puzzled him. She made it sound as if being good at what he did was a bad thing.

She bit her lip thoughtfully, her eyes fixed on his, glimmering in the scant moonlight that was filtering through the window. And damned if Daniel didn't find himself wanting to pull her into his arms and kiss her. But as much as it might have felt as if no time had passed since Del Mar, there were eight years between now and then. And eight years was a long time in the best of circumstances. For Daniel and Marnie, it was virtually a lifetime.

So Daniel turned and started for the door, then halted. He couldn't just walk away and leave things as they were, unsettled. He'd done that eight years ago and regretted it.

"It *was* good to see you again, Marnie," he said softly. And since he was being honest, he added, "I hope we see each other again."

She didn't say anything in response, only stood silhouetted against the window with her arms wrapped around her in a way that made him wonder whether she was doing it because she was cold, or if she just needed something—someone—to hold on to. In either case, Daniel understood. There was an emptiness clinging to him that he suspected would be there for a long time.

* * * * *

THOROUGHBRED LEGACY
coming soon wherever books are sold!

Silhouette Desire

Cole's Red-Hot Pursuit

Cole Westmoreland is a man who gets what he
wants. And he wants independent and sultry
Patrina Forman! She resists him—until a Montana
blizzard traps them together. For three delicious
nights, Cole indulges Patrina with his brand of
seduction. When the sun comes out, Cole and
Patrina are left to wonder—will this be the end of
the passion that storms between them?

Look for

COLE'S RED-HOT PURSUIT

by *USA TODAY* bestselling author

BRENDA JACKSON

Available in June 2008 wherever you buy books.

Always Powerful, Passionate and Provocative.

Silhouette®

Romantic
SUSPENSE

Sparked by Danger, Fueled by Passion.

Seduction Summer:
Seduction in the sand…and a killer on the beach.

Silhouette Romantic Suspense invites you to the hottest summer yet with three connected stories from some of our steamiest storytellers! Get ready for…

Killer Temptation
by Nina Bruhns;
a millionaire this tempting is worth a little danger.

Killer Passion
by Sheri WhiteFeather;
an FBI profiler's forbidden passion incites a killer's rage,

and

Killer Affair
by Cindy Dees;
this affair with a mystery man is to die for.

Look for

KILLER TEMPTATION by Nina Bruhns in June 2008
KILLER PASSION by Sheri WhiteFeather in July 2008
and
KILLER AFFAIR by Cindy Dees in August 2008.

Available wherever you buy books!

Visit Silhouette Books at www.eHarlequin.com   SRS27586

REQUEST YOUR FREE BOOKS!

Harlequin® Historical
Historical Romantic Adventure!

2 FREE NOVELS PLUS 2 FREE GIFTS!

YES! Please send me 2 FREE Harlequin® Historical novels and my 2 FREE gifts (gifts are worth about $10). After receiving them, if I don't wish to receive any more books, I can return the shipping statement marked "cancel". If I don't cancel, I will receive 6 brand-new novels every month and be billed just $4.94 per book in the U.S. or $5.49 per book in Canada, plus 25¢ shipping and handling per book and applicable taxes, if any*. That's a savings of 20% off the cover price! I understand that accepting the 2 free books and gifts places me under no obligation to buy anything. I can always return a shipment and cancel at any time. Even if I never buy another book, the two free books and gifts are mine to keep forever.

246 HDN ERUM 349 HDN ERUA

Name	(PLEASE PRINT)
Address	Apt. #
City	State/Prov.	Zip/Postal Code

Signature (if under 18, a parent or guardian must sign)

Mail to the **Harlequin Reader Service:**
IN U.S.A.: P.O. Box 1867, Buffalo, NY 14240-1867
IN CANADA: P.O. Box 609, Fort Erie, Ontario L2A 5X3

Not valid to current subscribers of Harlequin Historical books.

Want to try two free books from another line?
Call 1-800-873-8635 or visit www.morefreebooks.com.

* Terms and prices subject to change without notice. N.Y. residents add applicable sales tax. Canadian residents will be charged applicable provincial taxes and GST. This offer is limited to one order per household. All orders subject to approval. Credit or debit balances in a customer's account(s) may be offset by any other outstanding balance owed by or to the customer. Please allow 4 to 6 weeks for delivery. Offer available while quantities last.

Your Privacy: Harlequin Books is committed to protecting your privacy. Our Privacy Policy is available online at www.eHarlequin.com or upon request from the Reader Service. From time to time we make our lists of customers available to reputable third parties who may have a product or service of interest to you. If you would prefer we not share your name and address, please check here. ☐

HH08

Royal Seductions

Michelle Celmer delivers a powerful miniseries in
Royal Seductions; where two brothers fight for the
crown and discover love. In *The King's Convenient Bride,*
the king discovers his marriage of convenience to the
woman he's been promised to wed is turning all too
real. The playboy prince proposes a mock engagement
to defuse rumors circulating about him and restore
order to the kingdom…until his pretend fiancée
becomes pregnant in *The Illegitimate Prince's Baby.*

Look for

THE KING'S CONVENIENT BRIDE
&
THE ILLEGITIMATE PRINCE'S BABY

BY MICHELLE CELMER

Available in June 2008 wherever you buy books.

Always Powerful, Passionate and Provocative.

COMING NEXT MONTH FROM
HARLEQUIN®
HISTORICAL

- **THE LAST RAKE IN LONDON**
  by **Nicola Cornick**
  (Edwardian)
  Dangerous Jack Kestrel was the most sinfully sensual rogue she'd
  ever met, and the wicked glint in his eyes promised he'd take care of
  satisfying Sally's every need....
  Watch as the last rake in London meets his match!

- **AN IMPETUOUS ABDUCTION**
  by **Patricia Frances Rowell**
  (Regency)
  Persephone had stumbled into danger, and the only way to protect her
  was to abduct her! But what would Leo's beautiful prisoner do when he
  revealed his true identity?
  *Don't miss Patricia Frances Rowell's unique blend of passion spiced
  with danger!*

- **KIDNAPPED BY THE COWBOY**
  by **Pam Crooks**
  (Western)
  TJ Grier was determined to clear his name, even if his actions might
  cost him the woman he loved!
  Fall in love with Pam Crooks's honorable cowboy!

- **INNOCENCE UNVEILED**
  by **Blythe Gifford**
  (Medieval)
  With her flaming red hair, Katrine knew no man would be tempted
  by her. But Renard, a man of secrets, intended to break through her
  defenses....
  *Innocence and passion are an intoxicating mix in this emotional
  medieval tale.*

HHCNM0508